Six Students

Who took a college project and turned it into the conscience of a city, touching the soul of a generation.

Six People

Who meet again fifteen years later and discover the many choices and changes they have made, as screenwriter or social worker, university professor or maverick photographer, Manhattan executive or Washington insider.

Six Friends

Who remember the fads and the fashions, the politics and the music, of the sixties and seventies, who rekindle old relationships, spark new romances and reaffirm what matters most—their feelings for one another.

34

Books by Judith Arnold

HARLEQUIN AMERICAN ROMANCE

*KEEPING THE FAITH SUBSERIES

HARLEQUIN TEMPTATION

Don't miss any of our special offers. Write to us at the following address for information on our newest releases.

Harlequin Reader Service
901 Fuhrmann Blvd., P.O. Box 1397, Buffalo, NY 14240
Canadian address: P.O. Box 603,
Fort Erie, Ont. L2A 5X3

Promises
Judith Arnold

Harlequin Books

TORONTO • NEW YORK • LONDON
AMSTERDAM • PARIS • SYDNEY • HAMBURG
STOCKHOLM • ATHENS • TOKYO • MILAN

Published June 1987

First printing April 1987

ISBN 0-373-16201-4

Foreword

When I was coming of age, in the late sixties and early seventies, my friends and I were scornful about romance. The word conjured in our minds images of long-stemmed roses, candlelit dinners, midnight strolls with the man of our dreams. It implied a glittering engagement ring, a spectacular wedding, a cozy little house in the suburbs, two-point-two kids and a station wagon.

Romance? What could be cornier?

Besides, what could be more pointless than romance? How, after all, could we be worrying about trying to find Mr. Right and settling down, when there were so many more important matters to take care of? We were too busy changing the world to care about getting married. A war was raging far away, stealing the lives of our friends and brothers. At home we had to deal with racism, sexism, pollution, the outdated values of our elders. My generation was enormous and powerful. We understood that if we so much as sneezed in unison, we could shatter the universe.

There would be time for romance later, we resolved. But for the moment, while we had our youth and our energy, we would right all the wrongs, clean the air, end the war, demand equality for the victims of prejudice and fight for the constitutional integrity of our government. So we marched on Washington, signed petitions, staged sit-ins. We wore buttons, hung posters, flashed the peace sign, ate brown rice and sang the rock songs that became the anthems of our day. We wore blue jeans, army fatigues and love beads, let our hair grow long and declared that materialism was a sin.

Our world has come a long way since then, and so have I. Now I recognize that we were arguably the most romantic generation ever to fill the planet. What could be more romantic than believing that if enough people shouted enough slogans and signed enough letters we could make a difference?

Romance isn't really about flowers or moonlight. It's about listening to your heart, listening and then obeying what it tells you. Romance involves giving free rein to your feelings, having faith in yourself, believing in what is right and following the dictates of your soul. It means keeping promises, making commitments and chasing dreams. Sometimes romance entails the love of a man and a woman. Sometimes it entails the love of a country, a principle, an idea. But always it entails love.

In this trilogy called *Keeping the Faith*, I've created six characters who, like me, came of age during the turbulent late sixties and early seventies. Although they lived together through certain universal experiences of the time, each of them personalized those experiences, adapted to them as individuals and allowed their shared history to affect them in individual ways.

Laura Brodie absorbed from her youth the emphasis on brotherhood. She is in many ways an "earth mother," eager to save humanity, finding pleasure in the simple life. For Kimberly Belmont, reaching maturity during an age of rebellion gave her the strength to distance herself from the constricting conservatism of her family and to pursue a career in government, supporting a political leader in whom she believed. Julianne Robinson drew from the sixties the power of the feminist movement, which enabled her to succeed as a publishing executive who could use her magazine to expound her principles. Seth Stone took to heart the personal freedom celebrated in those days, the joy of "going for it," laughing at the universe and tweaking authority. In Andrew Collins's case, the sixties was a time when being armed with knowledge was considered the best defense; he chose a career in academia, where he could help mold the minds of a new generation. For Troy Bennett, the most significant aspect of the era was the war in Southeast Asia. The choices that war forced him to make both scarred and saved him. Like the other characters—like any of us from that era—he lives every day with the understanding of how his past has shaped his present.

There is a little of me in each of these characters. Like Laura, Kimberly and Julianne, I have struggled to reconcile a career and motherhood. I have lived on a commune. I have seen the difficulties faced by my divorced friends. I have benefited from the variety of possibilities the feminist movement opened to all women. Like Seth, Andrew and Troy, I have tried to "go for it," worked as a college professor and felt the repercussions of our nation's tragedy in Vietnam.

When I was young we used to say, "Never trust anybody over thirty." Now I, like the characters in *Keeping the Faith*, have passed the thirty-year mark—and survived. Laura, Seth, Kimberly, Andrew, Julianne and Troy aren't the same people they were fifteen years ago, but perhaps they're better people today than they were then. As their stories unfold in *Promises*, *Commitments*, and *Dreams*, they are finally able to acknowledge the romance of their past, and welcome the romances in their futures.

Just as it always has, romance still means listening to your heart and following your dreams. In *Keeping the Faith*, my characters listen, follow and triumph.

Chapter One

"I'm standing in the heart of a dream right now. Or, to be more accurate, the heart of the suite of offices that house Dream *magazine on the seventh floor of the Shelton Publications Building in midtown Manhattan. We're only a few miles from the Columbia University basement classroom where, exactly fifteen years ago today, a group of enterprising students decided to start an underground newspaper they called* The Dream. *But looking around at the elegant decor of* Dream's *headquarters, I can't help thinking that the distance* Dream *has traveled these past fifteen years is much farther than a few miles."*

Julianne's gaze circled the festively decorated reception lounge. Already the room was fairly crowded. Journalists, luminaries of the publishing world and advertising executives mingled and chattered softly, sipping champagne punch from plastic cups and nibbling on hors d'oeuvres. The guests of honor hadn't arrived yet, and she knew that checking the door every minute on the minute wouldn't make them arrive any faster. Yet staring at the door was easier on her eyes than staring at the glaring white light the television crew had set up.

Connie Simmons, the reporter from *Evening Potpourri*, stood in front of the table where the sheet cake sat, two candles in the shape of a one and a five protruding from its rich butter-cream frosting. Behind the cake a framed black-and-white photograph was on display. It was a picture of a very young Julianne and her fellow dreamers, clowning around outside the campus building where the cellar office that had housed their operation was located. Troy had taken the picture with a timer. Kimberly and Laura had hunched over Troy and the other men as they held Julianne, their editor in chief, across their laps, and in the photo she had managed to look not at all disturbed about the possibility that they might drop her. It had been a real possibility, since they had all been laughing so hard. All six of them had been dressed in the requisite scruffy jeans and shirts. All six of them had peered out at the camera from behind inordinate quantities of hair.

Usually Julianne kept the eight-by-ten photo in her office, hanging on the wall behind her desk. Looking at it, seeing how idealistic and bright-eyed they appeared, ought to have made her feel depressingly old. But aging wasn't the sort of thing that upset her. Time passed. It was something one simply had to accept.

She noticed that Connie was beckoning to her, and after patting her smooth brown page boy and adjusting the lightly padded shoulders of her royal-blue silk dress, she joined the reporter at the table. Standing at five feet nine inches, not to mention the two inches her high-heeled shoes added to her height, she towered over the petite young woman, who tilted her head upward and gave Julianne a winning smile. "Nervous?" Connie asked.

Julianne returned her smile. "About being on television? Not really." If she was nervous about anything, it was about reuniting with her old friends. And no, she wasn't nervous about that, either. Except perhaps seeing Troy...

"With me is Julianne Robinson, *Dream*'s editor in chief," Connie recited, facing the camera. "Julianne was one of those six Columbia and Barnard students who founded the newspaper, which has since evolved into a glossy hundred-page monthly with a national circulation in excess of half a million. Tell us, Julianne, was starting up a newspaper like one of those Judy Garland-Mickey Rooney movies? You know, where someone says, 'Hey, my uncle has a barn—let's put on a show!' "

Julianne peered down at Connie, who was still smiling warmly. "Actually, no," she replied, trying not to sound self-conscious as the television camera recorded her speech. "We were classmates in an advanced rhetoric and composition course, and we decided to pool our energies for a class assignment. We thought it would be interesting to put together a newsletter about a block of brownstones owned by the university in Morningside Heights, approaching that single subject from different angles. One of us wrote about some of the older tenants and one about the kids who used to hang out on the street. Another of our group wrote about the questionable condition of the buildings themselves, one about friction between the residents and the neighboring college students, and so on. Troy Bennett—one of the founders—had a camera, so he took some pictures. We ran off a bunch of copies and distributed it free. It created quite a sensation."

"The original name wasn't *Dream*, but *The Dream*," Connie commented. "How did you come up with that?"

"It was from Dr. Martin Luther King's 'I have a dream' speech. We were all big fans of his."

Connie turned to the camera and said, "To help celebrate *Dream*'s fifteenth birthday, Julianne Robinson and her publisher have invited the other five founders back for this gala celebration. We can't help but wonder, where are they now? What have they been doing since those heady, radical days when underground newspapers were all the rage?" She pivoted to Julianne again. "Any of them here yet?"

"Not yet," Julianne told her. "But they'll be here. At least, four of them will be. They telephoned me to let me know they'd be coming." The only one who hadn't called in response to her invitation was Troy. She wondered if the invitation had reached him, if he had thrown it out without reading it, if he was even still alive.... "They'll be here," she said, as much to assure herself as to assure Connie Simmons. "They wouldn't miss this party for anything."

"YUCK! You aren't gonna wear *that*, are you?" Rita squawked.

Laura rotated from the full-length mirror on the back of her bedroom door. She had rather liked what she'd seen. The Indian print wraparound skirt was a bit snugger about her waist than it had been when she'd bought it back in her college days, but it still fit. So did the lacy white peasant blouse, of the same vintage as her skirt. "What's wrong with what I'm wearing?" she asked her daughter.

"It's flaming bad, Ma. I don't like it."

Laura's gaze skimmed the thirteen-year-old girl who had marched into the bedroom to plop herself onto the double bed. Rita had on a baggy, loose-knit pink sweater that fell nearly to her knees—in Laura's day, such a garment could have passed as a dress by itself—and a pair of equally baggy powder-blue slacks that left her ankles exposed, as if she'd outgrown the pants. Rita's curly black hair was shorn short in a punkish style, and her ears were adorned with brassy triangular earrings. If Rita's attire was good, Laura was more than happy to look flaming bad.

"Do you know how old this skirt is?" she asked, moving to the bureau and reaching for her hairbrush.

"Older than you, probably," Rita mused, tearing her eyes from her mother to examine a chip on her copper-colored nail polish.

"Heavens, if it were *that* old, it would have disintegrated into dust by now," Laura said with a laugh. "I bought this skirt in college. It was the first nonminiskirt I ever bought myself."

"I bet it looked bad then, too. You look like a gypsy or something."

"What's wrong with looking like a gypsy?" Laura ran the brush through her long, rippling curls, then pulled two frizzy locks back from her face and clasped them behind her head with a silver comb. A gypsy. With her unmanageable brown hair and her dark eyes and olive complexion, Laura found herself agreeing with Rita. She put on her silver hoop earrings and a matching silver bangle bracelet. "There," she said, spinning around on the heels of her leather sandals. "I think I look wonderful."

"Yuck," Rita appraised her. The doorbell sounded, and she sprang from the bed to answer it. She returned to the bedroom with Courtney Gonzalez in tow. Courtney lived three floors below Laura and Rita. Half black and half Puerto Rican, Courtney was the product of a background as unconventional as Rita's. The two girls were best friends.

Like Rita, Courtney was wearing an oversize sweater and baggy slacks. "Hey, Laura, you look great," she said.

Laura shot Rita a triumphant look. "No wonder I love you, Courtney," she joked, reaching for her white crocheted shawl and flinging it around her shoulders. "All right, girls, you know the rules. I may not be home till midnight, so if you get tired, just go to sleep. Anything goes wrong, you call Courtney's mom. There's frozen yogurt in the fridge if you're hungry."

"Yuck," Rita grumbled. "Why can't we have ice cream like normal people?"

"Yogurt's better for you," Laura answered.

"I like frozen yogurt. It's good stuff," Courtney remarked. "Anyway, I gotta lose weight. So do you, lardo," she ribbed Rita.

Laura eyed her daughter's friend and then Rita. Both girls were built like string beans. Lord, but thirteen was an awful age to have to live through.

She lifted her purse from the bureau, opened it and counted the money in her wallet. It was still early enough to be safe taking the subway into Manhattan, and she had enough cash on hand for a cab ride home. "Okay," she said, heading for the bedroom door. "Do you want me to give you a call in a couple of hours and see how you're doing?"

"Ma-a," Rita groaned.

"All right," Laura conceded with another laugh. "I'm on my way. Stay out of trouble."

THE JET TOUCHED DOWN with a gentle thump. Seth opened his eyes and stared out the window as the plane taxied toward one of the terminals. It seemed as if they'd been in a landing pattern for hours, and he felt stiff from having sat with his seat in the upright position for so long.

He raked his hands through his short dirty-blond tufts of hair, then reached into the inner pocket of his white linen jacket for his sunglasses. It was nearly seven o'clock and dark outside, but the sunglasses were a gag. Their rounded lenses were one-way mirrors.

He didn't bother to tighten the narrow gray tie at his throat. When you were wearing a wrinkled white suit and a turquoise shirt—to say nothing of mirrored sunglasses—you weren't supposed to strangle yourself on your tie. He watched the much more conservatively dressed businessman in the next seat preen and adjust his collar. No class, Seth reflected.

The party was supposed to start at seven, which meant that even if Seth went straight from the airport to the Shelton Building without checking in at the hotel first he'd still be late. But what the hell, he'd rather be visiting with his old buddies than unpacking. In fact, he couldn't wait to see the gang. Winging in tedious figure eights above Long Island had just about driven him nuts. He'd get to the hotel later.

He was the first passenger to reach the cabin's makeshift closet when the airplane lurched to a halt, and he yanked his garment bag from the rod and bolted down the aisle, nearly knocking over a flight attendant who seemed to think his life depended on her bountiful expression of gratitude for his having chosen to fly United. *Fly United...* He remembered the obscene poster he had hung in his dorm room in college; it featured two mating geese in midair, with "Fly United" printed underneath them. He loved that poster, and the other one he had, depicting a very pregnant woman with the caption "Nixon's the One." And his Spiro Agnew dartboard. Interior design á la hippie cheap.

The white limousine was parked outside the terminal, along with cabs and buses and elongated station wagons that bore signs reading Connecticut Express. Seth had arranged for the limo as a joke. Back home he preferred to drive himself wherever he had to go. But nowadays the New York taxis charged an arm and a leg, and anyway, what the hell. He could afford the limo.

The driver, though—he looked barely out of diapers. He was leaning against the gleaming front bumper, but he rose to attention when he spotted Seth approaching him. "Are you Mr. Stone?" he asked, quickly slipping his uniform cap onto his head.

"Good guess," Seth said, handing him the garment bag and opening the back door for himself. The driver stowed the bag in the trunk, then took the wheel. Seth sank into the plush leather upholstery and sighed. "Skip the Sheraton," he instructed the driver. "Let's go straight to the Shelton Building."

"Whatever you say, Mr. Stone."

Mr. Stone. Seth grimaced, then chuckled. The kid was only being polite, doing his job.

He gazed through the tinted-glass side window long enough to become disgusted with the snarled traffic. Life was as crowded on the highway as it had been in the air above Kennedy Airport. He had a long trip ahead of him. "Are you old enough to drive this thing?" he asked the young man piloting the car.

"Yes, sir. I've been doing it for nearly a year."

"How old are you?"

"Twenty, sir."

Twenty. That was how old Seth had been when they'd gotten *The Dream* started fifteen years ago. What did twenty-year-olds do these days, besides go to the movies and chauffeur limos? "So tell me," he said, figuring that a conversation with the driver would make the trip pass more pleasantly. "What do you want to be when you grow up?"

The driver accepted Seth's question with equanimity. "Actually, I'm studying to become an actor," he confessed. "I take classes at the Neighborhood Playhouse."

"No kidding? Good for you," Seth praised him. "You know, I'm in the film business. I write screenplays."

He glimpsed the young man's thrilled smile in the rear-view mirror. "Do you really? That's terrific," the driver enthused. "Anything I might have heard of?"

"Only if you like junk," Seth said modestly. "I wrote *Victory of the Ninja Women*, *Coed Summer*, cowrote *Return of Ax Man* and *Ax Man: Final Cut*. Right now I'm working on *Ax Man Cuts Both Ways*."

"I thought *Ax Man: Final Cut* was the last one in the series," the driver remarked.

"It was supposed to be. But hey, people keep coming. Why spoil a good thing?"

"But Ax Man was killed in *Final Cut*," the driver protested. "They blew him up with a grenade, didn't they?"

A fan, Seth realized with a smug grin. Everybody was always quick enough to put down the schlock movies Seth wrote, but the theaters had to turn patrons away whenever one of Seth's movies was appearing. "Wait until *Cuts Both Ways* comes out. You'll learn more about resurrection than they ever taught you in Sunday school. So what's with this traffic? Are we going to get to Manhattan before the summer solstice?"

"It's Friday night," the driver said apologetically. "Big night in the Big Apple."

"Yeah," Seth grunted. "Right."

"I'll get you there as quickly as I can."

"As long as you don't break any laws," Seth admonished him. "I don't want to take a tour of the city jails."

THE THING ABOUT REUNIONS, as far as Kimberly could tell, was that it was bad form to attend one if you were a failure. When she and Julianne had attended their five-year reunion at Barnard, each and every classmate they'd encountered had been doing something utterly wonderful with her life. Sally Bolton was into her medical residency; Cathy Beck was a lawyer; Doreen O'Connell had just edited a coffee table book on Ireland; Brenda Slavin was on the verge of opening her second boutique; Melanie Fierberg was a marine biologist and happily married. When Kimberly had commented to Julianne about the exemplary lives their classmates were leading, Julianne had pointed out that the reason all the returning women they saw were successes was that failures weren't likely to attend class reunions.

Kimberly had been a success then, too. Happily married, rising fast at the public relations firm. She didn't consider herself a success anymore, and she was entertaining serious misgivings about having let Julianne talk her into attending this party to celebrate *Dream*.

Cars were backed up for half a mile from the toll booths leading into the Lincoln Tunnel. There was no way for Kimberly to turn around and drive back to Washington. All she could do was wait, creep the car forward an inch at a time, tap her manicured fingernails against the steering wheel and worry about what everyone would say if they found out what a mess she'd made of her life in the past fifteen years.

She lowered the sun visor above the windshield to check her reflection in the vanity mirror. Despite the fact that every gentle blond wave was in place, her eye makeup impeccable, her cheeks smooth and pink and the line of her jaw as clean and taut as it had ever been, she thought she looked old and haggard. *Blame it on the long drive,* she muttered silently. *Blame it on a hellish week at work. Blame it on anything but the fact that you've blown it.*

"Accentuate the positive." That was what Julianne was always telling her to do. "You've got a prestigious job. That's something you ought to be proud of." *Sure,* Kimberly answered her silently. *I work absurdly long hours, I'm underpaid, and so what if I can address the senator by his first name?* Even though Senator Milford had granted her permission to call him "Howard," she felt uncomfortable calling him anything but "The Senator." That was what all his senior staff people called him. And to work on The Senator's staff—well, that sounded exalted, too. But it wasn't as if Kimberly were actually making policy. She was only enunciating it, shaping it into orotund phrases that rolled trippingly off The Senator's tongue whenever he was on the stump. Which seemed to be most of the time.

She was tired. Tired of the Washington rat race, tired of struggling to pay the rent for her basement apartment in

Georgetown on the stingy salary she earned, tired of having
to think about dollars and cents. And lawyers. She'd finally obtained a competent divorce attorney to handle her
end of things. She had put off taking that step as long as she
could, not only because she needed to save money, but,
more important, because she didn't want to accept the fi-
nality of the situation. But it was final, no doubt about that.
Her marriage was a certifiable failure.

Only two more cars to go. She rummaged in her purse for
a couple of dollar bills, then moved forward, waiting her
turn to pay the toll. Once she had paid, she was able to shift
into high gear again, grateful for the sudden rush of humid
darkness as the tunnel swallowed her BMW.

At least she didn't look as old as she felt. People kept
telling her that. Whitney Brannigan had been constantly
pestering her for dates, practically from the day she'd moved
out of the house in Chevy Chase. "Good God, give me
some space," she'd complained. "I'm hoping that Todd and
I can work things out and get back together." *Ha,* she
grunted beneath her breath. *As if there had ever been a
chance of that.*

The car emerged in Manhattan, and she steered north to
Forty-second street. The sidewalks were crowded with
throngs of people milling about the rehabilitated pornog-
raphy houses that had been transformed into Theater Row,
an enclave of off-Broadway showcases. The road was
clogged with double-parked cars. So many people, Kimberly pondered, each of them a statistic. Just like her. A
pretty, well-educated woman for whom the world once
promised everything—except that she'd blown it and joined
the ranks of the losers, the statistics. The next time she filled
out a census form she would have to write "divorced."

She'd better do something about her frame of mind before she reached the Shelton Building. She would walk in
with her head held high, as if her entire life were proceed-

ing swimmingly, just as everyone had always predicted it would. Hadn't she been elected "Most Likely to Succeed" in high school?

She would march into the reunion like the conquering queen she was alleged to be. She still had her beloved BMW, she still had her figure—which Whitney, in one of his more expansive moments, had described as luscious—and she still had her pride. Nobody, other than Julianne, had to know about the mess with Todd. Kimberly could pretend she was a success for the duration of the evening, and then, when she returned to Julianne's apartment for the night, she could let down her guard and share with her good friend all the miserable details of her first meeting with the divorce lawyer.

"DON'T FORGET YOUR JACKET," Edith said, rushing ahead of Andrew to the coat closet and pulling the brown corduroy blazer from a hanger. "And here, let me straighten your tie. You look wonderful, Andrew. I'm sure you're going to have a fine time."

"Of course he is," Henry chimed in, hovering behind Edith as she adjusted the knot of Andrew's knit necktie and smoothed the button-down collar of his shirt.

"I love reunions," Edith babbled. "I just love them. And I'm so glad this one gave you the opportunity to visit us. You don't visit us often enough, Andrew."

He smiled faintly. It wasn't that he didn't want to visit Edith and Henry. It was just that whenever he did, they always looked so sad. No matter how much they beamed and laughed and fussed over him, their eyes always shimmered with unspent tears.

They meant well, and he cared for them a great deal. Every time he saw them, he promised that he wouldn't wait so long before the next visit. He knew that they still viewed him as a son, and he didn't mind that in the least.

But their eyes, always brimming, always bravely damming back the tears... It was hard, that was all. Hard seeing them, hard being forced to remember.

"The dinner was great, Edith," he said genuinely, adjusting his aviator-frame eyeglasses and feeling in the pocket of his khaki trousers for his keys. "I'll try not to get back too late."

"Don't be silly," Henry admonished him, pulling a house key from his own keyring. "Here, let yourself in. We won't wait up."

"If you're sure you don't mind..."

"Of course not. You'll probably want to spend half the night talking to your old friends. Come home when you come home. We'll let you sleep late tomorrow morning."

"You're really very generous," Andrew said, a half-hearted protest.

"Don't be silly," Edith echoed her husband. "It's our pleasure, Andrew. It always is. You look very handsome. Have a good time."

He strolled down the front walk without turning to wave goodbye. He knew Edith and Henry were lingering on the porch, watching his departure. He loved them, he really did, but sometimes they could be a bit overwhelming. They doted on him, practically smothered him with affection. He appreciated it, but it made him claustrophobic at times.

Once he'd driven down the cozy street of split-level houses and turned the corner, he began to unwind. Edith and Henry were much easier to love when he wasn't in the same room with them, forced to look at them, forced to acknowledge that, underlining their fondness for him, was that deep, pulsing sadness that would never go away.

He didn't plan to think about it anymore tonight. He couldn't help but think about it when he was with Edith and Henry, but now that he was on his way to the city, he could shunt his grief to the tiny corner of his mind reserved for it and concentrate on renewing his friendship with Julianne, Seth, Troy and Laura.

Oh, yes, and Kimberly, he added with a snort. Cutesy Kimberly, with her coquettish smile and her cheerleader approach to life. The others had all undoubtedly been doing interesting things with their lives. Laura had probably adopted a bunch of Asian orphans and was running a pig farm or something. Seth? If Seth hadn't fried his brains, Andrew would bet that Seth was engaged in some wonderfully frivolous enterprise—running a record shop, perhaps. Troy might be living out of a camper in the Sierra Nevada, taking breathtaking photographs, doing an impersonation of Ansel Adams. And Julianne... well, Andrew was a regular subscriber to *Dream*. He already knew that Julianne had parlayed their little newspaper into an illustrious magazine. But Kimberly Belmont, Southern belle *extraordinaire*... Married, Andrew decided. Mother of two, living in some pillared Atlanta mansion, active in the Junior League, chairwoman of the Red Cross Ball.

Trying to imagine what his old cronies would be like made the drive pass more easily. As for himself, Andrew suspected that the others wouldn't be much surprised by what they saw—except that they would see more of him than they'd ever seen before. None of them had known him before he'd grown his beard, back in his freshman year. He'd shaved the beard off six years ago, when a few strands of premature gray had infiltrated it and given him a Nestorian look that didn't sit well with him. Some gray had permeated his thick brown hair, too, but he wasn't about to shave his skull. He didn't need too many reminders of how old he was. The young, energetic students he faced every day were reminder enough.

He rarely drove down to New York City, but as he crossed the invisible boundary separating Westchester from the Bronx he felt a slight charge. Maybe he was spending too much time in his quiet little corner of western Massachusetts. Maybe he was becoming too remote. The sooty sting of the Bronx air resonated with teeming humanity. Andrew was glad for this excuse to venture back into the messy, disorganized, vital city that had been his home for four years. Returning to the past didn't always have to be a mournful experience.

Grinning, he crossed the bridge into Manhattan.

TROY STUBBED OUT his cigarette and stared through the pane of glass at the boxlike skyscraper across the street. Somewhere inside that building on an upper floor dozens of celebrants were drinking and congratulating themselves. Five of those dozens of celebrants were the special people with whom he'd come of age. One of those five special people was Julianne.

It was nearly eight o'clock. Sooner or later he would have to make up his mind whether to join them or to head back to Penn Station to catch the next train to Montreal.

"Care for a refill?" the waitress asked.

He turned from the window to acknowledge the plump young woman, who was holding a glass decanter full of coffee. He nodded, then reached into his shirt pocket and pulled out another cigarette.

The waitress spoke English, but Troy couldn't shake the feeling that he was in a foreign land. He supposed he was. The United States had become a foreign land to him on July 4, 1972. Independence Day, he recalled with a bitter laugh.

He lit his cigarette, then propped his head in his hand and stared through the window at the Shelton Building again. His overnight bag sat on the chair beside him; he'd already arranged to crash at Peter's apartment that night—if he decided to stay. If he did, if he made it to Peter's place, he might just throttle Peter for having forwarded the invitation to him. If only Julianne had sent the damned thing to his parents, instead, he would never have received it, and he wouldn't be sitting in this dingy coffee shop now, getting wired on caffeine and nicotine and wondering when the next Amtrak left the city.

Julianne wouldn't have invited him if she hadn't forgiven him. He'd left nearly fifteen years ago, and she wasn't the sort to hold grudges, to hang on. She was probably married by now, attached to some straight, law-abiding gentleman. Damn, he should have just telephoned her when he got the forwarded invitation, and saved himself the torment of traveling all this way without knowing what to expect.

He saw an extravagantly huge white limousine pull up to the curb in front of the building across the street, and he quickly turned away. If that was the kind of party it was, Troy was sure to stick out like a sore thumb, in his faded jeans, scuffed Western-style boots and brown leather bomber jacket. He'd worn the heavy jacket because Montreal was a great deal colder than New York in March. He'd worn the jeans because they were comfortable. He'd worn the boots because he always wore boots—when he wasn't photographing a wedding—and because Julianne always used to wear Western-style boots.

But that was a long time ago. Now she probably wore high-heeled shoes, panty hose, designer dresses, lipstick. Now she was a proper executive, writing letters of invitation to magazine birthday parties on fancy stationery with her name and title engraved along the left margin.

Hell, why did he come?

TURNING THE CORNER, Laura noticed the white limousine parked in front of the building and drew to a halt. A shy smile crept across her face as she wondered what famous celebrity would be emerging from the elongated vehicle. When she'd called Julianne after receiving her invitation,

Julianne had assured her that, no matter how resplendent the gala was going to be, as far as *The Dream*'s founders were concerned, the party was definitely a come-as-you-are type thing. Laura didn't feel inhibited by the luxurious car, or embarrassed about her "flaming bad" outfit. But she shrank back a step, awed and curious to see whom the car had carried to the party.

Before the nattily uniformed chauffeur could reach the passenger door, it swung open and a lanky man wearing ridiculous mirrored sunglasses stepped out onto the sidewalk. He had short, fluffy dark blond hair and he was dressed in a wrinkled white suit with a flamboyant turquoise shirt. Laura didn't recognize him, but, then, Rita was always deriding her for not knowing who all the latest stars were.

The man noticed Laura and froze in his tracks. Then his mouth spread in a broad, exuberant grin—an eerily familiar grin, Laura realized. "Laura?" he hooted. "Laura Brodie? Is that you?"

"*Stoned?*" she shrieked, racing over to him. "Seth *Stoned*? I don't believe it!"

He wrapped her in a lusty bear hug. "What don't you believe? It's me, all right. In the flesh. Look at you," he said, releasing her from his embrace and backing up to give her an intense perusal. "Something tells me this is going to be the cliché of the evening, but you haven't changed a bit."

"You have," she claimed, laughing. The last time she'd seen Seth Stone, his hair fell below his shoulders and his wardrobe consisted almost exclusively of T-shirts with off-color sentiments stenciled onto them and jeans with bizarre patches stitched on: an American flag across the seat of one pair, an appliquéd daisy on the knee of another. And always, even in the bitter dead of winter, he wore water buffalo sandals on his bare feet. Her gaze wandered down the length of his pleated white trousers to discover his feet enclosed in bright red high-tops. She was overcome by fresh laughter.

Seth didn't appear to be at all fazed by her reaction to him. He propped his sunglasses on the top of his head so she could see his sparkling, well-lashed hazel eyes. "Now tell me, Brodie, same eyes?"

She lifted her gaze to his face. "No, Seth," she answered, her laughter replaced by a delighted smile. "They don't look nearly as bloodshot as I remember them being."

"I rarely pull all-nighters anymore," he pointed out.

"All-nighters weren't what made them bloodshot," she reminded him.

He grinned. "I don't do much of that anymore, either. I could pass any blood test in town. But look at you! Man, you look fantastic."

"I love you, too," Laura said, giving him another impulsive hug. "But you're a liar. I've gained weight."

"Two pounds, three ounces," he estimated. "You used to be too skinny. God, look at all that hair," he said, gently stroking the thick, kinky locks that drizzled down her back. "At least one of us didn't get a haircut."

If she'd thought about it, Laura might have been amazed that she felt instantly comfortable with someone she hadn't seen in close to an eternity. She plucked his sunglasses off his head and tried them on. "These are absolutely stupid," she declared. "And that car, Seth—what possessed you to buy a limousine?"

"I didn't buy it," he told her. "Just rented it for the night. I thought it would be a gas. Same with the shades," he said, adjusting them on her nose and then chuckling at how she looked in them.

"You rented the sunglasses?"

"Yeah, right," he scoffed. "Laura, where I live the sun always shines. I've got more sunglasses than Imelda Marcos has shoes."

"Where do you live?" she asked.

"Topanga Canyon. Outside L.A. Listen, pal" he called over his shoulder to the chauffeur, "stick around, get some coffee or something across the street. I've just fallen in love, so I'll be a while." He slipped his arm around Laura's waist and escorted her to the revolving door that led into the lobby of the Shelton Building.

"If it's me you've fallen in love with," Laura said, removing the sunglasses and handing them back to Seth, "I'm very flattered."

"Believe me, my intentions are totally dishonorable." Seth ushered her to the guard posted by the elevators. He produced his invitation from an inner pocket of his jacket, and the guard directed them to the seventh floor. An elevator was waiting, and they entered it. "Let me warn you," Seth continued, donning his sunglasses, "I plan to march into the party and shout, 'I just flew in from the coast.' I want to make a grand entrance."

"You could make a grand entrance with your mouth shut," Laura chided him. "Those shoes are absolutely—"

"Outrageous," Seth completed with an impish grin. "So where did you fly in from?"

"Brooklyn. My daughter and I have an apartment in Flatbush."

"Your *daughter*?" He staggered backward in an exaggerated display of shock. "You have a *daughter*?"

Laura smiled and nodded. If Rita ever had the opportunity to meet Seth, she would probably consider his strange outfit flaming good. She would probably comb the city for a pair of mirror sunglasses just like his, and a weird-looking white suit and a Day-Glo blue shirt.

"So where's your husband?" he asked.

"I haven't got one."

"Divorced?"

Laura shook her head placidly. "No."

Seth's eyebrows rose. "Very interesting. I can't wait to hear about it."

But before he could question her further, the elevator door slid open, depositing them outside a double doorway that led into a reception area mobbed with revelers. Just inside the doorway stood a trio of people: a statuesque brown-haired woman in a classically styled blue silk dress, a curvaceous blonde in a cream-colored suit and a violet crepe-de-chine blouse and a tall, clean-shaven man in a preppy get-up—khaki pants, corduroy blazer, loafers.

"Oh, boy," Seth whispered to Laura. "Déjà Vu City."

"Laura! Seth!" Kimberly broke from the trio and collided with Seth and Laura in the doorway. "You're here! Did you two come together?"

"Hardly," Laura said with a chuckle. "He came in a limo. I came on the D train."

"No, no, wait a minute," Seth silenced her. He strode through the doorway and announced, "I just flew in from the coast."

"We know that," Kimberly prattled, Seth's broad pronouncement evidently having little effect on his friends. "Julianne already told us you live in California."

"Is that really you, Andrew Collins?" Laura inquired, turning to Andrew. "Is that really your face? I never knew you had a chin."

"I needed a chin to hold all the hair," he said mildly. "You're looking wonderful, Laura."

"She's got a *daughter*," Seth proclaimed. "Do you believe it? Laura is a mother."

"Of course she is," Kimberly confirmed. "She was always mothering us. It makes sense that she should be mothering someone else these days."

"Let me get you some drinks," Julianne offered. She eyed Seth's sunglasses and suppressed a guffaw. "You," she said, "look egregious. Make sure you wear those when Connie Simmons interviews you."

"Who's Connie Simmons?" Seth asked.

"A television reporter," Andrew replied as Julianne vanished in search of some champagne punch. "Julianne has been prepping us. We're going to be on *Evening Potpourri*."

"That tacky syndicated TV magazine?" Seth protested.

"It's good publicity for *Dream*," Kimberly explained. "They're doing a kind of before-and-after piece on us and *The Dream*. It's going to air in a couple of weeks. So behave yourself, Stoned."

"I *am* behaving myself," he insisted. "Where's Troy?"

"He hasn't gotten here yet," Kimberly informed him. "Julianne said she wasn't sure whether he'd show. He didn't respond to her invitation. Maybe he never got it. She sent it to him in care of some small-press owner who published a collection of Troy's photographs a few years ago."

"Troy published a book? I think I'm impressed," said Seth. "So, Andrew, what have you done that can top that?"

"I've published a book," Andrew answered before sipping his punch.

"What am I, illiterate?" Seth asked rhetorically, spinning around to Laura. "I haven't heard of any of these books. Have you heard of any of these books?"

"No, I haven't." She turned to Andrew. "What's your book about?"

"It's a text on political economics in Latin America," he answered. "Very dry, very boring. The sort of thing that's supposed to win me tenure down the road."

"You're a professor?" she asked, thinking that that was exactly what he looked like.

"Yes, I teach at Amherst College."

"Oh, man," Seth groaned good-naturedly. "Amherst College. And I thought I was going to impress people with my fancy-dancy sunglasses."

JULIANNE LOCATED a waiter carrying a tray of drinks and secured two cups. Through the swirling throng, she could see her friends clustered near the doorway, talking and laughing.

Kimberly had been the first to arrive, looking ravishing, although her eyes were wide with barely contained panic. She had corralled Julianne, dragged her into a corner and whispered, "Don't tell anyone about me and Todd, okay? We've gotten lawyers and my life's a disaster. But we'll talk later, Okay? Not a word to the gang."

Julianne had dutifully sworn that she wouldn't breathe a hint of Kimberly's marital difficulties to any of their school chums. And then Andrew had entered, cool and quiet, his hair longish but neatly groomed and his manner reserved. The panic in Kimberly's eyes had abruptly vanished, replaced by sedate control, and she'd abandoned Julianne to greet him.

Julianne had learned from Andrew's parents, whose address she'd ferreted out of the Columbia University Admissions Office, that he was an assistant professor at Amherst College, so he had been easy to reach. She'd already known about Seth's career as a writer of raunchy film scripts, since *Dream* regularly ran movie reviews and essays on contemporary culture, much like the "Kulchah Column" Seth used to write for *Dream* when it was a fledgling newspaper. And she'd tracked down Laura's current address from the Barnard Career Office. Julianne had been delighted to learn that Laura currently lived in Brooklyn and that they would be able to see more of each other than simply a formal reunion once every fifteen years.

Julianne was happy, happy to be with her friends, happy to see them having such a good time together, catching up. She was happy that the party—she had long ago come to think of it as *her* party, not the magazine's—was going smoothly. Only one thing would make her happier: seeing Troy.

As if a fairy godmother had heard her unspoken wish, Julianne suddenly spotted the tall, lean man in a worn leather jacket and jeans standing just outside the door. His hair was an unkempt mane of black waves and his upper lip was hidden beneath a thick mustache. His dark eyes were guarded, searching the room as he hung back. A tattered duffel bag rested on the floor at his feet.

Troy had come.

Chapter Two

"Are you sure you don't mind?" Laura asked.

Seth laughed and swung open the limousine's passenger door. "Don't be silly. The thing's already paid for, whether or not I use it. Why should we waste time looking for a cab for you?" He helped her into the car, then climbed in himself. "Besides, when was the last time you got to ride in a white limousine?"

"In a former incarnation, if ever," she said with a smile. She took in her surroundings: the spacious, well-appointed interior, the soft leather upholstery, the tinted windows, the carpet as thick as the carpeting in her apartment. The arm ledges protruding from the insides of the doors were covered with a mystifying array of buttons. She fingered them, but didn't dare to push any of them.

It was all so glamorous, so—so alien. Laura wasn't sure how she felt about traveling in such a ritzy vehicle. At thirty-five years of age, she had never even owned a car. Material possessions simply weren't a major part of her life.

However, riding home in Seth's rented limo beat having to try to flag down a cab at this late hour. And getting to spend a little more time with Seth was an added bonus. Or maybe the chance to spend more time with Seth was the real reason Laura had accepted his offer of a lift, and the limousine ride was the bonus.

The chauffeur set aside the book he was reading and donned his cap. "Where to, Mr. Stone? The Sheraton?"

"No, we're going to Brooklyn," Seth informed him. "We're taking my friend home first." He pressed one of the buttons by his elbow, and a glass panel rose behind the driver's seat, sealing Laura and Seth in privacy. "What do you think?" he asked her, observing her awestruck expression as the limo pulled away from the curb.

"If you hoped to impress me, you've succeeded," said Laura. "Except..." She smiled mischievously.

"Except what?"

"I always thought these things had TVs inside them."

"Well, there's just no pleasing some women," Seth muttered, feigning annoyance. Then he chuckled. "A lot of limos do. But I specifically asked for one that didn't. If there were a TV in here, I might feel obliged to use it. And if I turned it on, I might get stuck watching one of my own movies."

"Don't tell me they show movies like *Coed Summer* on television!"

"With extensive editing," Seth told her. "But you know, not everything I write is R-rated. I've done a few made-for-TV jobs—*Black Market Babies*, *Rich Intimacies*, *Barrio Warlords*...."

"What uplifting subjects," Laura teased him. "I hope they pay you well for writing such trash."

Seth accepted her criticism with a lackadaisical shrug. "I ain't kicking. The bottom line is, it's fun."

"I'm glad," Laura said. She meant it, too. Seth had always been one to pursue things for the sheer fun of it. She'd hate to think that he had turned into a mercenary, writing nonsensical film scripts only because he lusted after money.

She nestled into the deep cushions and sighed contentedly. Seth turned to her and absorbed her weary smile. "Tired?" he asked.

She nodded.

"The night is young, my love."

"In California, maybe," she conceded. "We're on Eastern time now. You'd better get used to it."

"By the time I get used to it I'll be on the plane back to L.A."

"How long are you planning to stay in New York?"

"Till Sunday afternoon. I figured I ought to spend at least one full day on the ground before heading for home. But jet lag never bothers me much," he assured her. "I can get by on only a few hours of sleep."

"Just like in college," Laura recalled. She compared the energetic, freewheeling, hirsute young Seth of her memory with the serene, dimple-smiled man seated beside her. Too many years might have passed since she'd last seen him, but his humor was just as infectious as it used to be, and his eyes still glinted with life, and his hair—in its abbreviated length—was still lustrous with pale blond streaks visible even in the darkened interior of the car. "I'm so glad you came tonight, Seth," she murmured. "I've missed you. We should have kept in touch over the years."

He nodded and brushed a stray lock of her hair back from her cheek. The gesture warmed her. She and Seth had always been close, close enough to touch each other without attaching any significance to the act. Sitting with him now in his rented limousine seemed as natural to her as sitting with him on an overcrowded chartered bus to Washington, or on a subway downtown to Greenwich Village, or on a bed in a dormitory room as they plotted a series of essays for *The Dream*.

"I'm a lousy letter writer," he said, responding to her wistful comment. "People who write for a living shouldn't have to write in their spare time, too."

"We could have kept in touch by telephone," Laura noted. "At least, you could have. My budget's tighter than yours."

"Yeah, and how many years were you living on that commune in the sticks? You said you didn't even have electricity up there, let alone a telephone."

"That's true," Laura conceded. "But even so...I wish it hadn't taken all of us fifteen years to get back together. It was so good seeing everybody." Her eyes glowed happily as she reflected on the reunion. "Everybody's doing such exciting things with their lives. You're out in Hollywood—"

"Writing trash," Seth reminded her.

"And having fun. And Julianne's got the magazine, and Andrew's a professor. Kimberly's working for Senator Milford. Troy's got his own photography studio...."

"And you're helping unwed mothers. That's exciting, too."

"No," Laura disagreed. "It's rewarding and it's fulfilling, but I wouldn't call it 'exciting.'" She didn't want to think about her own work. Yes, it was rewarding and fulfilling, but it could also be downright frustrating, and even depressing at times. Although she and Neil hadn't gotten married when she found out she was pregnant, at least she had been fairly mature and well educated, and she had wanted the baby. Most of the mothers she counseled in her job were teenagers, totally unprepared for the difficult tasks that motherhood entailed. Laura's clients hadn't become pregnant because they were bursting with love but for quite the opposite reason—because they were sorely in need of someone to love them. Their actions were grounded not in idealism but in carelessness and ignorance.

Laura knew she was doing something important in her work. But to write speeches for a senator, or editorials for a national magazine, or lectures for the young wizards who attended Amherst College, or, for that matter, screenplays for silly television movies like *Barrio Warlords*—such careers had to be more exciting than what she did.

"Didn't everyone look great?" she mused, preferring to concentrate on her friends rather than herself. "Kimberly is just as gorgeous as ever—"

"Once a prom queen, always a prom queen," Seth summed up. "I've got to admit, I was surprised she's still 'Belmont.' She didn't strike me as the sort of woman who'd keep her maiden name after she got married."

"I always knew she was a feminist," Laura remarked.

"Yeah, but whose initials did they use on the monogrammed silverware? That's the sort of thing that used to matter to Kim."

"You underestimate her," Laura scolded him. "You guys always did. Just because she married her hometown sweetheart doesn't mean she doesn't possess a healthy streak of independence."

"Uh-huh," Seth snorted dubiously. "So, what were you independent feminists cackling about when Andrew and Troy and I were dealing with that Connie Simmons person?"

"About how funny you looked in your sunglasses and about how clean-cut Andrew looked without his beard."

"What about Troy?" Seth goaded her. "How come you weren't laughing at him?"

Laura's smile waned. "He seemed so lost, Seth. Kim and I noticed it right away, that sadness in his eyes. Julianne didn't want to talk about it, though. She just kept saying, 'At least he came. At least he's here.' Did you know Kim's staying at Julianne's place tonight? I'm meeting them there for lunch tomorrow. God, I'm glad they're back in my life. I missed them."

"You must have known Julianne was living in the city when you moved to Brooklyn. Why haven't you contacted her before now?"

Laura shifted slightly in her seat. Why, indeed? It would have been easy enough. She knew that Julianne ran *Dream* magazine; she could have called their editorial office and asked to speak to the editor in chief.

But the move from Buffalo had been exhausting, and beginning a new job and getting Rita settled in at a new school... And then Laura had wondered whether Julianne would have wanted to see her. Julianne was a reputable executive, polished, elevated above the world Laura inhabited. Laura had had enough experience with childless professional women to know that she functioned on a different wavelength than they. When she had lunch with her unmarried colleagues at work, they either spent the entire time talking about shopping at Bloomingdale's, attending singles' weekends at resorts in the Catskills, refinishing antique chests of drawers—activities for which Laura lacked the time, the money and the interest—or else they focused the entire discussion on Rita, as if Rita were the only thing in Laura's life worth talking about. Women in positions like Julianne's didn't seem to understand Laura, and she usually avoided them.

She shouldn't have avoided Julianne, though. She shouldn't have assumed that Julianne wouldn't want to make time in her life for a harried single mother who made a career of counseling other harried single mothers. "Well," Laura resolved, "tomorrow we can start making up for lost time." She turned fully to Seth. "And what were you guys cackling about while we were dealing with Connie Simmons?"

"Mostly about how funny I looked in my sunglasses," Seth joked. "Actually, they were psyched to hear about all the little starlets I work with."

"Sure," Laura scoffed.

Seth abruptly grew solemn. "They've both had kind of a rough time of it, Laura. You're right. Troy isn't all that happy in Montreal. I told him he ought to come home, let bygones be bygones and move back to the States, but he said no, he didn't think he ever would. And Andrew..." Seth drifted off.

"What about Andrew?" Laura prodded him.

"Well, he told us about his wife. Kind of by accident, I think. I got the clear impression he really didn't want to talk about it, but—"

"His wife? Andrew's married?"

"Was. She died a few years ago. The truth was, we weren't cackling much at all."

"Oh, God." For a moment Laura couldn't think of anything else to say. "I wish he'd told me."

"Why? What would you have done?"

Laura ruminated. They'd all grown a lot in fifteen years, grown up, grown old. But to be widowed—were they really old enough to be widowed? "I would have put my arms around him and given him a big hug," she said.

"Why don't you give me a big hug, instead?" Seth suggested.

Laura slid close to him on the seat and he wrapped his arm comfortingly around her. She rested her head on his shoulder and sighed. The solid warmth of Seth's lean body was almost enough to dispel the chilly ache in the pit of her stomach at the thought of Andrew's loss. "He looked so good without the beard, and in those spiffy eyeglasses," she recalled. "Remember how he used to look in his old wire-rims?"

"He looked professorial," Seth remarked. "And now he's a hotshot professor. Don't get all mopey on me, Laura. He's doing just fine. And anyway, you lost a lover, too. I've lost thousands of them myself. *C'est la vie* and all that."

"I didn't lose a lover," Laura disputed him. "If you're talking about Rita's father, I didn't lose him. He just left."

Seth angled his head to view her. She wondered whether he was going to question her about Neil, the dynamic, ruggedly handsome man she'd met and fallen in love with when she was living on the commune. She had long ago stopped loving him, and she had forgiven him for his having fled from the commune shortly after Rita was born. Neil wasn't a bad man, only a weak one. Laura felt sorry for him; he had deliberately chosen to miss out on the special joy of raising a child. She pitied him and she forgave him. Forgiveness came easily to Laura.

But she didn't want to explain all that to Seth. She didn't know whether she could. People who knew about Neil were always getting on Laura's case. "Why don't you sue him for support money? Why don't you get a bloodthirsty lawyer to drag the bastard over the coals?" Laura wasn't vindictive, and she had no desire to force anything out of Neil. She didn't even know where he was living anymore.

She waited for Seth to speak, hoping that he wouldn't demand to hear the entire story of Rita's birth. She would tell Seth about it someday if he wanted, but not tonight, not while she was still savoring the pleasant shock of having seen all her old friends.

Blessedly, Seth refrained from probing. All he asked was "Is Rita going to be awake when we get to your place? I want to meet this daughter of yours."

Laura twisted Seth's arm to read his wristwatch. "It's nearly one o'clock. If she's still awake she's in big trouble."

The limousine had crossed the Manhattan Bridge into Brooklyn, and the driver rapped on the glass barrier with his knuckles. Seth dutifully pressed the button to lower the barrier. "Directions, Mr. Stone?" the driver requested.

"Listen to this guy," Seth whispered to Laura. "He sounds like he graduated from the London School of Genteel Servants."

"You get what you pay for," Laura teased him, once again surveying her plush environment and shaking her head in awe. She provided the driver with instructions on how to reach her address, then snuggled into Seth's shoulder. Perhaps Troy wasn't happy living in Montreal, and Andrew had lost his wife, but Seth at least was enjoying a fairy-tale existence. "Thousands of lovers, huh," she pondered. "Were they all starlets?"

"No," Seth answered with a straight face. "Probably no more than seven or eight hundred of them were starlets."

Laura laughed softly. "Seriously, Seth. Tell me what your life is like. I can't imagine ever having enough money to rent a limousine." If someday, by some fluke, she did have that much money, she doubted she'd spend it on a limousine. But she was awfully curious, in a detached, anthropological way, to hear what life could be like when one was rich and surrounded by starlets.

"I rarely travel in limousines," Seth confessed. "I own a Porsche 944, and I use it to zip around the canyon roads and give myself cheap thrills."

"What's your house like?" she asked. "Do you have a hot tub?"

Seth guffawed. "I don't have a hot tub, and I don't have a water bed, and I don't have a mirrored ceiling in my bedroom. I don't do cocaine. I don't play tennis. I don't kiss strangers. I don't own a sailboat or a tuxedo. And I don't call people 'sweetheart' if I can help it. Anything else you want to know?"

"You still haven't told me what your house is like," Laura commented.

"It's not too big—eight rooms, if you count the breakfast room separately from the kitchen. Modern. Stuck halfway up a hillside. If there's ever a mud slide in our neighborhood, it's Sayonara City," Seth told her. "I've got a huge doghouse in the backyard, where my dog, Barney, lives. And I've got a garage, where my Porsche lives.''

"Do you have a garden?'' she asked. She was trying her best to picture Seth's home, but it seemed as alien to her as the limousine.

He shook his head. ''I thought about starting one, and then in the nick of time I came to my senses and convinced myself that the canyon was too dry. Actually, it isn't—some of my neighbors have gardens—but keeping a garden going is too much effort, so I decided to pretend the climate was wrong for it.''

"So what do you have in the yard? Grass?''

"A little. Mostly scrub, ground cover, whatever doesn't take any work to maintain.'' He drew her more snugly to himself. The lapel of his jacket was surprisingly soft against her cheek, and his neck smelled faintly of a musky after-shave. ''You ought to come out to California and see the place for yourself, Laura,'' he said.

"Do you mean that?''

"Of course I mean it. What do you say? You could go swimming in the Pacific, get a genuine 'It Never Rains In Southern California' tan, and tool around town with me in the Porsche. I'll even throw in the 'Homes of the Stars' tour at no extra charge.''

"I'd love to,'' she said impetuously, not bothering to consider where she'd get the money to make such a trip, or whether she could secure some vacation time, or what she'd do with Rita while she was away. She hadn't told Seth that she *would* visit him, only that she'd love to. Which was the truth.

The driver brought her back to reality by asking, ''We're on Ocean Avenue now. Which building is yours, ma'am?''

Laura caught Seth's eye and stifled the urge to giggle. Hearing the driver call her ''ma'am'' was as jarring as hearing him call Seth "Mr. Stone." "It's the one by the fire hydrant, on the right," she informed the driver.

Seth peered at the massive old apartment building, its entry pillars and rococo embellishments contrasting with the spray-paint graffiti that marred one brownstone wall. The building—like the neighborhood—was clearly long past its heyday, not quite a slum but evolving in that direction. "Are you sure it's all right if I come up?" he asked Laura.

"Why wouldn't it be all right?"

"I don't know. What does your daughter think when you bring strange men to your apartment?"

Laura laughed. "She's a big girl, Seth. And you're a friend. Although you *are* pretty strange, I've got to admit."

He pretended to be offended. "Just for that," he warned Laura as he shoved open the door, "I'm going to embarrass you mercilessly in front of the kid."

"That shouldn't be difficult for you," Laura parried. "Just be yourself."

Seth faked a scowl and jammed his sunglasses onto his nose. By the time he and Laura had left the car, however, they were both laughing. He held the building's outer door for Laura and waited patiently while she dug her key out of her purse and unlocked the inner door to the foyer. A few dusty tables and a horsehair sofa stood in the dimly lit lobby. Laura wondered whether the place looked seedy to Seth. It looked seedy to her, but she was used to it.

That she should care about Seth's opinion of her home surprised her. She'd never been one to worry about keeping up with the Joneses; the fact that her school friends were more affluent than Laura didn't bother her. She was proud of what she'd accomplished, and there wasn't a single thing in her life that she would have done differently if she'd had the chance: not living on the commune, not becoming pregnant, not raising Rita by herself, not leaving the com-

mune and moving to Buffalo, earning her master's degree in
social work, then moving to Brooklyn. Not a thing she'd
want changed.

Except, perhaps, for a more brightly lit lobby in her
apartment building and a less nosy super than Mr. San-
tiago—who, Laura knew, was spying on her through the
peephole in his door as she escorted Seth into the building—and an elevator that didn't wheeze eerily between
floors two and three.

Seth removed his sunglasses when the elevator ground to
a halt on the fifth floor. The hallway smelled of onions;
Mrs. Cobb in Apartment 5-D had a tendency to cook casseroles at odd hours. Trying to ignore the strong odor, Laura
led Seth to the end of the corridor and unlocked the door.

Light streamed into the entry hall from the living room,
and Laura heard the muffled babble of the television set.
She wasn't the strictest disciplinarian in the world, but with
Seth by her side, she decided she ought to appear at least a
little bit miffed at the girls for having stayed up so late.
Pressing her lips together, she marched into the living
room—to discover Rita and Courtney both fast asleep on
the couch, Rita curled up in one corner and Courtney
sprawled dramatically across the cushions, her head balanced precariously against the sofa's arm. An empty container of frozen yogurt stood on the coffee table in front of
them, along with two gooey spoons.

"Which one's yours?" Seth asked impishly, drifting into
the room behind Laura and evidently finding the scene
amusing.

Laura couldn't deny that she was also amused. "I think
the one in the corner," she answered Seth as she crossed to
the television set and turned it off.

The sudden silence roused both girls, who stirred, grunted
and opened their eyes. "Hi, Ma," Rita mumbled groggily.
Then her gaze wandered to Seth and sharpened. She sat up

and stared at him for a long minute, giving him a detailed inspection before turning back to her mother. "Who's that?" she asked.

"*That*," Laura replied, slipping her hand through the bend in Seth's arm and leading him toward her daughter, "is Seth Stone, a school friend of mine. Seth, meet my daughter, Rita. And this is her friend Courtney."

Seth seemed bemused by the sight of Laura's daughter. Not that Rita was peculiar-looking—certainly no more peculiar-looking than most thirteen-year-old girls. But Laura suspected that he still hadn't come to terms with the fact that one of his contemporaries—one of his friends—could be the mother of a person, an adolescent-type person, who stood five feet four inches and wore metallic enamel on her fingernails.

Rita was undoubtedly equally bemused by Seth's presence. Laura rarely dated, even more rarely brought a man home to the apartment—and the men she introduced to Rita never wore white suits and red high-tops. Indeed, none of them looked even remotely as hip as Seth. Rita sized him up again and then glanced at Courtney. The two girls giggled.

"I guess I'd better go," Courtney said, as usual much more diplomatic than Rita. She eyed Seth, then covered her mouth with her hand and giggled some more. "I'll see you, Rita," she said as she stood.

"Hang on, Courtney. Let me take you home," Laura offered. "It's awfully late."

"I could give her a ride home in the limo," Seth suggested.

Laura started to explain that since Courtney lived on the second floor of the building the only vehicle she needed to ride home in was the elevator, but before she could speak, the two girls were shrieking. "A limo? Ma-a! Does he have a limo?"

Laura rolled her eyes and grinned reproachfully at Seth. "Now see what you've done," she muttered.

"What's wrong with what I did?" Seth protested. "I gave you a ride home. Why can't I give your daughter's friend a ride home?"

"She lives in this building," Laura informed him.

But it was too late. The girls were clamoring to see the limousine. "Come on, Ma," Rita begged. "Just let us look at it. Come on! I've never seen one, except at Grampa's funeral, and that doesn't count because it was a funeral. Okay? Just one spin around the block, okay?"

Laura opened her mouth to respond, but closed it when she saw Rita and Courtney racing toward the door. She turned to Seth. "Oh, come on, *Ma*," he whispered, taking her hand and dragging her out of the apartment with the girls.

The truth was, Laura wasn't much good at pretending to be angry. And she really wasn't angry about taking the girls outside to look at the limousine, even at the ungodly hour of 1:20 a.m. Tomorrow was Saturday; they'd all sleep late. And while looking at a limo wasn't high on Laura's list of important things one ought to do during the course of one's life, she knew that Rita probably wouldn't have another opportunity to see a limo—or ride in one—until Laura's mother passed away. Or Laura herself. Such eventualities, Laura hoped, were far, far in Rita's future. Feeling rather generous, she decided to let Seth take Rita and Courtney for a ride in the car.

The driver set down his book and smiled stoically as the two giddy, overtired girls darted to the limo and shrieked some more. "Look, Rita, it's white!" Courtney observed. "This is one radical car."

"What's she talking about?" Seth asked Laura. "I always thought the most radical car you could own was a VW van with a peace sign painted on the roof."

"'Radical' means cool," Laura translated. "If they call something 'radical,' they mean it's far-out."

"Uh-huh," Seth grunted. "And I thought people talked funny in Hollywood." He chivalrously opened the passenger door, then lifted the jump seats up from the floor for the girls. "Hop into my chariot, lovely ladies," he said, gesturing them inside.

Rita and Courtney giggled again. "Wait till I tell my mother about this," Courtney squealed.

"Forget your mother," Rita contradicted her. "Wait till we tell Becky LoCaffio!"

"Yeah! Can we drive past Becky's building?" Courtney asked Seth.

"At this hour," Laura pointed out dryly, sliding along the seat to make room for Seth, "I doubt that Becky will be awake."

"Who cares? She's such a flaming slime," Rita said brightly. "Let's drive past her building, anyway. This car is great, Seth. What are you, a drug dealer or something?"

"No," Seth replied calmly. "I'm not a drug dealer. Does your mother usually hang out with drug dealers?"

Rita shrugged. "So how come you've got this car?"

"He rented it," Laura explained, then called to the driver to cruise slowly around the block.

Rita seemed much too excited to care whether they actually drove past Becky LoCaffio's building. "You rented it? Just for the party?" She knelt on the jump seat to face her mother. "I told you you should have worn something nicer."

"What's wrong with what your mother's wearing?" Seth defended Laura. "I think she looks wonderful."

"Yuck," Rita grumbled. "So, did you and my mom go out in college?"

"Go out? As in 'date'?" Seth appeared to find Rita's tactless questions refreshing. "No truth to the rumor. We were just friends."

"Yeah," Rita concurred. "Ma's told me she dated mostly weenies in college."

"Did you?" Seth asked, turning to Laura. "You dated Mark Hofkiss. He wasn't a weenie. At least, I don't think he was. What's a weenie, anyway?"

"Mark Hofkiss wasn't one," Laura agreed. "But we only went out a few times. Most of them were weenies, Seth. Rita's right about that."

Courtney had discovered the control buttons on the door and was systematically trying them all out. The glass panel slid up and down; reading lights flickered on and off; music filled the compartment and then stopped. Seth laughed, and so did Laura. It was fun taking the girls for a brief drive.

And driving in the limousine gave Laura a few more minutes with Seth. She was exhausted, but she wasn't ready to say goodbye to him yet. The understanding that he was going to be back in California Sunday night saddened Laura more than she might have expected. They had only just renewed their friendship, after all. They had only just found each other again. She didn't want to have to wait another fifteen years before she got to spend time with him again.

"On a bus," he was telling the girls, and Laura directed her attention to the conversation. "It was a bus to Washington, D.C., one of the buses Columbia chartered. Right, Laura?"

"You mean, when we met?"

Seth looped his arm around Laura's shoulders and turned back to the girls, who were listening attentively. "The Moratorium, November of 1969. We wound up sitting together even though we didn't know each other. The bus left the city at some ghastly hour, and by the time we hit Newark, your mother had fallen asleep on my shoulder. Do you believe it? Never saw me before, and she was already sleeping with me." He winked at Laura. "Am I shocking your daughter?"

Laura chuckled, unconcerned. "Rita is basically unshockable."

"So what was this Moratorium thing?" Rita wanted to know.

"What was this Moratorium *thing*?" Seth echoed, astounded. "This Moratorium *thing*, as you call it, was a march on Washington to end the war."

"The Vietnam War," Laura supplied, aware that the history curriculum of Rita's school wasn't all that it ought to be. "It was a huge march, with folks pouring in from all over the country. They had National Guardsmen standing on the roofs of all the federal buildings, armed with rifles. Remember?"

Seth nodded. "And it was freezing cold. And Peter, Paul and Mary sang 'Blowing in the Wind.' And we marched and sang and drank some wine that someone was passing around, and then we all piled onto the bus and traveled back to New York."

"And the war went on for another four-odd years," Laura concluded with a bittersweet smile.

"Well, at least we got a friendship out of it," Seth reflected, giving Laura a squeeze. "So when we found ourselves stuck in the same rhetorics class a few years later, we were naturals for working together on a class project."

"*The Dream*," Rita said with exaggerated boredom. "Ma told me all about that already. Ever since she got invited to that party it's all she's been talking about."

"Well," said Laura, justifying herself, "I was excited about getting to see my old friends. If you and Courtney didn't see each other for fifteen years you'd be excited about a reunion, too."

"That'll never happen," Courtney swore. "We're going to share an apartment when we finish high school. We already worked it all out."

This was news to Laura, but she let it pass without comment. By next week, she suspected, that plan would be supplanted by a new plan: Rita and Courtney running off together to join a circus. Or moving to Puerto Rico together to live with Courtney's grandmother. Or applying to attend M.I.T. together. Or opening a clothing store in the East Village and making lots of money together.

"So what's your thing, Seth?" Rita asked bluntly. "How come you've got the bucks for a car like this?"

"She means, what do you do for a living?" Laura helpfully interpreted her daughter's question. Then she smiled at Rita and Courtney. "You're going to love this, girls. He writes screenplays."

"What do you mean, screenplays?" Courtney asked.

"For movies," Seth explained. "I write scripts for movies."

The girls shared a glance, not certain how to react. "What movies?" Rita asked.

"I've written some of the *Ax Man* movies," Seth told her.

"*Ax Man*? You wrote *Ax Man*?" Courtney and Rita squealed in unison.

"Not the original, but three of the sequels."

"Oh." The girls lapsed into a worshipful silence. Then Courtney turned to Rita. "I like your mom's friend," she declared in a stage whisper that caused Seth and Laura to laugh.

"As you can see, I know the way to a girl's heart," Seth murmured to Laura. "All it takes is one white limo and one fictional psychotic killer armed with a hatchet."

"You sure do know all the right moves," Laura concurred with a chuckle.

The limousine had returned to Laura's building and coasted to a halt in front of the fire hydrant. "Show's over, girls," Seth said, swinging the door open and helping the passengers out.

"Thank you, Seth," Courtney said, then elbowed Rita, who vocalized her thanks, as well. If Courtney wanted to share an apartment with Rita, Laura decided, she would give the girls her blessing. Courtney was definitely a good influence on her daughter.

"The pleasure's all mine," Seth said grandly.

He rode with them to the second floor, waiting in the elevator with Rita while Laura walked Courtney to the Gonzalez apartment and saw her safely inside. "I don't know what your plans are," Laura remarked as they continued up to the fifth floor, "but you're more than welcome to spend the night here. The living room sofa isn't that uncomfortable—Rita sleeps on it all the time," she couldn't resist adding. Her joke earned her a withering look from Rita.

"I've got a room reserved at the Sheraton Center in Manhattan," said Seth.

Laura nodded. Given that he was used to traveling in limousines—or in Porsche 944's—he probably would prefer to stay at a fancy hotel rather than in her homey but distinctly unluxurious apartment. "Well," she said as they entered the oniony hallway that led to her apartment, "then I guess this is goodbye." She hoped she didn't sound too glum.

If she did sound glum, Seth looked even glummer. He gazed at Laura for a long time, memorizing her upturned face, the sensuous waves of her hair and her dark, resonant eyes. Then his face brightened. "Screw the Sheraton," he decided. "I'll stay here."

Laura tried not to look too pleased as she unlocked the apartment door and opened it. Seth hovered in the doorway, then said, "Let me run downstairs to get my bag—it's in the trunk of the limo."

"Okay. Just buzz from the lobby and I'll let you back inside," Laura told him. She and Rita stood in the doorway, watching as the elevator carried Seth away. Then Laura turned to Rita. "You've got all of thirteen seconds to get ready for bed, toots," she said as sternly as she could.

Rita ignored her. "Are you sure he's sleeping on the couch?"

"Positive. I have to disappoint you, Ms. Buttinsky, but Seth wasn't kidding when he said we were just friends."

"You ought to give that some thought, Ma," Rita advised her as she headed toward her bedroom. "He wrote *Ax Man* and he rides around in a limo. He's definitely not a weenie."

"No, he's definitely not." Laura had to agree.

"He's got nice eyes, too," Rita called over her shoulder before shutting herself into her bedroom.

He does have nice eyes, Laura mused silently as she gathered up the sticky spoons and the yogurt container and carried them into the kitchen. Seth had always had nice eyes, even after he'd pulled an all-nighter or indulged in the sort of excesses that had won him the nickname "Stoned." His eyes, no matter how bloodshot or bleary, were always dancing with laughter, always sparkling with a dazzling multitude of colors. Laura was infinitely glad he was going to stay for the night.

She was on her way to the linen closet to get a sheet and a pillow for him, when she heard the buzz of the intercom. After she pressed the button that unlocked the door to the building's lobby, she fixed up the couch for him. Like all her furniture, the couch was old and battered, but she knew it was comfortable. She herself slept on it whenever her mother came for a visit.

Seth rang the doorbell as Laura was tucking the blanket around the cushions. Straightening, she noticed the line of light beneath Rita's bedroom door flicker out. There was no reason to feel relieved that Rita was in bed for the night, other than ordinary maternal concern for a daughter who had stayed up way past her bedtime. Yet Laura did feel relieved. Nothing was going to happen between her and Seth. But she didn't want her daughter to witness that nothing.

She moved to the entry hall and opened the door for him. He lingered in the doorway for a minute, one hand clutching a lightweight garment bag and the other the doorjamb. "Excuse me, is this the Sheraton?" he asked.

"Flatbush Annex," Laura said, playing along. "Your room is all ready, sir."

"'Sir,'" he snorted as he entered the apartment. "That's almost as bad as 'Mr. Stone.'" He set his bag down in the center of the living room and inspected the couch. "Would I be out of line if I asked where you're sleeping tonight?" he inquired, grinning mischievously.

Laura shrugged, refusing to read anything serious into his question. "I guess that depends on your reason for asking."

His gaze roamed the room, examining the mismatched but clean furnishings and the numerous potted plants adorning the windowsill and the end tables. Then he focused on Laura and his smile expanded. "Hey, you lived on a commune, don't forget. A guy can't help but be curious."

Laura knew Seth well enough to recognize that he was teasing her. "Even during my communal youth I was never an advocate of free love."

"Okay. How much do you charge?"

Laura gave him a playful shove. "If I'd known you were going to act like this, Seth, I never would have invited you to stay."

He captured her hands and drew them to his sides. Then he wrapped his arms around her and planted a gentle kiss on her forehead. "I'll be a good boy," he promised. "But you can't blame me for thinking these past fifteen years have done you good, lady. Even just holding you feels great."

Holding Seth felt great, too. Laura tilted her head back to view him, then lightly touched her lips to his. It was an impulsive action; she intended it only as a way of sealing their restored friendship. Yet his eyes seemed suddenly to brighten, and his hands held her just a touch more firmly.

"Uh-oh," he said ominously, unable to suppress his smile as he gazed down at Laura. "Is passion about to rear its ugly head?"

His remark prompted her to laugh. "Let's be grown-ups, Seth," she began.

"That's exactly what we *were* being," he noted.

"Yes, well..." She drew in another deep breath. "You're going to sleep on the couch and I'm going to sleep in my bedroom, so whatever you've got in mind had better accommodate that fact."

"You're hard, woman," he complained, though he was grinning. "Were you always this sensible?"

"Always," she insisted.

He reflected for a moment, then nodded. "I guess you were. Okay. Take your hands off me, and I might just let you go to sleep."

Laura complied, but not before giving him a good-night hug. She crossed to the hall, then hesitated. "Listen, Seth— I don't know if you brought pajamas with you, but if you didn't...please be discreet. Rita's at a funny age."

"So am I," he countered. "Don't worry, Brodie. From here on in I'll be the epitome of good taste."

"That'll be the day, Ax Man," she scoffed before vanishing into her bedroom.

Chapter Three

Someone was watching him.

There was a time in Seth's life when he believed that being paranoid was as essential to his sense of self as knowing all the lyrics to Bob Dylan's "Positively Fourth Street" or all of Dennis Hopper's lines in *Easy Rider*. There was a time when paranoia was as faddish as bell-bottom blue jeans, as hip as granola, as ubiquitous as Boone's Farm Apple Wine. You were supposed to be paranoid; before lighting a joint, you were supposed to look over your shoulder, fully expecting to see a cop standing there spying on you. You were supposed to call the cop a pig and hate him, and presume that he hated you, too. In retrospect, Seth couldn't shake the notion that smoking grass had been pretty boring in and of itself and that the high had actually come from the special thrill of paranoia, the giddy understanding that one of "them" might be right behind you, just waiting to blow your head off if you smiled the wrong way.

Until Laura had reminded him, he had all but forgotten about the armed National Guardsmen who had been posted on the roofs of downtown Washington buildings during the Moratorium march, perfect symbols of the paranoia prevalent at that time. What Seth had remembered was the numbingly cold weather, the gray, threatening sky, the frizzy-haired, friendly Barnard girl who had sat next to him on the bus. He had remembered the walk, too, the mass of humanity surging along Constitution Avenue and assembling on the Mall in the shadow of the Washington Monument. He had remembered everyone stepping back to make way for a group from Vietnam Veterans against the War. One of their number wore opaque-lens spectacles that marked him as blind and rode in a wheelchair bedecked with black flags.

Those were days designed for paranoia. But today Seth rarely suffered from that sort of "us" versus "them" neurosis. Today he called cops "officers," or sometimes even "peace officers," and experienced a twinge of relief whenever he saw one late at night. Today he rarely felt as if he were being watched.

Yet he sensed that someone was watching him now. Not quite asleep and not quite awake, he lay prostrate on the couch in Laura's living room, trying to muster either the strength to wake up fully or else the nerve to go right on sleeping while the day passed around him. He could easily justify such laziness—no matter how late it was in Brooklyn, it was three hours earlier in California, and nobody could possibly expect his inner clock to have adjusted to Eastern time yet. He was entitled to sleep in.

Only he wasn't at the hotel, and he wasn't alone. He was in Laura's apartment, in her home. Being watched.

He had enjoyed a montage of dreams during the night, but he couldn't remember any of the dreams specifically. All he remembered was that every dream had been pleasant, relaxing, delightful. Images of the previous evening's party had intermingled with memories of his college days, of writing exuberant articles critiquing popular songs, films and television shows for *The Dream*. But the most pleasant, delightful part of last night had been spending time with Laura. And that hadn't been a dream at all.

Aging had definitely improved her. He liked the mature curves of her body—she really had been too skinny in college—and the generous fullness of her face. Her nose seemed less prominent now, and her eyes rounder and darker. No one would ever mistake her for a Hollywood starlet, but so what? Starlets were like potato chips—tasty, fine for snacking, but they left you hungry. Laura was substantial. She was solid and ripe. She was strong, independent, self-sufficient, giving. She was a real woman, a mother.

A mother... Oh, no. Where the hell was the blanket? Why didn't he feel its weight on him? Had he kicked it off in his sleep? He was always shoving off his blanket at home; he liked to feel the fresh night air on his skin, and he invariably woke up to discover the blanket crumpled up at the foot of the bed or heaped on the floor. No doubt the blanket Laura had given him was on the floor now, and Seth was sprawled out on the sofa in his birthday suit for all the world to view. *Please,* he prayed silently, *please, if I'm being watched, let it be by Laura, not by Rita.*

He cautiously opened one eye. All he could see was the faded brown brocade of the fabric covering the arm of the couch. Inhaling for courage, he opened the other eye, then lifted himself from the cushion and glanced over his shoulder.

Rita slouched in the arched opening connecting the living room to the hall. She wore a pair of balloon-legged jeans with a floral pattern on the denim, a T-shirt and an enormous lime-green knit vest with armholes that reached nearly to her waist. Her dark hair was brushed upward to resemble a spiked helmet, and large silver trapezoids hung from her ears. Her eyes resembled Laura's, Seth observed. They were large and dark, and they were riveted on him.

He cringed and turned his gaze to the carpet beside the couch. Uh-huh. There was the blanket.

"So, Rita," he said as calmly as he could, dangling his arm over the edge of the sofa in an attempt to snare the blanket without exposing himself. "Have you taken any anatomy courses in school yet?"

Rita giggled.

"If you haven't—" he caught the blanket with his fingers and hoisted it up over his body "—let me explain to you what it was you just saw." He gathered the blanket around himself before sitting. "What you just saw was a very embarrassed man."

"You've got a cute tush," Rita told him.

If he had been embarrassed to start with, Rita's comment increased the feeling tenfold. "What on earth would a nice young lady like you know about men's tushes?" he asked, deciding that his best tactic was to act indignant.

"I know some stuff," Rita declared slyly. "You think you're the only naked man who's ever been in our home?"

"I think..." Seth faltered. He supposed he ought to assume that Laura had men visiting her from time to time. But in all honesty, he would rather not know about the other men in her life. "I think," he resumed, "that I'm probably the only man stupid enough to let your mother's daughter see his tush."

Rita giggled again. "Here, I'll show you something," she said, bounding across the room to a cabinet that held a record player and a shelf of records. She flipped through the records until she found the album she was looking for. Sliding it from the shelf, she carried it to Seth and dropped onto the sofa next to him.

Refusing to let Rita realize how disconcerted he was by the situation, he tucked the blanket securely about his waist and offered a weak smile before accepting the album from her. He recognized it at once: it was the three-record *Woodstock* album, complete with a blurry photograph on the jacket of a man and a woman skinny-dipping in a muddy pool beneath the leafy bough of a tree. The man's rear end was only partially visible in the picture, but Seth imagined that to a thirteen-year-old girl, the murky photograph represented the ultimate in smut.

"So, speaking tush-wise, I compare favorably to this yo-yo?" he asked Rita.

"You're all right, Seth," Rita solemnly told him. "I think sleeping nude is radical, but Ma says I've got to wear pajamas till I'm sixteen."

"Your mother says that?" Seth let out a surprised laugh. He was having enough difficulty reconciling himself to the fact that Laura had a teenage daughter. But to learn that Laura laid down rules and regulations just like a normal parent seemed incredible. "Why sixteen? What's supposed to happen when you're sixteen?"

Rita shrugged. "I don't know. But I want a big party. One of my friends, her sister had a sweet-sixteen party at a restaurant, and everybody got all duded up, and they even had a deejay. That's the kind of party I want."

This from a child born on a commune, Seth mused wryly. He set the *Woodstock* record on the coffee table and tried to figure out how he could get himself to the bathroom without embarrassing himself further. "Where's your mother?" he asked.

"She went out to buy some breakfast for you. Did you go to Woodstock?"

"Sort of," he said, settling against the cushions and drawing the blanket up over his shoulders like an imitation Indian chief. He couldn't see any way of escaping to the bathroom before Laura got home. He would just have to chat with Rita until then and pretend he didn't feel like a first-class jerk.

"What do you mean, 'sort of'?"

"My friends and I got as far as Goshen before we gave up. Everyone thinks of Woodstock as the ultimate concert—

which it was—and all those good vibes. But the *real* story of Woodstock is that it was the biggest traffic jam in the history of the world. They closed the New York Thruway, you know? We were all stuck on the road in the rain. Nobody could drive anywhere. So we strolled from car to car and rapped with the other kids.'' He gazed at the album and smiled in reminiscence. ''There was a truck in the middle of the mess, a farm truck filled with peaches. I guess the guy was trying to get them to market, but he realized he wasn't going to reach his destination on time, so he just climbed onto the back of the truck and started handing out the peaches to anyone who wanted one. There must have been dozens of us, hundreds of us, stuck on Route 17 with nowhere to go and no way to get there, eating these delicious peaches that had just been washed by the rain.''

Rita mulled over the scene he'd described and scowled. ''Peaches?'' she finally said.

He couldn't have expected her to understand. Even today, Seth had a special place in his heart for peaches. Everyone else might associate Woodstock with music, but Seth associated it with the sweetest, freshest, juiciest peaches he had ever eaten in his life.

''Ma didn't go to Woodstock,'' Rita told him. ''She said it was too far away.''

''She's originally from the Phillie area, isn't she?''

''King of Prussia. My grandmother lives there. Isn't that a dumb name for a town? King of Prussia. Tell me about where you live,'' Rita requested. ''Do you know lots of stars?''

Seth chuckled and shook his head. ''I'm a writer, not an actor. I work mostly in a secluded little office with a typewriter. Sometimes they'll drag me to the set when they need a scene rewritten—but, then, the actors who work in movies like *Victory of the Ninja Women* aren't exactly contenders for the Oscars.''

"Ma won't let me see violent movies," Rita complained.

"I don't blame her." Seth grinned. "Maybe when you're sixteen, when she lets you sleep à la raw, she'll also let you go to the theater and watch all kinds of blood and gore. You've got a lot to look forward to, lovely Rita."

"Yuck!" Rita leaped from the couch and glowered at him. "Don't!"

"Don't what?" he asked, bewildered.

"Don't sing that song. Ma named me after it and it makes me sick!"

"What song?" Seth puzzled over what he'd said, then nodded. "'Lovely Rita, Meter Maid.'"

Even though he hadn't sung it, Rita pressed her hands to her ears and groaned. "Yuck. Meter maid. I mean, is it sick? My mother named me after a *meter maid*."

"She named you after a song," Seth corrected her. "A terrific song, too. A Beatles song." He began to sing the refrain.

"Yuck!" Rita wrinkled her nose and stormed out of the room.

Whatever works, Seth pondered, standing and wrapping the blanket toga-style around his body. If he had known that a classic Beatles song was his ticket to the bathroom, he would have started singing much sooner.

He crossed to his garment bag, which he'd left open on an easy chair, and pulled out some clean underwear, a pair of jeans and a white cotton sweater with a series of red-and-black concentric circles decorating the front like a bull's eye-target. He often wore the sweater when he visited New York City, joking that he wanted to help the muggers and snipers out by offering them a clear target. Lifting his clothing, he headed toward the hall. The sound of a key in the front door lock caused him to halt, and he turned in time to see Laura enter the apartment, carrying a white paper bag.

"Good morning, lazybones!" she greeted him.

Seth momentarily forgot his awkward encounter with Rita. All he was aware of was an unexpected rush of joy at being in Laura's presence. She looked refreshed from her outing, her cheeks pink and her eyes sparkling, her smile contagious, her windblown hair tumbling in dense, dark curls past her shoulders. She wore a pair of brown corduroy slacks, and Seth found himself admiring the feminine spread of her hips, an asset the skirt she'd worn to the party had downplayed. Seth liked a solid bottom on a woman, and he considered Laura's weight gain, minimal though it appeared to be, a definite improvement over her boyish figure in college.

If he'd considered it, he might have been astonished by the fact that he was thinking of Laura in sexual terms. Yet from what he could see, Laura appeared to be a remarkably sexy woman. If you wanted to talk about cute tushes...

His mouth shaped a grim line as he recalled his recent humiliation beneath Rita's inquisitive eyes. Exhaling, he greeted Laura with the bad news. "I've traumatized your daughter."

Laura's smile waned. "What do you mean, you 'traumatized' her?" she asked warily as she carried the bag into the kitchen and set it on a counter.

"Well...I have this habit," he explained. "You know how some people are so selfish in bed, they hog the blanket and wrap themselves up in it like a mummy and leave their lovers freezing to death?"

Laura eyed him quizzically. "Is that a rhetorical question, Seth?"

He smiled nervously. "The point is, Laura I'm *not* one of those people. I'm kind of the opposite—"

"You aren't selfish in bed?" Laura smiled wickedly. "Sounds interesting, Seth. I'm all ears."

He drew in a deep breath, trying to ignore her teasing and the uncomfortably arousing effect it had on him. "I'm so unselfish,'' he continued, ''that I do the opposite with the blanket. I *don't* wrap myself up in it like a mummy. And...well...I guess I unwittingly gave Rita an up-close-and-personal demonstration of my utter selflessness....''

Laura rolled her eyes. ''You flashed her? Wonderful,'' she grunted. ''What did she say?''

''Do you want to know the truth?'' Seth smiled modestly. ''She said I had a 'cute tush.' Look, Laura, if the kid needs years and years of therapy to work it out, I'd be more than willing to foot the bills...''

But Laura was laughing too hard to hear him. '''A cute tush'? Is that what she said? Oh, she's something, all right.'' ''Yeah,'' Seth agreed. ''Just like her mother.''

''Well, go get dressed before you do any more damage,'' Laura ordered him, sniffling away her laughter. Seth nodded grumpily and pivoted on his bare foot. Before he could escape, Laura pulled a spatula from a wall rack and used it to lift the corner of the blanket. ''Rita's right. It *is* cute,'' she asserted before dissolving in fresh laughter.

Seth tried to appear annoyed, but he really wasn't. It was unfortunate that Rita had happened upon him that morning, but Laura...if she thought his rear end was cute, that was quite all right with him.

LAURA HAD BOUGHT THE BAGELS for Seth and Rita, and she didn't eat any herself. She had slept late, after all, and she had a one o'clock engagement for lunch with Julianne and Kimberly. Walking to the bakery on Flatbush Avenue just to buy fresh bagels hadn't been necessary; she could as easily have made toast for Seth, or served him cereal. But she had wanted to get something special for him; she had wanted to put forth a little extra effort for her old friend.

Laura knew that Rita didn't care one way or the other about having fresh bagels for breakfast. She and Courtney were planning to spend the afternoon at the Kings Plaza shopping mall, where they would alternately stuff their faces with pizza and ice cream and bemoan their imaginary blubber; the only foods Rita showed much enthusiasm for were foods that Laura urged her not to eat. As long as Laura had brought home bagels and not chocolate-covered doughnuts, Rita wasn't disposed to appreciate her mother's hike to the bakery.

But Seth did seem to appreciate it. He ate two entire bagels and part of a third, slathering them with cream cheese and describing the rarity of good New York-style bagels in Southern California. "There's one deli in downtown L.A.," he told them, "with genuine bagels, pickles, pastrami, lox . . . astronomical prices, but desperate ex-New Yorkers will pay almost anything for a taste of home," he explained. "Trouble is, it's a long drive from Topanga Canyon to downtown L.A. If I happen to be in the neighborhood, I'll stock up. But on a weekend morning, given a choice between fighting the traffic and rolling over and going back to sleep, I inevitably roll over."

Seth had appreciated the bagels, and Laura had wanted to do something he'd appreciate. She had also wanted to leave the apartment for a few minutes, to breathe in the crisp spring air, to clear her head and think things through.

She was reasonably sure that Seth wasn't angry at her for stranding him on the couch last night. He hadn't accepted her invitation to stay at her apartment because he expected anything to happen between them. When she'd kissed him good-night, she herself hadn't expected that the kiss would be taken as anything other than a gesture of friendship. And his suggestive questions about where Laura would be sleeping while he was on the couch—she was sure he had only been kidding.

She liked Seth, not just the Seth she'd known fifteen years ago, but the Seth he was today. She liked him a lot more than she liked most of the men she met. But he would be in town only for the weekend, and even if she found a way to visit him in California, that would be at most another week they might spend together. And then what? A transcontinental love affair was hardly what Laura was looking for.

Not that sleeping with Seth while he was in town would constitute a love affair. At issue was a few hours of pleasure, if anything, a few hours of closeness. Not a full-fledged capital *R* relationship. Hadn't Seth made that comment about free love?

Laura had never been an advocate of free love, even though she'd lived on a commune. What she had liked about the commune was its ethic: sharing, openness, a commitment to others. All the adult members had contributed what they could to the community: cooking, keeping the main house functioning, growing vegetables in the garden, or taking a job "outside," in the nearby town of Ithaca, to bring money into their closed community. Laura had found work transcribing tapes and proofreading manuscripts for a professor of sociology at Cornell University, but she'd quit the job just before Rita was born, choosing to remain full-time at the commune, where she could attend to her new daughter.

She had loved the flexibility and fluidity of the place. She'd loved the hard work, the rugged life, the bucolic environment, the philosophy of giving of oneself for the betterment of the larger family. She'd loved some of the people, too. But as far as free love went...no. Her relationship with Neil had been exclusive. It had also been unfortunately public, even before Laura had become pregnant. Everyone had known almost from the start that she and Neil were lovers; everyone had known when they were fighting, when they were getting along, even when they were anxious for privacy. "Leave Neil and Laura alone," someone would announce at dinnertime. "They want to be alone." Their attempts to find solitude became, ironically, a group concern. And then, of course, when Laura became pregnant, her pregnancy became another group concern. Rita became the group's baby.

After Neil left, Laura wasn't about to become involved with another man on the commune. To her, the only free love worth pursuing was a love that was free from outside interference.

She had no idea what Seth expected of her now—other than what he'd told her just before she left for Julianne's apartment. "I'm going to try to pick up some tickets to a show for tonight, Laura. So if you haven't already got plans for this evening, don't make any."

"I'll erase everything on my calendar," she had said, kissing his cheek on her way out the door.

She climbed the stairs leading from the subway station up into the glaring afternoon sunshine. Julianne's apartment was situated in a fairly new building in the East Seventies. If Laura hadn't already known that the residence was in the high-rent district, the doorman's uniform, a navy double-breasted coat trimmed with gold braid, would have proved it.

Shrugging the strap of her purse higher on her shoulder, Laura entered the swanky foyer and gave the doorman Julianne's name. He lifted the telephone receiver from an intercom console, announced Laura's arrival and then indicated with a nod that Laura was cleared to go upstairs.

What do magazine editors earn? Laura wondered as the mirror-and-chrome elevator car whisked her up to the seventeenth floor. Not that she cared about the exact figure, but... She couldn't shake off her memory of the dingy basement office in which *The Dream* had been born and from which it had been disseminated. Comparing that tomblike cubicle, with its grilled windows and continually buzzing fluorescent lighting, to Julianne's elegant apartment building—or to the equally elegant suite of offices where *Dream*'s birthday party had been held—pointed up to Laura how many times the earth had circled the sun since *The Dream* had first been hatched and how far it had carried her and her friends.

Julianne had her door open by the time Laura stepped out of the elevator. Seeing Julianne's wonderfully familiar face made Laura forget all about her affluent surroundings. She broke into a glowing smile and hurried down the hall.

"Come on in," Julianne greeted Laura, ushering her into the living room. Its decor communicated impeccable taste. The furnishings were understated, the colors—primarily beige and blue—muted, every oak tabletop polished to a high gloss. A vase holding six white tulips stood at the center of the elliptical coffee table. More than anything else in the room, the tulips appealed to Laura. Tulips seemed so like Julianne—tall and graceful, straightforward in their beauty, nothing showy or gaudy about them.

"This is fantastic," Laura said, turning to Julianne. Dressed in a neatly tailored shirt and pleated gray slacks, she looked as tasteful as her living room, her appearance polished and understated. "I feel like such a grown-up, having lunch with you and Kim." Laura was used to brown-bagging her lunches during the week and on the weekends either skipping lunch or grabbing a snack while she caught up on her reading or did her shopping. To attend a luncheon in such a fancy apartment, with only adult women present, was a rare treat.

Julianne laughed. "*I* feel like a baby. This morning Kim and I baked chocolate chip cookies and we fought over who would get to lick the bowl."

"Chocolate chip cookies." Laura sighed. Feeling the need to set a healthy example for Rita, she generally restricted her baking to such wholesome treats as whole-grain bread and carrot cake. But she couldn't deny that she had a soft spot in her heart for homemade cookies, especially chocolate chip ones. "Where is Kim, anyway? Shut up in the bedroom with the bowl?"

As if in answer, the bathroom door swung open and Kimberly emerged. Although she was smiling, her eyes were red rimmed and devoid of makeup, and her lush golden-blond hair was mussed. "Hi, Laura," she said, gliding into the living room. "Here I am, sans the bowl."

"You've been crying," Laura guessed, taken aback by Kimberly's dismal appearance. She realized at once that her comment wasn't exactly tactful, and she tried to soften it with a joke. "Did the cookie batter taste that bad?"

Kimberly smiled feebly and shrugged. "I cry a lot these days," she admitted. "Come on, let's eat. Let's drink, too. Julianne has wine, and I could surely use some." Slipping her arm around Laura's shoulders, Kimberly led her into the compact modern kitchen. "Julianne has everything, Laura. It's amazing. Do you know what she's got? Cloth table mats with matching linen napkins and napkin rings. Straight out of the pages of *Good Housekeeping*."

"Do you read *Good Housekeeping*?" Laura asked Julianne, who had slipped past them to pull an ironstone bowl containing a spinach salad from the refrigerator.

"Got to," Julianne admitted. "I've got to keep up with the competition."

"*Dream* isn't anything like *Good Housekeeping*," Laura argued. "I have yet to read a single article about how to set a table in your magazine."

"There's one in the upcoming July issue," Julianne warned her with a chuckle. "Not exactly about how to set a table, but it's an article on how our eating habits reflect our prejudices. Interesting piece. I'm betting on lots of mail in reaction to it." She pulled another bowl from the refrigerator, this one filled with crabmeat salad. She carried the two bowls from the kitchen to the dining table in one corner of the living room.

Laura sighed again. Crabmeat salad. Matching table mats and napkins. "Don't you have matching napkins, too?" she asked Kimberly. "I always thought you were the matching-napkins type."

"I was, once upon a time," Kimberly said. Her eyes seemed to water, and she averted her face, concentrating on peeling the lead from the top of a bottle of imported white wine.

"And then what happened?" Laura asked, figuring that there was no need for tact when someone you cared about was on the verge of weeping.

"It's a long story," Kimberly groaned dramatically.

"It's a short story, Kim," Julianne chided her in a matter-of-fact tone. "She's getting a divorce."

"Oh," said Laura. She touched Kimberly's shoulder. "I'm sorry."

"Thanks for being supportive," Kimberly said, forcing another crooked smile.

Laura laughed. "I'm not being supportive. All I said was I'm sorry. If you want to know the truth, I hate the word 'supportive.'"

"And you call yourself a social worker," Kimberly sniffed. "What's wrong with supportive?"

"It sounds so trendy." Laura followed Kimberly to the table, where each of the matching blue place mats was set with a beige ironstone plate and a large crystal goblet. She watched for a moment as Kimberly poured the wine, but was distracted by a framed photograph now standing on the window ledge by the table. She had noticed the photo at the party last night, but hadn't had a chance to examine it closely. Moving closer, she reached for it and picked it up.

"This is a scream, Julianne. I can't believe you unearthed this for the party."

Julianne joined Laura and gazed at the picture. "I didn't dig it up. I keep it hanging over my desk in my office all the time."

"Why?" Laura asked with a laugh. The photo's six subjects looked barely out of puberty—which, Laura supposed, was what they were. Julianne seemed impossibly fresh scrubbed, the epitome of a wholesome midwestern girl, despite her waist-length hair and the stencil adorning her T-shirt: a clenched fist enclosed within a "Woman" symbol. Kimberly's hair, too, was long, lusciously wavy, and her blue work shirt appeared recently pressed. The guys all looked much scruffier, as did Laura. In fact, she looked rather like a scarecrow, quite bony, her face slightly drawn and surrounded by a thundercloud of bushy curls. "If I were you, Julianne, I'd burn this thing. And the negative, too."

"Nonsense," Julianne said, indicating with a wave of her hand where Laura was to sit at the table. "I think it's important to remember one's origins."

"If you buy Darwin, our origins are the apes. There are certain things I'd just as soon not remember," Laura maintained, though she was still laughing. She set down the photograph and took her seat. When Kimberly and Julianne were also seated, Laura lifted her goblet. "Let's drink a toast to Kim's newfound freedom."

"Hear, hear," Julianne chimed in.

Kimberly grinned pathetically, but she raised her glass and clinked it against the others. "I don't feel particularly free," she declared as the bowls of salad were passed around. "I don't know how you handled the split with your daughter's father, Laura, but things have got to be a whole lot easier when you circumvent the law. I mean, it's mortifying to have to reveal all your heartache to an utter stranger who's billing you by the hour." She speared a chunk of crabmeat with her fork and smiled bravely. "Let's not talk about me," she decided. "I'm too depressing. Let's talk about the men."

"What about them?" Julianne asked.

Kimberly's large hazel eyes glittered impishly. "What do you think was the best thing about Seth last night?"

Laura permitted herself a private smile. The best thing about Seth had been giving him a friendly kiss, holding him, feeling his arms around her. But she wasn't about to tell that to Kimberly and Julianne. Nor was she going to admit that another very nice thing about him was his rear end—the truth was, she hadn't gotten to see how nice it was until that morning, and the question Kimberly had posed referred specifically to the previous night.

"His red high-tops," she answered.

Julianne contemplated Laura's reply and nodded. "Yes. They added a great deal of style to his ensemble. In fact, they added a great deal of style to the party."

Kimberly nodded, too. "And what do you think was the worst thing about Seth? What's the worst thing the past fifteen years have done to him?"

"He writes trash," Laura said, not even having to think.

"How do you know it's trash?" Julianne asked. "Have you seen the *Ax Man* movies? According to *Dream*'s film critic, there's a certain *film noir* quality about them."

"Spare me," Laura grunted. "They're trash because Seth told me they're trash, and he wouldn't lie about it." She sipped her wine, then lowered her glass and shook her head. "Remember those impassioned critiques he used to write for the newspaper? Analyzing the political implications of every movie, every song? Remember that in-depth piece he wrote on *All in the Family* as a barometer of American culture? And now he's writing film scripts about psychopaths with hatchets."

"And making a bundle," Kimberly mused.

"So what? Is making money that important?" Laura challenged her. Then she bit her lip. Here she was, sitting at a beautiful dining table, eating crabmeat and sipping an expensive wine. Here she was, having lunch with a successful magazine editor and a senator's speech writer, each of them wearing upward of one hundred dollars' worth of clothing.

It was all very impressive, just as impressive as riding in Seth's rented limousine had been. But while Laura could enjoy such things, and could admire them, and could even wonder, every now and then, whether her life might be improved if it had a few material niceties in it, being in possession of abundant wealth wasn't vital to her.

She had no right to judge Seth, but she was disappointed that he was writing trash. He had been a fine writer in his youth, full of passions and ideals. Surely he oughtn't to have abandoned those passions and ideals for the mere rewards of money. He was too decent a person to have sold out so totally.

The possibility that he had was disheartening, and she distracted herself by asking, "What do you think was the best thing about Andrew last night?"

"His chin," Julianne said quickly.

"Do you like his chin?" Kimberly debated her. "I thought it jutted too much."

"I liked his eyeglasses," Laura remarked. "I thought they made him look very intellectual."

"He doesn't need eyeglasses to make him look intellectual," Kimberly argued, her tone laced with sarcasm. "I bet he looks intellectual even when he's going to the bathroom."

Laura sipped her wine. Kimberly and Andrew had always been antagonists, even when they'd been collaborating on *The Dream*. Andrew *had* been an intellectual, and he had always been putting Kimberly down for not being intellectual enough. Kimberly was smart, but she wasn't given to pondering the universe or wearing her knowledge on her sleeve. She had always been bouncy, full of constructive energy, cheering on the newspaper staff as fervently as she had once cheered her high school's football team to victory. She could even turn a discussion about their reunion into a game: what's the best thing, what's the worst thing. Laura found Kimberly's spirit endearing.

She gauged Kimberly's acidic tone when talking about Andrew and asked, "What do you think was the worst thing about him?"

"His control," Kimberly said.

"What control?"

"He holds everything back," Kimberly explained. "He always did. He still does. He's an emotional miser. Don't you think so, Julianne?"

"He's reserved," Julianne allowed.

"He's a widower," Laura announced.

Julianne and Kimberly turned to her, aghast. "Where did you hear that?" Julianne asked.

"Seth told me. Andrew got married and then his wife died. Seth said it slipped out, and Andrew didn't want to talk about it."

"Oh, Lord," Julianne said with a deep sigh. "That's terrible."

"I'd rather be a widow than a divorcee," Kimberly commented thoughtfully. "Not that I wish Todd would die, although sometimes... No, as vile a creature as he is, I truly don't wish he would die. But Andrew...he'll never hate the woman he lost. He can go on loving her forever and remember his marriage as something beautiful. I mean, I feel sorry for Andrew, but—"

"But you feel sorrier for yourself," Julianne concluded. "Drink some more wine, Kim. I like you better when you're drunk than when you're maudlin."

"If you insist," Kimberly complied, polishing off the wine in her goblet and refilling it. She eyed Laura, and they both giggled. Julianne was a born boss. She was forever telling people what to do, and she was invariably right. It was no wonder she'd become *The Dream's* editor in chief by acclamation.

"How about Troy? What's the best thing about him?" Laura asked.

"He's gorgeous," Kimberly said at once. "Don't you think so?"

"He always was a knockout," Laura concurred. "I never knew what bedroom eyes were until I met him."

"What do you think, Julianne?" Kimberly asked. "Is he still gorgeous?"

"Yes," said Julianne, sipping her wine. "Still gorgeous."

"And what's the worst thing about him?"

Julianne's gaze moved from Kimberly to Laura and then past them to one of the bookshelves built into a wall of her living room. She rose from the table and pulled a notebook-sized paperback from one of the shelves. "Do you want to know the worst thing about Troy?" she asked the others. "It's right here."

She handed the book to Laura, and Kimberly slid her chair closer so she could see the book, as well. It was entitled *Maritime*, and it was a collection of stark black-and-white photographs, mostly of fishermen, laborers, impoverished children and weary women, and a few of landscapes. Each picture was striking, unsentimental but moving. The portraits in particular captured frozen moments of unvoiced pain, deprivation, yearning.

"This is his book," Laura murmured. "The small-press book Kim was talking about last night."

Julianne nodded. "He took most of the photos on Cape Breton Island."

"It's wonderful," Laura exclaimed, poring over the photographs. "How can you say this is the worst thing about him?"

"It's the worst thing about him because—" Julianne inhaled. Laura could tell she was bristling with emotion, which was unusual for someone as self-possessed as Julianne. "A man who can take photographs like that is supporting himself by snapping pictures of wedding parties."

"All right." Kimberly shrugged. "Seth writes *Ax Man* movies. Troy takes pictures of brides. Welcome to the real world."

"At least Seth is making a fortune writing *Ax Man* movies. And apparently enjoying it," Julianne pointed out. "Troy doesn't enjoy taking pictures of brides, and all he's making is a living. He could make a living doing photojournalism if he wanted. Not putting out small-press books like this one, granted. But I bet *Dream* could pay him more for doing magazine photos than he's making in his studio in Canada."

"So offer him a job," Laura suggested.

Julianne pressed her lips together, then took the book and set it aside. "He wouldn't accept it," she said quietly. "I know he wouldn't. He has too much pride."

Laura wanted to question Julianne further, but she didn't dare. With Kimberly she could be tactless, but not with Julianne. She detected pain in Julianne's lucid blue eyes, pain and conflict, something that demanded respect, that begged for distance. If Julianne wanted to talk about it, she would. And if she didn't, Laura would never ask.

Fortunately Kimberly decided that she wanted to talk about her divorce, after all, so Laura asked her about that, instead. They emptied the bottle of wine into their glasses, and Julianne's eyes came into focus again as she gave Kimberly plenty of her typically clearheaded advice. Julianne spoke in defense of lawyers, and Laura spoke in defense of

Kimberly's inner strength and her emotional resources. It was marvelous talking with women about something real, not about shopping and not about Rita, but about how to steer through life and avoid the shoals.

She didn't want to leave, but at four o'clock, after promising to call both Julianne and Kimberly soon, Laura made her departure. She felt as if she had just found two long-lost sisters; she swore to herself that she would never lose them again.

And in the meantime, she was about to spend an evening with another long-lost friend. But not a brother. After kissing Seth last night, however briefly, however casually, she would never be able to think of him as a brother.

After kissing him, she would definitely never want to.

Chapter Four

"Okay, they can close the show now," Laura joked as she and Seth emerged from the theater into the chilly night. "I've finally seen it. They don't have to keep it running anymore."

Turning up the collar of his white suit jacket, which he'd worn over his bull's-eye sweater, Seth laughed and steered Laura through the throng of theater goers crowding Shubert Alley. "You think the only reason *A Chorus Line* is still running is that they didn't want to close it until you'd had a chance to see it?"

"Of course," Laura answered with a straight face. "I'm sure the producers got together and said, 'Say, if we can keep Laura Brodie away from our play for ten years or so, we might just wind up with a hit on our hands.'"

"The fact that it's a good play has nothing to do with it, I suppose," said Seth.

"It *is* a good play," Laura readily agreed, no longer joking. "Thank you for taking me to see it, Seth. I really enjoyed it."

"I figured, since we've already seen the longest running off-off-Broadway show together, we ought to see the longest running Broadway show together, too."

"We weren't exactly 'together' when we saw *The Fantasticks*," Laura recalled.

"Sure we were."

"I was with Mark Hofkiss," she corrected him, "and you were with . . . Meryl Banks, wasn't it?"

"You've got a good memory," Seth praised her.

"So do you." Until Seth had mentioned it, Laura had all but forgotten about the double date they'd gone on in college. They had decided to see *The Fantasticks*, in part because the tickets were cheap, in part because the musical had been written by two Columbia alumni, but mostly because the minuscule theater where the show was being staged was located in Greenwich Village, the Mecca of New York hippies.

The four of them had taken the subway down to West Fourth Street one afternoon after their final classes of the day. They'd sauntered around Washington Square, which at that time had been appealingly rundown, a point of convergence for panhandlers, N.Y.U. students, elderly men in cardigans playing chess, self-defined *artistes*, free-lance vendors of tooled leather belts, silver jewelry and marijuana and folk singers strumming guitars and vying to become the next Bob Dylan or Joan Baez or Richie Havens. Seth and Laura and their dates had journeyed from the carnivallike atmosphere of the park to MacDougall Street, where they'd browsed in the head shops and bookstores and poster emporiums, and from there they'd gone to dinner at an amazingly inexpensive Italian restaurant. Then they'd seen *The Fantasticks*, splurged on ice-cream cones afterward and, at midnight, taken the subway back to the Columbia campus on the opposite end of Manhattan, singing "Try To Remember" and arguing over the lyrics. In those days one could still ride on the subway at midnight—even sing on the subway, if one felt like it—without fearing for one's life.

That outing seemed much further in Laura's past than sixteen years ago. She had been a different person then, practically a child. She'd been so eager for experience that she rarely allowed herself the luxury of reflecting, of pausing to digest what it was she was experiencing. Now she was older, more mature, less interested in accumulating new experiences than in savoring whatever was occurring in the present. In the theater tonight, she had been acutely aware of everything: the solid, enveloping darkness before the curtain rose, the distinctively musty aroma of the air, the muted tapping sounds the dancers' feet made on the stage, the glittering row of top hats in the final, gloriously strutting song. The fuzzy texture of Seth's sweater against her fingers as she slipped her hand around his elbow on the armrest between their seats. The lingering scent of his shampoo. The sharp angle of his jaw in profile as he watched the performers dance.

"Wanna go out for a drink or something?" he asked as they ambled toward Broadway, hand in hand.

"Not really," Laura replied. She wasn't sure what would happen when she and Seth got to her apartment, but her uncertainty wasn't much of a reason to delay their getting there. She felt comfortable enough with Seth to want to remain sober, no matter how their night would progress.

At the corner of Broadway, Seth scouted for a cab. "No limo tonight, love," he said apologetically as the cab he signaled sped past them, its Off Duty light glowing. "We're going to have to rough it."

Laura chuckled. "Taking a cab is hardly what I'd call roughing it."

Seth eyed her with spurious annoyance. "That's easy for you to say. *I'm* the one standing in the middle of the road waving my hands like a maniac," he pointed out before spotting another cab and trying to flag it down. It, too, cruised past Seth without slowing. "What is this?" he muttered. "Do I have bad breath?"

"Be patient," Laura chided him affectionately. "Sooner or later we'll get a cab."

"Later," Seth griped. "Sooner is already out of the question."

After several traffic-light changes, an on-duty taxi coasted to a halt in front of Seth. He had to leap backward onto the curb to avoid having his toes crushed under the car's wheels, and Laura smiled as she glimpsed his bright red sneakers. His sputtering curses concerning the driver's homicidal bent only caused Laura's smile to widen.

He was still grumbling when they climbed into the back seat, but as soon as Laura guided his arm around her shoulders and snuggled against him, he softened. "Ocean Avenue in Brooklyn," he called to the driver. Then he settled back in the seat and entangled his fingers in Laura's thick, flowing mane. "It's all right if we go straight to your place?" he half asked.

"Why wouldn't it be all right?"

She felt his fingers digging through the mass of her hair in search of the back of her neck. He found it and gently stroked the warm skin. "Because...maybe this is an off-the-wall idea, Brodie, but..."

"But...?"

"The God's honest truth is, the minute we get there, I'm going to want to do something very carnal with you."

"Carnal, huh." She laughed quietly. For some reason, the idea didn't seem particularly off the wall to her. Impractical, impulsive, imprudent, maybe, but not outlandish. "I hate to break the news to you, Seth," she warned him, "but the minute we get to my place, we're probably going to have to make small talk with Rita."

"We can give her a quarter and send her to the movies."

"If anyone should know how much movies cost these days it's you," Laura reproached him.

Seth touched his lips to the crown of Laura's head. "Okay, pal. Give it to me straight. What's the best strategy for getting the mother of a teenage girl into bed?"

"I'm not sure," Laura played along. "But I've got to tell you, Seth, exposing your naked body to the teenage girl doesn't win you points with her mother."

"Would it help if I told you you're beautiful?"

He sounded so sincere that Laura chose to believe that he wasn't simply feeding her a line. But, then, Seth would never feed her lines. They had known each other too long, too well. "Telling me I'm beautiful definitely wins you points," she granted.

"Yeah? How many?" His thumb located her earlobe and traced its curve, causing Laura to sigh. "Look, I'm trying to be reasonable," he defended himself in a hushed voice. "I've been thinking about you all day, Laura, thinking about you and getting turned on."

"That's very intriguing," Laura said, unsure of how to react. At least her words were honest. She *was* intrigued. She was intrigued by the constant shimmer in his eyes, by the sensation of his thumb stroking the skin behind her ear, by his nearness, his bluntness.

"What are you going to do about it?" he asked, his question less a challenge than an expression of genuine curiosity.

She contemplated the situation. She hadn't been seriously involved with a man since moving to Brooklyn over three years ago, and she might have explained her interest in Seth as nothing more than the arousal of a lonely woman in the presence of an attractive man. Except that she wasn't lonely; she had enough opportunities to date, and the lack of a serious relationship in her life was Laura's choice.

Besides, she wasn't simply responding to an attractive man. She was responding to Seth, her friend, her old, trusted buddy. "I'm not sure," she finally answered.

He kissed her brow again. "If you're planning to say no to me, the least you can do is tell me whether you're saying no because of Rita or because of me."

"I don't know what I'm planning," Laura confessed. "In all honesty, Seth, I don't think I'm planning at all."

"In that case, let me do the planning," he offered, cupping his free hand beneath her chin and angling her face to his. His mouth covered hers, and his tongue gently coaxed her lips apart.

Laura twisted on the seat to face him and slid her fingers upward to caress his cheek. His skin was slightly scratchy; he hadn't shaved since late that morning, and a hint of his beard had broken through. She molded her palm to the bristly surface and deepened the kiss.

Their tongues moved slowly, one against the other, in a sensuous exploration. As arousing as it was to kiss Seth, she was equally aroused by what he had just told her. She was aroused by his forthright expression of desire for her: *I've been thinking about you all day and getting turned on.* There was nothing subtle in Seth's statement, nothing sneaky about it. And if anything could turn Laura on more than a kiss like the one she was sharing with him right now, it was directness and honesty.

His hand tensed at the back of her head for a moment, then relaxed. He drew his mouth from hers, grazing her cheek and then her temple with his lips. "God, this is fun," he said, slightly out of breath. "I haven't necked in the back seat of a car since I was a kid. I forgot how much fun it could be."

"Maybe when you return to California you can get back into the habit of it," Laura proposed.

Seth shook his head. "Porsche 944's are pretty underendowed in the back-seat department. And anyway," he added, brushing his lips against her temple again, "it wouldn't be much fun if you weren't there." His mouth found hers and lingered, his tongue darting inside only long enough to tease hers. Then he tucked her head into the hollow of his neck and wrapped his arms snugly around her.

His comment had struck a nerve. Once more she was forced to acknowledge the fact that he would be leaving for home the following day and she would be staying in Brooklyn, and that whatever was occurring between them now would be finite, its conclusion already written. She didn't want to have a one-night stand with Seth. She didn't want to be a one-night stand for him.

But she didn't want to let go of him, either. She wanted to remain cuddled close to him, breathing in his clean, masculine fragrance, tasting the underside of his chin with her lips. She wanted him to keep holding her. She wanted to pull off his garish sweater, his gaudy sneakers, to touch the lean contours of the chest she'd barely glimpsed behind the shield of his blanket that morning and—sure, why not?—to get a closer look at his cute tush.

Amazing as it seemed, she wanted Seth as much as he wanted her.

"Let's go home," she murmured, closing her eyes and hugging him tightly.

He glanced out the window, then shouted to the driver, "Step on it!" Bowing his head to Laura's ear, he whispered, "I've always wanted to say that to a taxi driver."

"This has been quite a weekend for you," Laura mused. "First you got to say 'I just flew in from the coast,' and now this. I bet you're just dying to order the driver, 'Follow that car!'"

"You've got me down pretty well," Seth conceded with a laugh. His fingers slipped inside her collar to stroke the skin of her shoulder. "Give me half a chance, lady, and I could probably fall in love with you."

"I doubt that," Laura said, only partly in jest. Seth was much too carefree to fall in love with someone who lived a

continent away from him. Long-distance love was complicated, difficult. If Seth were truly looking for complicated,
difficult challenges in his life, he wouldn't be writing *Ax
Man* movies for the fun of it. He wouldn't be frittering his
professional energy on trash and his emotional energy on
seven hundred starlets.

Unnerved by the direction her thoughts had taken, she
inched away from him and sat upright. Seth didn't comment on her movement. Undoubtedly he interpreted it as her
way of composing herself for their arrival at her home,
where her daughter was waiting. The cab had reached her
block, and Seth indicated the building to the driver.

After paying the fare, he escorted Laura into the building. "Maybe we can give Rita a quarter and send her downstairs to her friend's apartment," he suggested.

"Maybe we can behave responsibly," Laura retorted. She
bit her lip, trying to smother her apprehension. Rita wasn't
Laura's primary concern. What was gnawing at her was the
understanding that, even if Seth didn't give her half a
chance, she could probably fall in love with him. And she
honestly didn't think that was a good idea. She simply didn't
believe there was much promise in pursuing a deep relationship with Seth.

When they entered the apartment, they found Rita
watching television, two incriminating candy wrappers lying
on the coffee table. Seeing her mother, Rita sprang off the
couch and crumpled the wrappers into a ball. "You're home
early," she announced with a sheepish grin as she scam-
pered into the kitchen to toss the evidence into the trash can.

Laura smiled in resignation. "Stuff your mouth with
junk, Rita, if that's what you want to do. But don't blame
me if you turn into a blimp."

Rita spun from the trash can and shrugged. "See, Courtney bought a ten-pack at Kings Plaza, but she didn't want
to bring the whole package home because then her brother

would eat them and he's got zits," she explained vaguely. Then she turned to Seth. "So," she said brightly, "how was the show?"

"Terrific," he reported.

"What was it about?"

Laura rummaged in her handbag for her *Playbill* and handed it to Rita. "It's about a bunch of struggling dancers auditioning for parts in a musical," she told her daughter.

"And then what happens?" Rita asked.

"Some of them get parts and some of them don't."

Rita issued an exaggerated yawn. "Sounds exciting," she said sarcastically.

"It was," Seth claimed, helping Laura off with her jacket and then removing his blazer. "The auditioners each do a song or a dance and they get you involved in their lives, and then you start rooting for them, hoping for them. It's heartbreaking when some of them don't get cast in the show."

Rita eyed him dubiously. "Don't lose sleep over it, Seth. They already *are* in the show."

"She tends to operate on a very literal level at times," Laura said, explaining her daughter. "Well, Ms. Candy Bar, speaking of losing sleep, it's eleven thirty. Your pillow awaits."

"So does yours, Ma," Rita said, shooting Seth another knowing look before confronting her mother. "Be careful, all right? You're too old to have any more kids."

Laura faked an openhanded swat at Rita's backside, and Rita danced out of reach. Giggling, she scurried down the hall to her bedroom and shut herself inside.

Her arms folded across her chest, Laura glowered for a moment at her daughter's closed door, then permitted herself a reluctant chuckle. "Too old to have kids, huh," she muttered. "Somebody ought to explain the facts of life to her."

"Yeah, like her mother," Seth suggested before succumbing to laughter. He planted his hands on Laura's shoulders and rotated her to face him. "If you ask me, she's got the facts pretty well sorted out. Let's be careful, okay?"

"Seth..." Taking a deep breath, Laura averted her gaze. She wished he weren't looking at her so seductively. She wished his eyes weren't quite so radiant, his smile quite so sexy. She wished his hair weren't glittering with golden highlights below the circular ceiling light. She wished his hands didn't feel so strong and confident on her. "Seth, can we—can we just talk?"

He appeared surprised, but not particularly upset. "We can do whatever you want, Laura," he said earnestly.

"You—you wouldn't be bummed out if we didn't go any further than that?"

His eyebrows quirked upward as he considered his response. "Other than the fact that I'll probably wind up walking bowlegged and talking in a funny, squeaky voice for the rest of my life, why should I be bummed out?"

"Oh, Seth." Laura grinned wistfully. It was more than his eyes, his smile, his hair and his hands on her that made her want him. It was his ability to find comedy in what surely had to be a frustrating situation. "I don't want to turn you into a soprano," she swore, arching her arms around his waist. "Let's . . . let's just talk for a while and see what happens."

"Okay by me," he agreed in a piping falsetto, causing her to laugh. In his normal voice he continued, "Let's talk dirty. I've got a way with words—maybe I'll get you in the mood."

"I'm already in the mood," Laura confessed, unwilling to be dishonest with Seth when he was accepting her decision with such civility.

"Good," he murmured. "Let's go talk on your bed."

"With our clothing on," she insisted. She knew that allowing Seth onto her bed was foolhardy, but she was unable to resist his mischievous humor.

He took her hand, and she led him into her bedroom. Like the living room, it was furnished with mismatched pieces, cast-offs, she'd accumulated over the years. But the double bed was made with fresh linen and the patchwork quilt covering it was a source of great pride to Laura. She herself had sewn it when she was living on the commune.

Seth kicked off his sneakers and dove onto the mattress as she turned the lamp on the night table to its brightest setting. He extended his arms to her, and she lowered herself onto the bed next to him, stretching out on her side and propping her head in her hand. "Go ahead, talk dirty," she dared him, grinning.

"Soot," he complied good-naturedly. "Cigarette butts. Sweat stains. Axle grease."

"Boy, am I ever in the mood!" Laura hooted.

"All right, I'll talk clean, then," he decided. He scooped a thick lock of her hair off the pillow and toyed with it, tracing the convoluted whirls and coils of the waves with his index finger. "I didn't come to New York looking for a roll in the hay, you know," he said solemnly.

"I know," Laura assured him.

"And I sure didn't come to New York figuring I'd make a pass at one of the old gang. I mean, talk about your farfetched ideas!" He snorted and shook his head. "I'm a big boy. I've got a good life in L.A. Nothing for the record books, but I'm content. I don't have to prove anything. My idea of fun and games is the Mets versus the Dodgers. I'm not on the make. Lying in bed with you—even with all my clothes on—is not what I expected to happen this weekend. But I'm not telling you anything you don't already know."

How like Seth not to drown her in sentimental claptrap. She smiled tenderly, touched by his candor. "Who do you root for, the Dodgers or the Mets?" she asked.

He chuckled. "Maybe it's all your fault, Laura. I mean, why do you have to look so great? Why couldn't you have gotten all fat and wrinkled or something?"

"I *have* gotten fat," she argued.

"What you've gotten are breasts, which I don't think you had fifteen years ago."

"I did so!"

"Not that I ever noticed." Letting her hair fall back to the pillow, he ran his hand lightly over the full swell of her bosom.

Laura allowed herself to enjoy his provocative exploration for only a moment before covering his hand with hers and lifting it to her lips. She kissed his fingertips, then pinned his hand safely beneath hers on the pillow between them. "Let's talk about *A Chorus Line*," she said.

If Seth was nonplussed by her choice of topic, he hid it well. "Okay, let's talk about it," he said. "You go first."

Laura studied his hand. Next to his long, graceful fingers, her own hand looked short and stubby. She had stopped trying to cultivate well-shaped nails when she moved to the commune, where her manicures were constantly being destroyed by gardening, sweeping the kitchen and typing notes for the Cornell University professor on her sticky manual typewriter. But now, lying beside Seth, she wished her hands were prettier. His starlets in California probably had beautiful hands.

She didn't want to think about his other women or his West Coast life. What she wanted was to remind herself why she wasn't at that very moment making love with Seth. "You know that song from the show, 'What I Did For Love'? I've heard it a million times on the radio, and I always assumed that it was a love song, something a woman is singing about a man. I never knew until tonight that it was about a woman's decision to become a Broadway dancer.''

"There's women's lib for you,'' Seth scoffed. "Nowadays a woman can belt out a love song about her career that's just as schmaltzy as any of the love songs women used to sing about their men.''

"That song could have been sung by a man,'' Laura declared. "What it's about is having so much faith in your talent and your dreams that you never take the easy way out. You just keep pursuing your goal.'' She twined her fingers through Seth's, seeking the strength to continue. She had no right to say what she was about to say; she had no right to sit in judgment of him and of the choices he'd made. But he deserved to know why she was backing off from him, when she desired him as much as he desired her. "Seth.'' She took a deep breath, then addressed his hand. "You have so much talent, such a good mind, so many things to say to the world. Why are you writing trash?''

"Uh-oh,'' Seth intoned. His eyes were sparkling, though, and despite the absence of a smile, his cheeks were marked with dimples. "Am I about to get chewed out?''

"No,'' Laura swore. Then she smiled sheepishly. "Maybe,'' she admitted. "It really—Seth, it bothers me that you're writing scripts about a madman who hacks nude baby-sitters and camp counselors into little pieces, when you could be writing scripts that have some value.''

"My scripts have value,'' Seth maintained amiably. "If they didn't have value, do you think I'd own a Topanga Canyon house and a Porsche 944 right now?''

"That's just it,'' said Laura. "They've got a monetary value, period. And you've got a fancy house and a fancy car. Is owning a house and a car so important to you?''

Seth chuckled. "If you ever saw the dive I was living in when I first moved to L.A., you would never have asked that question. We're talking 'Hotel California,' Laura.

Sleazeball City. And as far as a car, well, there's no such
animal as the D train out there. If you don't own a car
you've got three choices—walk, hitch, or don't go. I tried
to make do with a bicycle, but the bad news was, it *did* rain
in Southern California, and it always rained when I was
riding from here to there with a script under my arm. So yes,
I'm into good housing and an enclosed vehicle.''

"That's fine, Seth," she said, smiling gently. "I don't
want you getting pneumonia. But is it really necessary to sell
your talent short in order to keep from getting rained on?''

"Sell my talent short?" He rolled his eyes. "Laura, let me
explain to you the facts of life in Hollywood. For every five
hundred or so screenplays that get written, maybe one gets
bought. For every fifty or so that get bought, maybe one
gets into production. For every twenty that get into production, maybe one makes it into distribution. For me to
write a screenplay that actually survives all the way to distribution is a small miracle. Believe me, I'm not selling my
talent short.''

"If you've got enough talent to be able to write a screenplay that survives," Laura asserted, "then couldn't you put
that talent to work writing screenplays that can make the
world a better place?''

"Spare me, Brodie," Seth grunted. "We can't all be social workers, you know.''

"You don't have to be a social worker to do good," Laura
countered, her eyes aglow as she considered Seth's powerful situation. She was excited by the possibilities of what
Seth could accomplish if he put his mind—and his writing
gifts—to the task. "You're in a position to do a whole lot
more good than most social workers. Think of it, Seth. I
meet with only twenty-five clients a week. Your screenplays
can reach thousands and thousands of people in a single
day!''

"They can't if they aren't produced," Seth reminded her.

Laura eased onto her back and studied the ceiling. She was vexed by what Seth was saying, even though she knew it was probably true. That he had achieved so much in such a tough field was cause for congratulations, not criticism.

Yet she couldn't help being critical. Once again she reminded herself that it wasn't fair of her to judge Seth—and certainly not to judge him against the standards they'd lived by fifteen years ago. Ideals often had to give way to reality; that was a simple fact of growing up. Laura herself would rather be living in a rural environment than in overcrowded Brooklyn, but she had a daughter to support, and New York City paid its social workers much more than most rural counties did. So Laura worked for the city.

But Seth did have choices. He was an artist, abundantly talented, and his only dependent was his pet dog. Perhaps he needed a car, but he didn't need a Porsche. Perhaps he needed a house, but he didn't need an eight-room palace perched on a hillside in an affluent suburb of Los Angeles. Given his unique skill at molding words and enunciating ideas, shouldn't he be putting himself at the service of those less fortunate? Laura could help only a few single mothers, but Seth . . . he was blessed with the ability to move others through his words.

And what had he done with his ability? Zilch.

"Laura." He peered down at her, obviously aware of her disapproval. His jaw moved as he contemplated his words, and the corners of his mouth twitched upward. "Have you ever seen any of my movies?"

"I—" Laura pressed her lips together. Lord, how presumptuous she was! "No," she confessed. "I never have."

"No big deal," he reassured her. "They aren't made with audiences like you in mind. But . . . you know, I'm not as much of a sellout as you seem to think I am. I do sneak little messages into my movies sometimes."

"You do?" She gazed up at him hopefully.

"Sure. Take *Victory of the Ninja Women*, for instance. You wouldn't believe the hoops I had to jump through to get that flick made. Seems Ninjas are supposed to be pure macho. Oh, an occasional Ninja woman is all right, sure. Let her kick her feet a bit, throw a saber once or twice and screw around with the hero—and then make sure she gets killed so the hero can be hell-bent on revenge. But to have an entire squad of female Ninjas running around beating the living daylights out of all those bad guys—well, you would have thought I was trying to pitch the studio on Betty Friedan's life story, the way they were carrying on."

"If you could sell them on female Ninjas, I bet you could sell them on Betty Friedan's life story, too," Laura posed.

"Uh-huh. With Jane Fonda playing the lead. Give me a break, will you?" His patience was beginning to wear thin, and his dimples vanished. "You wanna know the truth, pal? If I were dirt poor—and I'm speaking from experience, because I *was* dirt poor when I was first getting started—if I were dirt poor, the last thing I'd want to see, if I got up a few bucks and decided to blow them on a movie, is some film about people who are dirt poor. Right? What movies did people go to see during the depression? Busby Berkeley. Fred Astaire and Ginger Rogers. Screwball comedies."

"*The Grapes of Wrath*," said Laura.

"All right. One *Grapes of Wrath* versus hundreds of screwball comedies. People go to the movies because they want to escape. They don't want to be harangued."

"And you give them what they want, Seth. You give the people what they want, and in return you get a hotshot sports car."

"Damn it, Laura—" He sat up and stared at the scratched chest of drawers that stood against the far wall. He bent his knees to his chest, rested his forearms across them and simmered.

Laura had never seen Seth angry before. Oh, sure, he'd been angry about the big issues back in their past, angry about the war, censorship, the first tiny hints of the Watergate scandal that were leaking out even before Nixon's reelection. But she had never seen him angry with a person before, and she felt extremely guilty.

Maybe she'd been too hard on him. Maybe she'd been too hard on him because if she hadn't been hard on him, she would have fallen in love with him.

She sat up, too, and cautiously touched his arm. "I'm sorry, Seth."

"Don't be," he said curtly.

"I'm in no position to pass judgment on you." She ran her fingers up to his shoulder and squeezed it. "Do you hate me?"

He twisted to look at her. A crooked smile flickered across his lips. "If I *did* hate you, Brodie, it would be because we're sitting here fully clothed instead of having the time of our lives. But, no, I don't hate you." He turned fully to her and kissed her lips lightly. "If anyone is in a position to pass judgment on me, lady, it's you. You haven't sold out, Laura. You're still trying to save the world. And I love you for it. I mean that." He kissed her again, another light kiss, more friendly than passionate. Then he reached behind her and clicked off the lamp. "Let's catch some z's, okay?"

He lay back down and pulled Laura into his arms. She cushioned her head with his shoulder and closed her eyes. She was glad that he would be spending the night in her bed, even if they had all their clothing on.

Especially if they had all their clothing on. She wasn't feeling particularly romantic anymore, but she didn't want Seth to leave her. She wanted the reassurance of his arms around her, the warmth of his lanky body next to hers. With their clothing on, they could lie together as friends, bound by trust rather than lust. And that was what she wanted right now—Seth's trust, his friendship.

HE COULD PRETEND that the problem was the time zones. It was only ten-thirty Pacific time, and he rarely crashed that early. He could pretend that his inner clock was skewed, that his nervous system was keyed to to the wrong longitude.

Or he could pretend that Laura's mere presence was keeping him awake. Not that she snored, not that her head was too heavy on his arm, not that he found the pressure of her knees against his particularly annoying. Nor was it that her closeness was causing him to suffer the agonies of unfulfilled passion. She looked utterly beautiful to him, her long, dark lashes visible against her cheeks even in the room's shadows, her mouth unmoving, her hair tumbling wildly about her face and shoulders, but lying beside her while she slept and not making love to her wasn't truly going to render him bowlegged for the rest of his life.

He could pretend a lot of things, but the truth was, he was awake because Laura was right. He had sold out.

A sellout. When Seth was younger, labeling someone a sellout was just about the worst thing you could call him, worse than an SOB, a fascist pig, a hawk, a brownnose. You weren't supposed to trust anyone over thirty because, chances were, people over thirty were sellouts.

Take a bow, Seth, he muttered silently. *This one's for you.*

It wasn't as if he had abandoned his principles. It wasn't as if he no longer cared about the needy, nuclear proliferation, racism, the greenhouse effect . . . But honest to God, nobody wanted to see movies about that sort of stuff. Sure, once in a while you could get something like *The China Syndrome* made, or *Roots*, or *Apocalypse Now*. But it wasn't as if every producer in town were currently ready to do armed battle over the rights to *The Mother Theresa Story*.

Seth had done his best. He had honestly given it the old college try. In one of the file cabinets in his office he had a drawer filled with his early efforts: one screenplay about a racial incident in a supposedly enlightened town, another about a small village that discovers its water supply tainted with carcinogens and another one about ethnic clashes among inner-city gangs. Seth had ultimately cannibalized that one for *Barrio Warlords*, but the original offered some keen insights into racial and cultural conflicts.

The first writing job he had landed when he arrived in Los Angeles was pure hack: contributing to the joke-filled scripts of a syndicated game show. The job paid dreadfully, and eventually Seth obtained a better job cranking out dialogue for a soap opera. But from the start, even before he'd snared the game-show position, he had labored at odd hours, on weekends and late into the night on noble, important screenplays, scripts that would undoubtedly bring tears to Laura's eyes. He had pedaled around town on his bicycle, conniving his way into the offices of agents and producers, cajoling receptionists, begging anyone and everyone to read his noble, important scripts.

"You've got a genuine sensitivity, kid," they used to say, "but I'm overbooked at the moment." Or "Interesting, but it doesn't work for me," or "Racial themes are out this year." An agent named Melinda Greiss, a blunt, gum-chewing woman working out of a downtown skyscraper, read all of Seth's scripts and invited him to her office for a chat. "Okay," she said. "If you're willing to write violence I'll represent you."

At the time Seth had been chagrined. Four years later, when the soap opera ceased production and he was down to his last dollar, he decided he was ready to write violence. Melinda Greiss signed him on.

It hadn't been an easy decision. Seth had been far from overjoyed by the first assignment she obtained for him—an anonymous rewrite on a made-for-television script about a Ph.D. candidate in archaeology who has to support her child by working nights as a topless dancer in a go-go bar. Real high art, Seth recalled with a snort. But the bottom line was the bottom line—he had gotten paid for the job, paid enough to be able to buy a used but reliable Volkswagen Beetle.

Then Melinda scored him another anonymous rewrite job, and that one enabled Seth to pay back some of the money he owed his parents. He actually got a screen credit on his third job, paid back the rest of his debt to his folks and moved to a safer neighborhood. He began to live like a human being, eating real food, wearing real clothes. It was fun.

And it was still fun today. *Ax Man* movies were a kick to write not because Seth loved blood and gore, but because he enjoyed knowing that he was reaching millions of people with his words, entertaining them, distracting them from their own miseries for ninety minutes on a Friday night. And he derived private pleasure from sneaking in his little messages: the speech he gave the psychologist in *Final Cut* about how greed is the root of all evil and the subplot in *Return of Ax Man* about the herbicide being used on poison ivy that caused a skin rash identical to the rash caused by the poison ivy itself. And the feminist slant of *Ninja Women. Coed Summer* had no little messages to redeem it, but who needed messages in a movie costarring those two delectable actresses with the matching Kewpie-doll smiles....

Sellout, he berated himself.

What the hell. If the past fifteen years had a lesson to teach, it was that no one individual could save the world. You did what you could, sure, but the truth was, no matter what sort of scripts Seth wrote, he couldn't stop the earth from turning. He couldn't stop world leaders from making fools of themselves. He couldn't stop anyone from falling in love with the wrong person or falling out of love with the right person. No matter what Seth wrote, crazed street thugs would still prey on elderly widows. Crazed parents would still abuse their children. Crazed assassins would still shoot heads of state.

But at least it was possible that, for a short time, in a darkened theater, with a tub of popcorn in your lap and a friend by your side, you could forget about all the real crazies and lose yourself in the travails of a beautiful psychologist doing battle with a fictitious murderer. You could, for a few minutes, put out of your mind all the horrors of the world, all the horrors of your own life.

Maybe Seth had sold out. But maybe, just maybe, he was doing what he could to help others. People needed more than peace, love and freedom to keep them going day to day. They needed laughs, phony scares, visceral thrills, a chance to escape every once and a while.

That was what Seth contributed to the world: a chance to escape. And damn it, that was important, too.

Chapter Five

"Let's be real, Zeke," Seth argued. "The grenade blew off his arm, so now he needs an artificial limb. We're agreed on that. But this isn't the *Six Million Dollar Man* we're making here—it's *Ax Man*. Sure, he can wield an ax with an artificial arm, but firing bullets out of a bionic index finger? No way, José."

Smiling smugly, Zeke rubbed his scented black cigarette out in the ashtray Seth kept on hand for him. He was seated in the leather La-Z-Boy in Seth's in-home office, his legs crossed at the ankles, the sleeves of his patterned silk shirt rolled up to his elbows, his silver hair so smoothly combed it almost looked like tempered metal. "Imagination, Seth," he said calmly. "Think big."

"I can think big," Seth maintained. "But let's be real. Let's talk motivation. Granted, the technician who designs the limb is under pressure—"

"Pressure?" Zeke laughed at Seth's understatement. "Ax Man has all but destroyed the lab. He's wrought havoc. He has the technician's scantily clad assistant under his thumb, so to speak, and—"

"Ax Man doesn't *have* a thumb at this point," Seth grumbled. "Sure, he can pressure the technician to make him a limb. But a limb that fires bullets is way out of line, Zeke. I stand by my original proposal—that the technician manages to build a blade into the side of the hand so that whenever Ax Man karates somebody he cuts the guy to ribbons. But no shooting fingers, Zeke. It destroys the entire concept."

"You're going to instruct me on concept? Who's directing this mother, anyway?"

Seth ground his teeth and turned back to the electric typewriter on his desk. "All I'm saying is, motivation, Zeke. Where's the technician's motivation? Building a prosthesis that can fire bullets is above and beyond."

"You're saying motivation. *I'm* saying imagination. Let's not be so psychologically constrained, chump. We need the bullets for the big climactic scene. That's a beautiful scene you wrote, Seth, that gorgeous shoot-out at the little suburban house, with the inferno at the end. Where did you come up with that image, anyway?"

"Patty Hearst," Seth told him. "Remember when Cincque's house was surrounded by feds and blasted to hell? Talk about special effects—and that was for real, man, right there on the six o'clock news." Closing his eyes, he indulged in a memory of the spectacular public shoot-out at the modest house where the kidnapped heiress had been held for a while. He had seen the replay numerous times on various news reports, and he'd considered that shoot-out almost obscene. Indeed, it was just the sort of imagery that made the *Ax Man* movies what they were.

Opening his eyes again, he was confronted by the sight of his director seated too comfortably in Seth's favorite chair, and he added, "Cincque didn't have any ammo popping out of his fingertips, Zeke. What he had—if I can refresh your memory—was a good old gun. Why can't we give Ax Man a gun and leave it at that?"

"There's no imagination in a gun," Zeke disputed him placidly. "Humor me, Seth. I promise you, however you write it, I can make it work."

Staring at the typewriter, Seth grinned reluctantly. After having composed so many film scripts, he ought to have been used to writing scenes to order.

And out of chronological order. Zeke had already begun secondary shooting on *Ax Man Cuts Both Ways*—sex scenes, mostly. Sex scenes could always be spliced in, no matter what plot finally emerged from Seth's typewriter. Whatever motivation the sex scenes needed was more than amply supplied by the very appearance of the actresses Zeke had already hired for the film. Darla Dupree, for instance, with her big eyes and her cute little button nose and her 38-C bra size.... The way she looked in a bikini was all the motivation anyone could ask for in a sex scene.

"All right," he capitulated with a sigh. Why should he care? Given the fee plus points he had coming to him on this picture, he ought to be a professional and write whatever idiotic crap his director requested of him. "You want bullets in his finger? You've got bullets in his finger. But give me a chance to build up to it. Maybe Ax Man can torture the scantily clad assistant first."

"Torture?" Zeke echoed, intrigued. "What kind of torture can he do? He hasn't got an arm yet, don't forget."

"Try this on for size," Seth suggested, his thoughts taking a new tack. "Ax Man barges into the lab and finds the technician and the assistant in flagrante delicto."

"All she's got on under her lab coat is some filmy underwear," Zeke chimed in, eagerly adopting the spirit of Seth's idea.

"Whatever," Seth said with a shrug. "The technician is in love with the assistant. The assistant is married to the technician's boss. The technician will do *anything* to keep her old man from finding out that he's been diddling her."

"Perfect," Zeke agreed, chuckling with satisfaction. "Good old-fashioned blackmail, with as much kink as possible thrown in. There's your motivation."

"I'll have the scene in your hands by tomorrow morning," Seth promised.

"Beautiful." Zeke stacked his papers into a tidy pile and kicked down the footrest of the chair. "Meanwhile we'll sub these pages for the original scenes twenty-four through twenty-seven. This is good stuff, Seth. You're a genius."

"I wouldn't go that far," Seth said with false modesty. He supposed that anyone who could come up with a decent justification for Ax Man's ability to fire bullets out of his finger probably possessed some sort of grotesque genius.

He escorted Zeke through the rambling ranch house to the front door. As soon as he opened it, Barney bounded inside from the yard, panting and drooling. Zeke leaped out of the huge dalmatian's path and fastidiously dusted his designer jeans. "God, I hate that creature," he grumbled.

"And he hates you, too," Seth countered cheerfully. He curled his fingers around Barney's collar to keep the dog from attempting to hug Zeke. They remained in the open doorway as Zeke left the house, climbed into his fire-engine-red Lotus and peeled down the driveway. "What a jerk," Seth whispered to Barney as they watched the dust settle along the driveway in the sports car's wake. "Bullets out of an artificial finger. The guy's got oatmeal for brains." Barney expressed his agreement with a gleeful bark.

After shutting the door, Seth shambled back to his office with Barney doing his darnedest to get underfoot. In the office the dog circled the earthen-hued Navaho rug several times before curling up on it and settling down for a nap. Seth dropped onto the swivel chair by the desk, glared at his typewriter and switched it off with an impatient grunt.

He wasn't in the mood to write the revised scene. He had to get it done by tomorrow, and he would, even if it meant pulling an all-nighter. Given his habit of procrastinating, a habit that harkened back to his college days, Seth was no stranger to all-nighters. He was too old to forgo sleep as often as he did in his youth, but if he had to, he could do it. As always, he'd get his scene written by deadline.

But right now he didn't feel like tackling it. Shoving aside his folder of notes, he lifted the oversize paperback book he'd been examining when Zeke had arrived an hour ago. Seth had found the book that morning at his favorite new-and-used bookstore. It was a collection of photographs of Nova Scotia, its people and scenery. *Maritime*, it was called.

Seth opened the book for the fourth time that day, and for the fourth time that day, he wondered. If Troy Bennett could produce stuff as exciting as this, why the hell was he wasting his time taking wedding pictures?

Seth pored over each of the book's photographs, dazzled by Troy's mastery of natural light, his ability to convey texture and celebrate nuance. How in God's name could Troy work with prissy little brides and panic-stricken grooms, when he was capable of magic like the photos in *Maritime*?

His gaze lingered on a photograph of a young boy standing beside a grizzled fisherman who was repairing a net. The fisherman sat hunched over his work, evidently oblivious of the photographer, but the child stared directly at the camera, his eyes large and haunting, curiously accusing. He was too young ever to have seen any of Seth's movies, but even if the boy had been older, Seth would have hoped that he didn't blow the contents of his piggy bank on trashy films. It wasn't for kids like him that Seth was writing.

Nor was it for the girls Laura worked with, girls barely a few years older than Rita, already on welfare, already saddled with babies, oppressed beyond belief. What little money they had ought to be earmarked for food, rent, diapers—and books. Not cinematic junk.

Who was Seth kidding? The only people his scripts were designed to reach were people who had the wherewithal to find healthier ways to escape. Why lose yourself in an *Ax*

Man movie when you could lose yourself in a five-mile jog or a Dickens novel?

And, more important, why should Seth be wasting his time and exhausting his creative energy trying to find a rationale for the firepower of Ax Man's mechanical arm, when he could be writing something that would touch pregnant inner-city teenagers and lonely yearning youngsters in Nova Scotia?

It wasn't as if Laura had suffused him with guilt. It wasn't as if she didn't understand the need people felt to escape. She was as in need of escaping every now and then as any of the people who flocked to Seth's movies.

In a way, Seth realized, the weekend he and Laura had spent together was an escape for both of them. He knew she didn't often get to attend Broadway shows. Nor, he imagined, did she make a habit of visiting Prospect Park with Rita. When Seth had suggested that the three of them take a trip to the park on Sunday morning, Laura had welcomed the idea with genuine excitement.

Prospect Park was only a dozen blocks from her apartment. A sprawling oasis in the heart of Brooklyn, it rivaled Central Park as a respite from the city's overcrowded neighborhoods. At ten o'clock on Sunday morning the park was relatively empty.

Initially Rita had balked at riding on the carousel. "I'm too old," she'd complained. "What if someone from school sees me or something?"

"If someone from school sees you, they'll be jealous," Seth had predicted. "Look how old your mother is. If she can ride on a merry-go-round, so can you. Right, Brodie?"

Laura had pretended to be insulted by Seth's crack about her age, but she had happily climbed onto the ride and selected a black pony with a white mane and gilt saddle to sit on. Seth had chosen the horse beside hers, and Rita had reluctantly climbed on board, as well, making a great show of being blasé about the ride and deliberately choosing a horse several rows ahead of her mother's and Seth's so she could act as if she didn't know who they were.

That had been fine with Seth. He had wanted to concentrate fully on Laura, watching as she clasped the brass pole with her small, graceful hand, watching as her thick, dark hair streamed back from her face. Watching her face, illuminated with pleasure as her pony carried her away.

Lord, but she was beautiful. She had seemed so peaceful, relaxing in the rhythm of the ride, giggling at Seth's antics as he kicked his sneaker heels into his horse's rump and chided it for its leisurely gait, shrieking when he leaned far out over the side of the platform in search of a gold ring. If he had won one, he would have made her wear it.

She had looked equally beautiful when they'd abandoned the carousel for the zoo. Seth's behavior around animals was to get down to their level, to scratch his armpits in front of the gorilla cage, to roar and strut for the lions and caw nasally for the tropical birds, to clap his hands for the sea lions. Whether or not he was communicating with the beasts, he believed that it was a sign of respect to meet them on their own ground.

Despite her disdainful expression, Rita had clearly been amused by Seth's mimicry. Laura, however, had dealt with the animals quite differently. Instead of roaring and prowling in tandem with the lion, she had leaned over the railing and cooed to it, humming a lullaby, soothing it with her sweet song. At the elephant cage she had insisted on buying a bag of peanuts and feeding the lumbering gray animals. At the monkey house she had asked each of the monkeys if it knew where Curious George might be. When she, Rita and Seth finally left the zoo, she had sighed wistfully and remarked that she wished the animals didn't have to live in cages.

How like her, Seth mused. How like her to empathize with animals, to overflow with love for them. How like her to try to reach every creature, human or otherwise, with her kindness. It had been agony leaving her after they had gotten back to her apartment. It had been a kind of torture saying good-bye and summoning a cab to take him to the airport. He'd spent the entire flight back to Los Angeles staring blankly out the window and hearing her soft, mellifluous voice crooning "Hush, Little Baby" to the lion.

She needed escape just like anyone else. But even in escape she never lost track of who she was. She would never find movies like Seth's a valid way of escaping. And while he didn't think she would begrudge other people the escape Seth's films offered, he knew she believed that Seth himself was capable of something more. Even scratching your arm pits and screeching with the apes was a superior way of escaping when compared to watching gory flicks.

Setting down the book, he lifted the receiver of his desk phone and began to dial Laura's number. Halfway through he hung up. He had already called her twice in the four days since he'd left Brooklyn. The first time it had been after ten o'clock in New York and he'd awakened her. She had been too drowsy to talk coherently, so he'd made the call brief, promising that he would phone again soon. The second time he had called earlier in the evening, and Rita had informed him that her mother was out leading a weekly group therapy session for pregnant high school students. Seth had had a pleasant chat with Rita, but chatting pleasantly with Rita hadn't been his purpose in calling.

If he called now, he might or might not reach Laura. And if he did reach her, he wouldn't know what to say, other than that he hadn't stopped thinking about her since he'd left New York the previous Sunday. He hadn't stopped thinking about her dark, shimmering eyes and the captivating lushness of her hair, about the way her breath had caught in her throat when he'd stroked her breast. More than once since returning to California he had found himself puzzling over whether he was angrier about her indictment of his work or about her refusal to make love with him.

These were not the sort of subjects he wished to discuss with Rita while her mother was leading some after-hours group therapy session.

He flipped back and forth through his phone book until he located the business card Troy had given him at the *Dream* party. It was a plain white rectangle with Troy's name and the address and telephone number of his studio printed in block letters, and along the bottom *Portraits, Parties, Passports.* Passports, Seth mused with a snort of disgust. The genius responsible for a book like *Maritime* was doing passport photos. All was not right with the world.

He dialed the number, listened to the electronic clicks as the long-distance call was connected and then heard a woman's voice recite crisply, "Bennett-Chartier Photography Studio, can I help you?"

Belatedly Seth checked his wristwatch. Quarter to four—that made it quarter to seven in Montreal. Photographers must work at odd hours, like scriptwriters. "Is Troy Bennett in?" he asked.

"Who's calling?"

"Seth Stone."

"Well, he's just on his way out," the woman reported. "Let me see if I can catch him."

Seth started to protest that his call wasn't that important, but before he could get very far, he realized that she had put him on hold. Within ten seconds Troy was on the line. "Stoned? Is it you?"

"Last time I looked it was," Seth joked. "I need a passport. Do you do U.S. passports, or only Canadian ones?"

"Hey, as long as you aren't calling me on a wedding. I'm booked up to here with those jobbers."

Troy didn't sound as if he were on his way out, but Seth courteously said, "Listen, if you can't talk now, I can try you some other time. Your secretary just told me you were about to take off."

"I'm always about to take off," Troy said wryly. "It's the story of my life."

"Do you want me to call back later?"

"Nah. It's just some retirement party I'm supposed to shoot. The guy's worked at the firm for forty-one years. He can wait a few more minutes before scoring his gold wristwatch." He paused for a moment, then said, "So? To what do I owe the honor?"

"Well..." Seth fingered the book on the desk. "I was at a bookstore this morning, and while I was scrounging around, I found a big paperback on a back shelf. It was a little dusty, but none the worse for wear. A terrific book, if you want to know the truth. Maybe you've heard of it. It's called *Maritime*."

After a brief silence Troy said, "Dusty, huh?"

"The thing's dated 1982," Seth noted, opening the book to the copyright page. "And what the hell is Voyager Press? I never heard of it before."

"It's a small, independent press run by a guy named Peter Dubin. He publishes a lot of poetry, monographs, stuff like that. He doesn't do much photography because it costs too much to print. I guess I lucked out—he decided to do a limited run of my C.B.I. photos."

"C.B.I.?"

"Cape Breton Island," said Troy.

"Yeah, well, I'd say *I'm* the one who lucked out, getting my hands on a book like this," Seth claimed as he thumbed through the book's pages. "These photos are strong, Troy, really excellent work. Right now you'd never guess what I'm supposed to be doing, but instead, here I am, staring at this picture of a little kid and an old man fixing a net.''

"All right, I'll never guess," Troy said with a laugh. "What are you supposed to be doing?"

"I'm supposed to be writing a scene that explains how the resurrected Ax Man manages to get an artificial arm that can fire bullets out of its index finger."

"Its index finger?" Troy guffawed. "Why the index finger? Why not get gross, Seth, and have him fire out of his middle finger? Or better yet, skip the euphemistic fingers altogether and have him fire out of his—"

"Whoa!" Seth cut him off before joining him in laughter. "And I thought *I* was perverted!"

"Face it, Stoned, what are guns?" Troy contended. "Phallic symbols, am I right? Why not extend the metaphor to its ultimate expression?"

"Sick," Seth groaned. "You're sick, Troy. Why are you wasting your life up there in Moose City? With a brain like yours you could make it big in Hollywood."

"Is that a compliment?"

Seth chuckled. "No, Troy, it's not. Forget I ever said it." His gaze fell once more to the photograph of the fisherman and the boy, and his laughter faded. "Look, I don't want to keep you from your work—"

"No problem, Seth," Troy assured him. "It's not like I can't wait to take pictures of a bunch of drunks making long-winded speeches about what a swell ol' guy the guest of honor is."

Seth digested Troy's remark. "Why do you do it?" he asked. "I mean, why aren't you out on Cape Breton Island, doing photographic essays about grizzled fishermen and little kids? The photos in *Maritime* are so good, Troy. Why aren't you doing more stuff like that?"

"In ten words or less?" Troy shot back. "Because I'm old and I've got rent to pay. Do you know how much I earned making *Maritime*?"

"A few hundred dollars?" Seth guessed. He had no idea of what small press publications brought in.

"Try nothing," Troy told him. "Actually, if you count travel expenses, I lost money on it. What Pete paid me barely covered the cost of the film and chemicals. Fun is fun, Seth, but you can't eat fun."

"Laura thinks I've sold out," Seth confessed.

"Laura?" Troy hesitated, trying to follow Seth's apparent change of topic. "Laura Brodie?"

"I spent a lot of time with her last weekend. We took in a show together, I met her kid, the whole trip. And we talked, Troy. It was so good talking to her." He sighed. "Saturday night she lit into me for not doing something worthwhile with my life. I gave her the same story you just gave me, about how I like to eat food on a regular basis, and she made me feel as if I'd sold out."

"What does she understand about eating food?" Troy posed. "She lived on a commune for years. She probably learned how to thrive on twigs and pebbles."

"Come on, Troy, I'm being serious. Have we sold out? Does taking pictures of a drunken guy getting a gold watch mean you've sold out? Does writing *Ax Man* movies mean I've sold out?"

Troy laughed. "You've sold out for a much better price, if that signifies anything."

"It doesn't," Seth said. "The bottom line is, Laura *hasn't* sold out."

"Laura doesn't have to," Troy opined. "She's an earth mother. A nurturer. Everything she does is at one with the universe." He ruminated for a minute. "Remember when we used to have our staff meetings at *The Dream* and she would always arrive downstairs in the office with a huge bag of Good Shepherd Granola and a stack of paper cups? And she'd divvy up the granola among all of us and make sure everyone got the same number of raisins."

Seth chuckled at the memory. "That was Laura, all right," he agreed.

"The issue," Troy went on, "was never, where did Laura get all that Good Shepherd Granola and how did she pay for it? You know the kind of person Laura is. If someone were walking down the street pushing a wheelbarrow filled with Good Shepherd Granola and he saw her he would say, 'She can do more good with this than I can,' and he'd give it to her. That's the way she is. Some women have a baby out of wedlock and their lives fall apart. Laura has a baby out of wedlock and she's so together she winds up making it her job to pick up the lives of all the other unwed mothers and put them back together, too. Don't compare us to her," he concluded. "She's in a class by herself."

"Maybe," Seth allowed. He agreed with Troy's assessment of Laura. But to agree too wholeheartedly would mean to accept that Seth and Troy were in a much lower class, beyond redemption. If someone with a wheelbarrow full of granola saw both Seth and Laura, he would undoubtedly give it to Laura. But at the very least, Seth wanted to believe that if *he* were the one with the wheelbarrow, he'd have the decency to give it to someone like her.

"My secretary just appeared in the doorway and did a pantomime involving her wristwatch, a steering wheel and a strangulation," Troy said. "I think she's trying to tell me that if I don't get it together and leave for the retirement party I'm dead."

"Right." Seth closed the book of photographs and sat up straighter. "It was good talking to you, Troy."

"Take my advice," Troy said by way of parting. "Have Ax Man fire bullets through his fly. Make a statement with it."

"I'm not sure I want to know exactly what statement that makes," Seth remarked with a smile. "Take it easy, Troy."

"You, too, Stoned."

Seth hung up the phone. He swiveled from the desk when he heard Barney making a whimpering noise. The dog stood, marched in a wide oval and curled up on the rug again, facing the opposite direction. Then he closed his eyes, yawned and fell back to sleep. A sentimental warmth filled Seth as he gazed at his beloved dog.

His lips shaping a pensive smile, he turned back to his telephone and dialed Laura's number. He heard a busy signal and hung up. Then he inhaled deeply, clicked on his typewriter and typed:

INT. LAB. MLS—camera tracks slowly through the room. Off-camera sound of grunts and pants—a man and a woman engaged in torrid lovemaking. Camera tracks to door, stops. Door opens silently. Enter Ax Man.

"WHAT DO YOU MEAN, a story about me?" Laura tucked the telephone receiver more securely between her chin and shoulder and wrestled with the silverware drawer. The drawers in her kitchen were constructed of thick wood, with several drippy layers of paint slathered on. On damp days the drawers always stuck. "It's bad enough that, thanks to you, I'm going to be on that *Evening Potpourri* show. I don't think I can handle any more fame at the moment."

"*Evening Potpourri* is just a PR thing for the magazine," Julianne explained calmly. "Kim told me to milk the birthday for as much publicity as I could, and given that she's got a background in public relations, I urged my publisher to heed her advice."

"Exploiting your old friends in the process," Laura muttered, though she was laughing. With a final, vicious jerk, she succeeded in wrenching the drawer open. She sagged against the counter to catch her breath. "All right. Explain this brainstorm of yours to me."

"What I have in mind is an article about the people you work with—teenagers who are unwed mothers. Not a dry, statistical piece, not a tear-stained heart-warmer. Just a day-in-the-life sort of story with you as the focal point and a few of your clients as the spin-offs. I have a wonderful reporter in mind for the article, and we'll illustrate it with a few photographs, if we can get permission from your clients." Julianne sounded utterly sure of herself, the epitome of a confident, successful editor in chief. But that was the way Julianne was—always on top of things, always in possession of herself. Laura would be willing to bet good money that the drawers in Julianne's well-appointed kitchen never got stuck.

Her proposal interested Laura, not because she wanted to be the subject of a magazine essay that would be read nationally, but because she wanted to see the issue of teenage pregnancy discussed dispassionately in the media, as often as possible, until ways were found to solve the problem. Most of the time stories on unwed mothers dealt with the matter in a sensational way. But if anyone could produce the right sort of essay, presenting the subject in a thoughtful and comprehensive manner, it was Julianne.

"Some of my clients treasure their privacy," Laura warned her, handing Rita some forks and pointing her in the direction of the table. "I can't make any promises on their behalf."

"We could change names, of course," Julianne assured her. "And we wouldn't photograph anyone indiscriminately. We're not out to pillory these girls—or their boyfriends, for that matter. We just want our readers to know what it's like trying to make it as a fifteen-year-old single mother. Social issues are a mainstay of *Dream*."

"I know. I'm a regular reader," Laura reminded Julianne, her gaze following Rita as she haphazardly set the table.

"Then it's all right with you if I pass your name along to the reporter?" Julianne asked.

"Sure. Let me give you my work number." Laura recited the phone number for Julianne, then called to Rita, "Not the steak knives. We're having cheese-and-spinach loaf." Rita curled her lip and put the serrated knives back into the silverware tray. "Sorry," Laura apologized into the telephone. "As usual, I'm doing fourteen things at once."

"I'm so impressed by how you manage," Julianne said genuinely. "A career and a daughter. *Dream* has done the subject of Superwomen to death, but if we ever decide to do another story on women juggling careers and families, I'll be sure to put your name on the list."

Laura laughed incredulously. The last word she'd used to describe herself was "super." "Frankly, Julianne, I'm amazed that you wouldn't rather do an article on Kim. She's right there, in the heart of the nation's power structure—"

"The powerful have plenty of journals singing their praises. I'd rather run stories about the powerless. Teenage motherhood is just the sort of thing I like."

"Napkins," Laura reminded Rita, then apologized again to Julianne. "I'd better get off. I've got to teach my Superdaughter how to juggle the table settings."

"All right, I'll let you go," Julianne said. "We'll talk soon. And thanks, Laura. It's so great to be working with you again."

"It's so great to be *talking* with you again," Laura replied. "And working, too. If I've got to have my life blue-penciled and God isn't available, I would be honored to have you edit me, Julianne. I'll talk to you later."

After setting the receiver in place on the kitchen's wall phone, she pulled the casserole dish out of the oven and carried it to the table. She had prepared it the previous evening and baked it halfway, so it only needed fifteen minutes in the oven that night. One didn't have to be a Superwoman to have learned how to get dinner on the table within thirty minutes of one's arrival home from work.

She carried the salad bowl to the table, paused and then went back to the refrigerator to pour herself a glass of white wine. She wasn't a big drinker, but until Julianne's call, Laura's day had been reasonably lousy. She deserved a glass of wine.

Rita flopped onto her chair, and despite the face she'd made when Laura had told her what was for dinner, she spooned an enormous portion of the spinach and cheese concoction onto her plate. "What was that all about?" she asked, nodding toward the telephone.

"My old friend Julianne wants to do a magazine article about me."

"How come? Because you're friends with a famous movie writer?"

Laura smiled wanly. Rita somehow found a way to introduce Seth into every conversation they had. Laura was glad that Rita liked Seth, but she couldn't shake the suspicion that what Rita liked best about him were the most inconsequential aspects of his character: that he had access to limousines, that he favored chic attire, that what he wrote could only be considered the cinematic equivalent of Snickers bars.

Furthermore, Rita's constant mention of Seth made Laura fearful that her daughter might be expecting too much of his friendship with Laura. He had spent a couple of days at their apartment and he had telephoned a couple of times, but Rita kept behaving as if she expected a world-class love affair to blossom between her mother and Seth.

If a world-class love affair had been fated to blossom between them, Laura believed, it would have blossomed when Seth was in her bed. But there hadn't been any blossoms that night. Only some good, solid commonsensical friend-to-friend talk. For which Laura had to take the blame—or the credit.

"The article is going to be about teenage mothers," Laura told her daughter. "How was school today?"

"The usual. Do you think Seth is going to call tonight?"

"I don't want to talk about him," Laura said, a touch too sharply. She sighed, then managed a contrite smile. "I'm sorry, Rita, but I'd really much rather hear about your day in school."

"You wanna know the truth?" Rita took a swig of milk, then lowered her glass. "It stank. I got a ninety-three on my algebra test."

"A ninety-three?" Laura's face lit up with maternal pride. "Rita, that's wonderful! Thank goodness you didn't inherit my math ability. Or should I say, my math *in*ability."

Rita shrugged, feigning nonchalance about her grade. But Laura knew her daughter too well to be taken in by Rita's attitude. Laura recognized the glimmer of satisfaction in Rita's dark eyes. "Yeah, well, the test was easy. I don't know why everybody else did so bad on it."

"They did badly because it *wasn't* easy," Laura praised her. "And you did well because you're brilliant." Rita snorted bashfully, but again Laura had no trouble discerning her daughter's pleasure at her high grade. "So," she inquired, "what's so stinky about being a budding Einstein?"

"That wasn't the stinky part. What stinks is, Becky LoCaffio's getting cable. Everybody's getting it, Ma. I'm the only kid in the whole school who doesn't get MTV."

"We've already discussed this," Laura said wearily. "The cable subscription is much too expensive. And anyway, Courtney lets you watch at her house."

"Yeah, except now it's baseball season and her brother wants to watch baseball all the time. We can't even watch *The Monkees*."

"*The Monkees*?" Laura's fork clattered to her plate and her eyebrows shot up. "As in, 'Hey—hey, we're the Monkees'?" she asked, singing a few bars of the old television show's theme song.

"See, if we got cable here," Rita pressed on, "Courtney could watch *The Monkees* with me up here, and her brother could watch his dumb ball games at their place. I honestly don't think it's fair that I should always have to watch TV at the Gonzalezes'," she concluded piously.

"You don't always have to watch TV at the Gonzalezes'," Laura pointed out. "You could do other things there—read books, play cards, help Courtney's mother with the dishes...."

Rita rolled her eyes disdainfully.

"*The Monkees*, huh," Laura reflected, smiling nostalgically. "I used to watch that show all the time."

"It's a radical show," Rita declared. "They're so cute. All that mod clothing and stuff, the funny bell-bottoms and paisley shirts. And the music is neat, too. Which Monkee was your favorite?"

"The blond one," Laura answered at once. "I think his name was Peter something—or—other."

"Tork," Rita informed her. "Peter Tork. He's the weenie of the band, Ma. I think Mickey Dolenz is much cuter."

"I guess my taste always ran to weenies," Laura said with a whimsical shrug. She had been a big fan of *The Monkees* during its first run on network television, back when she wasn't much older than Rita was now. The fact that the show was currently being rebroadcast on cable television was almost reason enough to subscribe to a cable service.

"I guess if your taste runs to weenies, you aren't going to get together with Seth, huh," Rita predicted. "He isn't a weenie."

"He's blond," Laura noted, not bothering to resist Rita's reintroduction of Seth into the conversation. "His hair is about the same color as Peter Tork's. And when I first knew Seth it was as long as Peter Tork's. Even longer. He used to wear it down past his shoulders. Sometimes he'd even fasten it in a ponytail."

"Those were weird times," Rita remarked philosophically.

"I suppose they were."

"But Peter Tork's hair is kind of nice. I bet Seth looked cute with long hair."

"He did," Laura confirmed.

"He still looks cute," said Rita. "If I were you—"

"You aren't me," Laura cut her off, deciding that the discussion had gone on long enough. "Finish your supper."

HE CALLED an hour later. Rita was in the living room, doing her homework to the raucous accompaniment of the television. Laura had refilled her glass with wine and was lounging on her bed, reading the *New York Times* and getting depressed about all the bad news that filled its pages. The ringing of the telephone came as a relief to Laura; she was more than ready to toss aside the newspaper and pretend for a few minutes that the world wasn't falling apart.

"Hello?"

"Hi, Laura, it's me," Seth said.

A warm smile brightened her face at the familiar sound of his voice. She still hadn't forgiven herself for having not been at home the last time he had called, and for having been grouchy and muddled the time before. She still hadn't forgiven herself for having come down on him so hard the Saturday night they'd spent together.

She hadn't forgiven herself, but obviously Seth had forgiven her. If he hadn't, he wouldn't keep calling her.

"Hello, Seth," she greeted him. "How are you?"

"Other than going through a minor life crisis, I'm fine," he reported. "How are you?"

Her own dreary mood went forgotten as a wave of concern washed over her. "Minor life crisis?" she asked.

"Yeah. The way I figure it, my only chance of survival is if you come out to California and visit me."

He sounded on the verge of laughter, and Laura's panic abated. "What kind of life crisis?" she asked politely.

"Just the usual. I've got a scene due tomorrow and I don't feel like writing it. It's an incredibly dumb scene, complete with sex, violence and crude dialogue. I wrote about four lines, and I'm already sick of it."

"Oh, that sounds really major to me," Laura commented with pretended dismay.

"Remember when we were working on *The Dream,* and I used to get blocked while I was trying to write my 'Kulchah Column'? How did I handle it?"

"You ordered a pizza and stuffed your face," Laura reminisced with a grin.

"As I recall, I started by listening to Grateful Dead music in order to mellow out," Seth asserted. "Then I'd telephone you, and you'd suggest a new slant for the column. You'd share your insights with me. You've got a whole lot of insight, Laura. It's no wonder you're such a good social worker."

"I'm not," she argued, her smile fading. "I'm pretty ordinary as social workers go." She reached for her glass of wine and took a sip to silence herself. She didn't want to bore Seth with her travails at work. She didn't want to burden him. "Julianne wants to run a story in the magazine on the girls I work with. I doubt she'd want to do a story about me if I wasn't representative."

"A story about you in *Dream*?" Seth exclaimed, ignoring Laura's modest explanation for Julianne's interest in her as the subject of an article. "Wow, that's fantastic."

"I don't know..." She sighed.

"What don't you know?" he asked gently.

She meditated for a moment. Perhaps it was just the raw, drizzly weather that had gotten her down, or mere exhaustion. She didn't want to whine to Seth.

Yet he had asked. He wouldn't have asked if he wasn't willing to listen. And if he was willing to listen, the least she could do was talk. "Seth, one of my clients is pregnant again. I went to her apartment today, and there she was, with her baby on her hip and this stupid smirk plastered across her face. She's sixteen years old, Seth, and I've been working with her for months, trying to teach her about birth control, about responsibility. And what was her excuse for her current predicament? 'My boyfriend called on me,' she said, 'and he's got this way about him and I just can't say no.'" Laura shuddered. "A guy's got a way about him, and all the months I've been knocking myself out trying to counsel some common sense into this girl—it all goes right down the tubes. I think I'm in the wrong line of work, Seth."

She hadn't intended to go into all that with Seth, and her spate of words surprised her. She was in the habit of keeping her frustrations to herself. She had seen too many of the single mothers who were her clients take their frustrations out on their children, or else rely too much on their children for emotional support because no one else was around to talk to.

Laura did her best to avoid unloading her tensions on Rita. She had become so adept at it that she rarely shared her professional problems with anyone. When Julianne had called earlier that evening, it hadn't even occurred to Laura to mention her irritation about Sandra Miller's new pregnancy.

Yet she *had* mentioned it to Seth. More than mentioned it—she had released her exasperation in an uncontrolled spurt. She took a moment to assess what she'd done, and discovered that sharing her frustration with Seth was far more therapeutic than consuming a glass and a half of wine. For the first time since she'd left Sandra Miller's apartment in Bedford-Stuyvesant, Laura felt genuinely relaxed. Even a supposedly good social worker like her needed to unload every now and then.

Apparently Seth found nothing remarkable about Laura's having poured out her anger to him. "Don't be so hard on her," he said placatingly. "Accidents happen. Maybe the girl just lost track or something—"

"It wasn't an accident," Laura informed Seth, not bothering to question whether he was in any way qualified to discuss a client with her. She felt such relief in simply talking about the girl with another intelligent adult. "She said her boyfriend likes what he calls 'pure sex,' and he's got this way about him, so she took a chance. And now another baby's going to be born into that mess. On days like this, Seth, I wonder why I bother at all."

Her statement obviously took him aback. He didn't speak right away, and when he did, he sounded solemn. "You bother, Laura, because you care."

"Do I really?" She fingered her wineglass, then set it down without drinking.

"Of course you do. You've had a rough day, that's all. Maybe you need a break."

"What did you have in mind, Dr. Stone?"

"I already told you what I had in mind. Come to California. Play with Barney. I read somewhere once that petting dogs is supposed to lower your blood pressure."

"My blood pressure is normal," Laura said, laughing.

"Mine always spikes when I have to write sex and violence on a deadline," Seth revealed. "Why don't you come out here and watch *me* pet Barney?"

"Oh, Seth." She sighed again. The idea of flying out to California, even if only to watch Seth pet his dog, was so tempting that she had to smother the urge to say yes at once. "When?" she said, instead. "When should I come?"

"Now. This minute. This very instant," Seth answered exuberantly. "The second I hang up the phone, I want you to walk through my front door."

"Barring the impossible, that won't happen," Laura warned him.

"Then when can you come?" he asked. When she hesitated, he said, "The airfare is my treat, by the way."

"Seth—"

"That isn't open to discussion," he silenced her. "I've got money. I'll pay."

"You really want to see me, don't you?" Laura murmured, appreciating the unspoken compliment in his offer.

"No," he responded sarcastically. "I always pay the airfare for someone I don't want to see. Of course I want to see you. When can you get here?"

"Well..." She closed her eyes and let her head settle comfortably into the pillow. She wanted to see Seth, too. Not only for romantic reasons, but because for the first time in aeons, she had found someone she could confide in, someone she could complain to. She had spent so much of her life taking care of others, helping others to work out their problems, that she had neglected her own desire to be taken care of. If anyone could take care of her, it was Seth.

She could talk to him. She could share her difficulties with him.

"Tomorrow?" he suggested.

"I work for a bureaucracy," she reminded him. "Finagling some vacation time isn't as easy as all that."

"What vacation time? Trade with someone and forget the bureaucracy. Rules were made to be broken."

She grinned. She could probably negotiate something with a couple of the other case workers in her department. They could cover for her for a week, and she could cover for them sometime down the road. "What about Rita?" she asked.

"Bring her along."

"No," Laura said firmly. If this trip was going to be a genuine break for her, then it ought to be a break from the pressures of motherhood as well as the pressures of work. She wanted time alone with Seth, without having to worry about entertaining Rita or making sure that Seth was always fully clothed in Rita's presence. "I'll talk to Courtney's mother and see if Rita can stay with them for a few days. Rita's got school, after all."

"Okay. Terrific. The minute you've got it all worked out, Laura, let me know and I'll arrange for a ticket for you."

"Are you sure you want to pay for it?" she asked. She didn't doubt his generosity, but she didn't believe that she was truly going to be visiting him, either.

"Is Columbia the gem of the ocean? I'm rich, lovely Laura. I'll pay for the ticket, and then you can come here and scold me for being so extravagant. Doesn't that sound like fun?"

"Tons of fun, Seth. I'll give you a call after I rearrange my entire life."

"I'll be waiting with bated breath," he promised before hanging up.

Laura lowered the receiver and stared at the telephone. Her gaze wandered to her wineglass, and she lifted it in the phone's direction, offering a silent toast to Seth before she sipped. Once her wine was gone, she would worry about rearranging her life, working out the many details that would make her trip to California possible. Glenda Gonzalez would probably agree to let Rita stay with Courtney for the week. And Laura would do whatever was necessary to wrangle some time off from work. If she couldn't trade around with her colleagues for some leave time, she would tell her supervisor that she was suffering from a temporary case of burnout. Given how furious Laura had been with Sandra Miller that day, such a diagnosis wouldn't be much of an exaggeration.

The pieces would fall into place. If they didn't, Laura would force them into place. She wanted to see Seth, and she would see him. No matter what.

Chapter Six

She ought to have felt free. An entire week away from home stretched ahead, as clear as the cloudless sky surrounding the airplane. An entire week during which Laura wouldn't have to hear the words "weenie" or "everybody else does." A week away from Rita, and a week away from Sandra Miller and all Laura's other clients, those troubled, thoughtless girls who claimed with astounding certainty that they had heard from a reliable source that you couldn't get pregnant if, one, you had your period, or two, you went on top, or three, you took an aspirin immediately afterward.

Laura ought to have felt free, but she didn't. As she was learning, cloudless skies didn't guarantee a smooth flight. The wide-bodied jet kept bucking and trembling as it hit invisible pockets of turbulence, and each jolt caused Laura's stomach to lurch up toward her throat. She wasn't the most seasoned of air travelers.

She probably should have taken an inner seat and slept throughout the trip. But she had requested a window seat, and, turbulence notwithstanding, she couldn't fight the compulsion to stare out the window at the miniature world below, the green-and-brown checkerboard of farmland, the hairbreadth threads of rivers, the dense, shadowy blur of a forest. She wasn't sentimental enough to romanticize the glorious vista. She knew that some, if not most, of those impressive checkerboard farms were owned by families teetering on the brink of financial collapse and that somewhere, in the back seat of a car parked beside one of those meandering silver threads of water, a seventeen-year-old boy was busy convincing his sixteen-year-old girlfriend that if she went on top she wouldn't get pregnant.

It wasn't that Laura was a pessimist. She had enormous faith in the human race, in the capacity of ordinary people to conduct their lives with decency and love. All they needed was knowledge, sensitivity to others and a willingness to accept responsibility—precisely the characteristics she sought to instill in her clients. Social work wasn't for cynics.

Yet she was glad to get away from her job for a few days. Maybe she *was* burning out just a little bit; maybe she was getting old, her supply of patience running dangerously low.

The hell with her job. What she was getting away from wasn't nearly as important as what she was traveling toward. She was excited about seeing Seth.

Excited, and a touch anxious. She tried to convince herself that her primary reason for seeing him was that he was a friend, but she knew better. She knew that she was seeing him because his eyes were hypnotic and his smile was irresistible, because, even though they'd done little but talk the night they'd spent in her bed, she was overwhelmingly attracted to him.

And that was what made her nervous. As she'd recognized when he was in Brooklyn, it would be quite easy for her to fall in love with him. Not only because of his eyes and his smile, not only because of his lean, sexy body, but because he had the sensitivity to comprehend how desperately she needed a break from her daily worries—and because he had the strength to demand that she take that break. He had the perception to understand that she needed a good dose of playtime to regain her perspective on things.

She could fall in love with him, but she questioned whether she should. Deep in her heart, she questioned whether he could truly return her love. That doubt, as much as the plane's bumps and jumps, contributed heavily to her queasiness.

A steward came to remove Laura's lunch tray. All Laura had consumed was a glass of milk and a few bites of something called a "nature treat," which seemed to be little more than a glorified candy bar with some rolled oats mixed in with the sugar and chocolate. The rest of the meal had looked too unappetizing to taste. She was happy to have the fresh-scrubbed young man take the food away.

As soon as the steward left, Laura turned her attention to the window again. The rolling hills that marked the beginning of the continent's incline to the Rockies reminded her of the hills near Ithaca, where the commune had been located.

She had learned about the place from a college friend in the fall of her senior year. After graduation, Laura and her friend had traveled up to Ithaca to visit the commune. Her friend had left after a couple of weeks, but Laura had remained.

It wasn't merely the warmth and generosity of the commune's residents that had persuaded Laura to stay, or the charmingly decrepit farmhouse, or the barn that a few of the men had skillfully converted into additional living quarters, or the flourishing garden, or the rustic beauty of the region. Nor was it Neil, although the attraction he and Laura felt for each other had been instant and intense. All those things contributed to her decision to join the commune, but the main reason she chose to live there was theoretical. She loved the idea of it.

She loved learning how to cook dinner for twenty hungry people and how to put up homemade preserves. She loved walking into the bustling kitchen shortly after sunrise each day and hearing three different people shout "Good morning!" She loved pitching in, doing chores, stacking split logs in the shed for the winter, hiking five miles with a bucket to pick wild blueberries and then hiking five miles back to the farmhouse with her harvest. She loved the two young children who lived on the commune with their parents. She loved the camaraderie, the sense of family. As an only child, and one who, like so many of her generation, had rebelled against her parents' traditional views, Laura had been delighted to adopt the communal family as her own.

It seemed only natural that she would want a child, to extend her sense of family even further. When she broached the subject with Neil, he greeted it with enthusiasm. She hadn't expected to conceive so quickly, but when she did, she was secretly pleased by her fertility. Being pregnant made her feel wholesome, womanly, rich in mysterious ways.

She took the job assisting the sociology professor at Cornell because she figured she'd need some extra money for the baby, and Neil kept his job at a food co-op because it provided medical insurance. Laura gave birth to Rita at the farmhouse, with only Neil and a midwife in attendance, which was exactly as Laura had wanted it.

She was shocked that Neil decided to leave the commune when Rita was less than six months old. Other commune residents had moved away and were replaced by newcomers, and each departure had disturbed Laura to a certain extent. But she had been positive that Neil would want to stay, even if he fell out of love with Laura. She had assumed that he would want to be near his daughter.

As he had explained it, the last person he wanted to be near was Rita. He hadn't fallen out of love with Laura; he honestly didn't want to leave her. But being a father wasn't at all what he had expected. It was too much work, with too little immediate return. He felt trapped.

"You aren't trapped," Laura had told him. She wouldn't ask him to stay if he wanted to go. The last thing she would ever want to do was trap a man. "There's the door," she had said, dry eyed and resolved. "It's unlocked."

And he'd left.

Perhaps it was then that Laura had first learned to keep her feelings to herself. Neil's abrupt departure became the major focus of Laura's communal family. They fretted over her and Rita—in part because they were genuinely worried about how she would manage, but mostly because Neil's abandonment of his daughter was the most exciting thing to occur at the generally uneventful commune for some time. Laura soon came to realize that, in the guise of concern, her companions were simply gossips, delighting in a scandal. So she kept her mouth shut, shaped into a passive smile. The commune was based on shared possessions, but Laura's feelings belonged to herself.

"There's the Grand Canyon," the elderly man beside Laura announced, nudging her ribs and then reaching across her body to point out the sight.

She blinked herself back into the present and gazed down through the window. A few tufted clouds momentarily obscured her view, and then she saw what appeared to be a wrinkled brown gash in the earth. "This is the first time I've ever seen it," she confessed, thrilled by the sight, even though it was too remote to be breathtaking.

"First time? You ought to get a look at it up close," the man advised her. "Take one of the burros down. It makes you feel insignificant, I'll tell you."

"I'm not sure I want to feel insignificant," Laura said with a laugh.

She chatted with the man for the remainder of the flight, delighted to be distracted from thoughts of her past, as well as from thoughts of her immediate future. She didn't know what was going to happen when she saw Seth. But everytime she allowed herself to think that her time with him would proceed smoothly, the plane hit another pocket of turbulence and reminded her that a rough ride was sometimes impossible to foresee.

The bumpiness of the flight ended once they passed over the Santa Ana Mountains and entered a new weather system. But if Laura had hoped to relax and feel her stomach settle back into its proper place for the final stretch of the journey, she was disappointed. The gentleman beside her regaled her with detailed accounts of the last few times he'd flown to California. "Last year, for instance, we were coming in to San Jose, and they had seventy-mile-an-hour wind shears. Although I hear it's worse taking off in a wind shear than landing in one. Still, I'll tell you, it wasn't much fun. Or the time a few months ago, I was on a jet landing at San Francisco and it nearly missed the runway and dropped into the Bay. Swooped up at the last minute and circled again. What a scare. You could practically feel the water splashing against the underside of the plane."

Laura swallowed and eyed the discomfort bag in the seat pocket in front of her. Forget about her immediate future. If by some miracle she survived the flight to California, what did she have to look forward to but a return flight to New York? Maybe she would cash in her return ticket and take a train back. Or maybe she wouldn't go back at all. Maybe she'd stay with Seth forever. That was a surprisingly consoling thought.

"You look a little peaked" were Seth's first words when, twenty minutes later, after the plane had made a perfectly safe, ordinary landing, Laura staggered off the craft and into the terminal. Seth was standing just beyond the security gates, waving frantically. She stumbled into his arms and issued a shaky sigh. "What happened?" he asked. "Was it a bad flight?"

"I'm alive, so I guess it couldn't have been all that bad," she conceded, smiling sheepishly and tilting her head back to see Seth. He happened to look wonderful, his hazel eyes radiant, his pale hair windblown and glistening with golden streaks, his dimples cutting deep lines into his sun-bronzed cheeks. But even if he had looked horrendous, Laura would have considered him the most wonderful sight in the world—infinitely more inspiring than the Grand Canyon from eighty thousand feet.

He appraised her thoughtfully, then frowned. "Then what's wrong? You're as white as a sheet, and you look as if you tried to eat your lower lip for lunch."

She laughed. "There was this man sitting next to me, Seth . . ." Her laughter increased as she realized how absurd her fear had been. "He looked like someone's grandfather, so sweet and Santa Clausy. In fact, he probably *is* someone's grandfather. Anyway, he spent the last hour of the flight telling me about every near miss in history. There he is," she said, angling her head toward the cherubic-faced man in the crowd swarming from her plane's gate.

"Sadist," Seth muttered under his breath. Laura's laughter increased, dispelling the last of her anxiety. "You've got to watch out for those Santa Claus look-alikes," Seth confided, slipping his arm around her waist and ushering her down the corridor to the baggage claim area. "Never trust anyone who looks sweet."

"Maybe I shouldn't trust you," Laura mused.

"Me? I don't look sweet." Seth twisted around to face her and bared his teeth menacingly. He emitted a growl from the back of his throat, then winked. "See? I'm trustworthy."

"Very, I'm sure," Laura played along.

He planted an affectionate kiss on her cheek. "Maybe *I* shouldn't trust *you*," he remarked. "Other than looking a little green, you're a sight for sore eyes."

HARLEQUIN

 **PRESENTS**

A Real Sweetheart of a Deal!

7 FREE GIFTS

PEEL BACK
THIS CARD
AND SEE
WHAT YOU
CAN GET!
THEN...

Complete the Hand Inside →

It's easy! To play your cards right, just match this card with the cards inside.

Turn over for more details . . .

Incredible isn't it? Deal yourself in <u>right now</u> and get 7 fabulous gifts. ABSOLUTELY FREE.

1. 4 BRAND NEW HARLEQUIN AMERICAN ROMANCE NOVELS – FREE!
Sit back and enjoy the excitement, romance and thrills of fou
fantastic novels. You'll receive them as part of this winning streak

2. A BEAUTIFUL AND PRACTICAL PEN AND WATCH – FREE
This watch with its leather strap and digital read-out certainly look
elegant – but it is also extremely practical. Its quartz crystal move
ment keeps precision time! And the pen with its slim good looks wi
make writing a pleasure.

3. AN EXCITING MYSTERY BONUS – FREE!
And still your luck holds! You'll also receive a special mystery bonu
You'll be thrilled with this surprise gift. It will be the source of man
compliments as well as a useful and attractive addition to your home

PLUS

**THERE'S MORE. THE DECK IS STACKED IN YOUR FAVOR. HER
ARE THREE MORE WINNING POINTS. YOU'LL ALSO RECEIVE:**

4. A MONTHLY NEWSLETTER – FREE!
It's "Heart to Heart" – the insider's privileged look at our most popula
writers, upcoming books and even recipes from your favorit
authors.

5. CONVENIENT HOME DELIVERY
Imagine how you'll enjoy having the chance to preview the roman
tic adventures of our Harlequin heroines in the convenience of you
own home at less than retail prices! Here's how it works. Every mont
we'll deliver 4 new books right to your door. There's no obligation and
if you decide to keep them, they'll be yours for only $2.49! That's 26
less per book than what you pay in stores. And there's no extra charg
for shipping and handling.

6. MORE GIFTS FROM TIME TO TIME – FREE!
It's easy to see why you have the winning hand. In addition to all th
other special deals available only to our home subscribers, you ca
look forward to additional free gifts throughout the year.

SO DEAL YOURSELF IN – YOU CAN'T HELP BUT WIN

Remember! To win this hand, all you have to do is place your
sticker inside and DETACH AND MAIL THE CARD BELOW.
You'll get four free books, a free pen and watch and an
exciting mystery bonus.

BUT DON'T DELAY! MAIL US YOUR LUCKY CARD TODAY!

If card has been removed write to: Harlequin Reader Service,
901 Fuhrmann Blvd., P.O. Box 1394, Buffalo, N.Y. 14240-1394

"You mean, looking at me makes your eyes sore?" she teased.

"I mean, lovely Laura, that looking at you makes my eyes very, very happy." He kissed her again. "If your flight was all that scary, I don't suppose you'll want me to show off my Porsche on the winding back roads." He scanned the bags as they slid down the chute to the carousel. "Which one's yours?"

Laura spotted her battered suitcase and reached for it. Seth chivalrously lifted it from the carousel, then took her hand and led her out of the terminal. The sun was high and hot above them, and she realized that late March in Los Angeles was a drastically different season from late March in Brooklyn. "I'm overdressed," she murmured.

Seth surveyed her outfit: a pair of evenly faded jeans, a long-sleeved blouse, a lightweight Windbreaker, socks and loafers. He was also wearing jeans, but his Hawaiian-print shirt had short sleeves, and he didn't have a jacket. Instead of his red high-tops, he was wearing water buffalo sandals. Laura tried to remember the last time she'd seen someone wearing sandals like his. In college, she recalled. On Seth's feet.

"Sure you're overdressed," he ribbed her. "All of us oddballs in Southern California are really closet nudists."

His car, which was parked in a short-term lot, was black, streamlined and low to the ground. "This is it, huh," she said, wondering exactly how impressed she was supposed to be.

"This is my baby, all right," Seth announced with the sort of pride Laura felt ought to be reserved for one's offspring. "I'd let you take it for a spin yourself, but you look like you're about to pass out, and frankly, I don't want you keeling over when you're at the wheel."

"You're all heart, Seth," Laura muttered. "I just know it's my well-being, and not your car, that you're thinking of."

He chuckled and unlocked the passenger-side door for her. "Well, it's too late to rent a limo. Rumor has it that all the limos in L.A. County are currently in the shop, being tuned up for the Academy Awards next week. So you're stuck with good ol' Chauffeur Stoned."

The Academy Awards. She really was in Lotusland. She waited until Seth had tossed her suitcase into the back seat and taken the wheel before asking, with as much nonchalance as she could muster, "Are you going to attend the awards?"

He tossed back his head and guffawed. "Me? Mr. Counterculture?" He twisted the ignition key, and the engine emitted a surprisingly quiet hum. "If you want to know the truth," he admitted, steering carefully through the crowded lot, "I did try to go once, the first year I was out here. I had this brainstorm that I would write a daring exposé about it and sell it to some muckraking magazine."

"What happened?"

Seth braked at the exit gate to pay the attendant the parking fee. "What happened? I found out that getting a ticket to the awards isn't exactly like getting a ticket to a Rolling Stones concert. Everybody and his second cousin tries to palm himself off as a journalist in order to get within ten feet of the Dorothy Chandler Pavilion. In addition to regular press credentials—which I didn't have at the time— I think you've got to submit a urine sample and three character witnesses." He pocketed his change, rolled up his window and hit the air-condition button on his dashboard as he pulled away from the gate.

"I bet you get an engraved invitation to the awards ceremony now," Laura noted. "Surely the author of *Ax Man* movies must be a revered member of the Hollywood community.''

"Revered?" He shrugged again. "I get an invitation because I'm a member of the Screen Writers' Guild. But if I decided to go, I'd have to fork over some ridiculous premium for tickets for myself and a date, and then I'd have to rent a monkey suit, pay some jacked-up parking cost—or rent a limo—and run the gantlet of all those screaming meemies who hang out in front of the theater, looking for stars. And then, to add insult to injury, I'd have to sit still for three-plus hours while the director of the best animated short subject wipes the tears from his eyes and thanks his wet nurse for making it all possible. Thanks, but I can think of better ways to spend a Monday evening."

Laura grinned. It was reassuring to hear Seth talk like this. The film industry may have made him richer, but deep in his heart he was still irreverent and antiestablishment, still able to view the monuments of contemporary culture with a jaundiced eye.

He manipulated the gear stick deftly as the car cruised away from the airport, and once the traffic began to thin, he fidgeted with the stereo console. An old Jefferson Airplane tape began to play. "I like your car," Laura said. "It has good taste in music."

He smiled and released the gear stick to squeeze Laura's hand. "I'm glad you could work things out and come, Laura," he told her earnestly. "I've missed you. And if anyone could use a good California suntan, it's you."

"The only reason I look so pale is that I'm still recovering from the flight," she reminded him, but her matching smile communicated that she was as glad as he was that she had come.

He steered onto the Pacific Coast Highway. It wasn't nearly as dramatic as she'd expected, but when she commented on that, Seth informed her that the spectacular scenery—the cliff-hugging hairpin turns—were located farther north, outside the city. Laura didn't really need any cliff-hugging hairpin turns after her bumpy plane trip, and she was content simply to view the pounding gray ocean that stretched toward the horizon to the west.

Just outside the city, Seth steered away from the water, taking a road that surely rivaled the coast highway. Low, dusty shrubs and dwarfed trees lined the road, and here and there she spotted a house clinging to the steep slopes. The houses seemed, for the most part, to be camouflaged by their surroundings.

It was a vastly different environment from the lush greenery of the East, but Laura found the tan, brown and olive-drab hues of the landscape strangely appealing. Before long, she was bravely peering down the slopes, enjoying the roller-coaster ruggedness of the terrain.

Eventually Seth turned off the road onto a driveway of packed dirt and loose gravel. The driveway they were on wove between dense clusters of red-barked bushes, which Seth identified as manzanita, before ending in front of a flat-roofed structure of fieldstone, wood and glass. "Be it ever so humble," he announced before shutting off the engine and swinging his door open.

A large, gangly dalmatian sprang out of nowhere and hurled itself at Seth, who miraculously remained upright under the animal's weight. "Barney!" Seth gave the dog a vigorous scratching behind its ears, then shoved it off himself and led it around the car to meet Laura. "Barney, this is Laura," he said, opening her door for her. "Take it from me, she smells good. So I'll thank you not to sniff her in unseemly parts of her anatomy."

"I know how to handle dogs," Laura assured Seth, extending her hand to Barney. He investigated it with his nose, then lifted his head so she could stroke him under his chin. He barked his approval.

"Phew!" Seth exhaled with exaggerated relief. "If he didn't like you, I'd have to put you on the next plane back to New York." He reached into the back seat to get Laura's bag, then escorted her into the house.

It hadn't appeared that big from the outside, but the interior spaciousness delighted her. Granted, she was used to cramped quarters—apartments in Brooklyn, and in Buffalo before that, and the low-ceilinged attic room she'd shared with Rita at the farmhouse on the commune. She waltzed through the vast living room, with its floor-to-ceiling windows on two walls, a cut-stone fireplace on a third wall and polished wood floors decorated with rust-and-gray woven rugs. "I love it," she said.

Seth seemed extraordinarily pleased. "Do you? I fixed it up myself."

"You've got the heart of an artist," she praised him, admiring the plump beige sofa and matching chairs, the teak tables, the abstract soapstone sculpture on a shelf built into one wall. The living room opened onto a dining room, which looked out on the overgrown backyard. Outcroppings of rock and tangled underbrush extended beyond the railed wooden deck to a cluster of trees that climbed the hill behind the house. "This is beautiful!" she exclaimed.

Seth smiled modestly. "Some people don't like it," he said. "It's practically a desert here, so brown and dusty. A lot of easterners find they can't adjust to life without crabgrass."

"I don't know about crabgrass, but I'd take this over concrete any day," she said, thinking not of the East Coast suburbs but of her densely built community of Flatbush. She wandered ahead of Seth into the kitchen. It was messier than the other rooms, with a dirty pot soaking in the sink and a stack of newspapers cluttering one counter, but Laura found it an infinite improvement over her own kitchen with its sticky drawers and archaic appliances. She crossed to the microwave oven, opened it and peered inside. "Fancy gear you've got here, Seth. Do you know how to use it?"

"Do I look like I'm starving?" he countered, attempting unsuccessfully to puff out his flat stomach. Laura burst into laughter, and Seth joined her. "All right, I haven't exactly mastered beef Wellington. But I do know how to make a baked potato in seven minutes flat."

"The rich are different from you and me," Laura quoted. "They don't have to wait a whole hour when they're in the mood for a potato."

"Money does have its compensations," Seth agreed, deadpan. He peeked into the sink, wrinkled his nose at the sudsy pot and headed out of the kitchen and down a back hall, with Laura following him.

The room they entered was clearly his office. A professional L-shaped desk stood in one corner by the broad window, a Selectric typewriter set up on the shorter surface and a thick black loose-leaf binder open on the longer surface, next to the telephone and an answering machine. Wall shelves held books and a number of other black binders, each spine labeled with a typewritten title. One wall was devoted to file cabinets. A leather reclining chair occupied a corner. Another beautiful handwoven rug covered the floor.

"So, this is where all that microwave money gets made," said Laura, drifting to one of the shelves and reading the titles on the binders: *Coed Summer*, *Barrio Warlords*, *Rich Intimacies*.

"This is where it happens," Seth confirmed, crossing to his desk and switching on his answering machine. "Let me scope my messages, and then we'll continue with the grand tour."

Nodding vaguely, Laura pulled one of the bound manuscripts from the shelf and opened it. The pages were nearly indecipherable to her, their contents typed in small clustered paragraphs with varying margins, bordered by numbers and unfamiliar abbreviations: "L.S." "C.U." "F/X." She slid the binder back into place on the shelf.

"Seth? Melinda," a voice said from the answering machine. "An update on that check New World still owes you. They assured me that it's in the mail. Ha, ha, if you catch my drift. I'll be in touch."

"That's my agent," Seth informed Laura as the tape whirled.

After a few clicks another woman's voice came on, this one soft and alluring: "Seth? It's me, Darla Dupree. I hate to bother you about this, but I'm having a real problem. It's this stuff about taking off my swimsuit before I go into the Jacuzzi. You know what I'm talking about, right? I mean, I'm still not clear on why I don't keep my swimsuit on. Zeke and I have been fighting about it, but you know him. Can you help me out maybe? I'll love you forever."

"A good friend of yours, I take it," Laura muttered wryly.

Seth offered a feeble smile and shut off the machine. "An actress," he said.

"One of your seven hundred starlets?"

Seth's smile widened. "Do I detect a smidgen of jealousy, lovely Laura?"

"Of course not," she retorted, irked that she might have sounded jealous. Whether or not Seth's lady friends went into Jacuzzis while wearing their swimsuits ought to have been of little concern to Laura.

That it evidently did concern her seemed to amuse Seth. He allowed her to stew for a moment before explaining, "She's starring in *Ax Man Cuts Both Ways*, and she's questioning her motivation for stripping in the Jacuzzi scene."

Laura forced a brittle smile. The truth was, she *was* jealous. She was jealous of Seth's glamorous life, his lovely home—and the existence of other women in his life. Even if the woman on the answering machine's tape was only a professional acquaintance of Seth's, Laura was jealous of her. She had never been a jealous person, and the realization that she was suffering from such uncharacteristic envy disconcerted her. Too rattled to speak, she pivoted and walked back into the hallway.

Seth picked up her suitcase on his way out of the office. They strolled down the hall to another open door, and he gestured her into the room. "This is the guest bedroom," he said as Laura took in the neatly made double bed and the clear-topped chest of drawers. She moved to the window and gazed out at a dark-leafed orange tree growing by the side of the house. Seth's silence prompted her to turn back to him. He stood hesitantly near the door, her suitcase still in his hand. "Do...uh...do you want me to leave this in here?" he asked, lifting the bag toward her.

He didn't exactly look awkward, but the question obviously made him feel a bit uncomfortable. Laura wasn't entirely sure what answer he expected—or wanted. If he had hoped for her to stay in his bed, wouldn't he have mentioned that when he had invited her? Yet if he didn't want her in his bed, he would have just dropped her suitcase and said, "This room's yours."

Apparently he hadn't made up his mind about where he wanted Laura to spend the night, so he was allowing her to make up his mind for him. She was touched, but like him a bit uncomfortable. Things would have been much simpler if they had worked the sleeping arrangements out beforehand.

On the other hand, there was that velvet-voiced woman on the answering machine, perhaps one of seven hundred. "I'll stay here," Laura decided. Better safe than sorry, she added silently, though she didn't want to think about why she might have been sorry if she had chosen to stay in Seth's room, instead.

He smiled enigmatically. "Okay," he said, setting down the suitcase by the bed. He studied her for a minute, and his smile grew gentle. "Would you like to sack out for a while? You really look bushed."

"That bad, huh." Laura glimpsed herself in the mirror above the bureau. Her hair was mussed, but given its curly, unpruned state, that wasn't worth mentioning. She did appear wan, but compared to Seth's burnished California complexion, any New Yorker would look wan. However, her flight hadn't been the most rejuvenating of experiences. Maybe a nap would do her some good. "What are you going to do while I rest?"

"Rewrite the Jacuzzi scene," he told her.

"Then I'll sleep for hours," she promised. "I don't want to interfere with your work."

He opened his mouth, then shut it. "Bathroom's across the hall," he told her as he backed out of the room. "There are fresh towels on the rack, so help yourself." Before Laura could say anything, he was gone.

YOU DO WANT TO INTERFERE with my work, Seth silently accused her. He stood in the doorway to his office, staring down the hall, imagining Laura opening her suitcase, brushing her hair, stretching out on the bed and closing her eyes. He was so happy she had come, so happy she was here with him, and yet . . .

Much as he wanted to, he couldn't blame Darla Dupree's poorly timed message for his uneasiness. It was his own fault for having turned on the answering machine while Laura was in the office. As soon as he'd heard Darla purring petulantly about having to strip off her clothes, he could almost feel condemnation oozing out of Laura.

Well, sure, *Cuts Both Ways* was a stupid flick. He wouldn't argue the point. But that didn't give Laura the right to be so damned sanctimonious about it. If it weren't

for a fictional madman armed with a hatchet, who would
have paid for Laura's airfare out West, anyway?

He stalked across the room to the desk and sank into his
swivel chair. After leafing through the manuscript in front
of him until he found the Jacuzzi scene, he rested his chin
in his hands and perused what he'd written. "Ugh," he
grunted softly.

Laura hadn't been sanctimonious. She hadn't been so
terribly critical. It was Seth's own doubts about what he was
doing that made him defensive around her.

He used to enjoy doing this sort of thing, didn't he? He
used to enjoy concocting foolish plots, with all the flesh and
gore a director like Zeke could dream of. Seth even used to
enjoy rewriting scenes to satisfy the actors and actresses. He
enjoyed satisfying them with his writing, just as he enjoyed
the knowledge that what he wrote would ultimately satisfy
an audience.

But he didn't want to be doing it now. He wanted to
march into the guest room, shake Laura's shoulders and say,
"You're right. Tell me what to do with my life, and I'll do
it."

He wanted more than that. He wanted to march into the
guest room, fling himself onto the bed and make love to
Laura. He wanted to pull off her clothing and kiss her softly
curved body from tip to toe, to bury his soul within her.

He wanted her. But like a first-class idiot, he had offered
her the guest room. And she'd accepted the offer, damn it.
When they were giving out the awards for the Academy of
Twinkies, they'd have to save a special statuette for her. And
one for him, too.

What was wrong with them? They were two mature, responsible adults. Seth hadn't imagined the magnetic pull
they'd felt for each other in New York, or in the airport just
hours ago, the moment they'd seen each other. Yet here they

were, tiptoeing around each other like a couple of smitten kids.

They were adults, and more important, they were friends. They were supposed to be honest with each other.

Maybe Laura honestly *didn't* want him the way he wanted her. Maybe it wasn't his occupation that turned her off so much as his doubts and confusion. Maybe she had simply expected him to take charge, to make demands and determine the course of their relationship.

Seth wasn't particularly macho, and he preferred women who met him halfway. That was the problem, though. Laura hadn't met him halfway. She'd chosen the guest room.

All he needed now was a wacky character with an ax to chop down the wall separating Laura's room from his. All he needed was the nerve to chop down the intangible but definite wall separating Laura from him.

Chapter Seven

Laura woke up, disoriented and vaguely expectant. A muted gray light seeped through the thin drapes drawn shut across the open window. The semisheer fabric billowed inward on a gentle breeze that carried a tangy, unfamiliar fragrance into the room.

She sat, adjusting the shoulder straps of her nightgown, and gazed around her. She felt supremely well rested, which wasn't much of a surprise, given how much sleep she'd gotten the previous evening.

That evening was something of a muddle. She remembered stretching out on the bed in the afternoon for what she had thought would be a brief snooze. Then Seth had awakened her for dinner. They'd sat in the glass-wrapped breakfast area of the kitchen, looking out on the descending night, eating the broiled chicken and salad Seth had prepared and sharing a bottle of wine. Laura was pretty sure she hadn't drunk much wine—as groggy as she was, she probably shouldn't have had any—and shortly thereafter she'd stumbled back to bed for the night.

Maybe Seth could handle jet lag, but Laura obviously couldn't.

She groped on the night table for her wristwatch and read that it was seven-fifteen. Kicking off the lightweight blanket, she padded barefoot to the window to open the drapes.

The sky outside the window was an incandescent grayish pink, a faint, predawn hue. She wondered why the sun hadn't risen yet, and then recalled that Seth's house was set within a canyon whose walls undoubtedly blocked the early rays. The orange tree beside the house was covered with delicate buds; it was their delightful perfume that Laura smelled.

She had no idea what time Seth had finally retired for the night, and she didn't want to disturb him if he was sleeping in. Silently she made her way down the hall to the kitchen, where a quick search located an open can of coffee and filters for his coffee maker. She set a pot to brewing, then wandered into the living room.

The openness of the space appealed to her. No curtains blocked the windows; given that the only building visible through the glass was Barney's doghouse, Seth didn't need curtains to ensure his privacy. She gazed out at the thick brush climbing the slope behind the house and smiled. *The rich are different,* she mused, reflecting on the fact that, in the eighteen years since she had left her parents' suburban home for college, she had never lived in a house all her own. There had been the noisy, active dormitory at Barnard and then the swarming farmhouse on the commune, the stuffy apartment near the SUNY-Buffalo campus when she was studying for her master's degree in social work and the slightly larger apartment she and Rita had moved to once she'd completed her graduate schooling and landed a decent-paying job, and then her current home in Brooklyn. She wasn't complaining; she knew all too well that in New York City, adequate housing—let alone an affordable two-bedroom apartment only a couple of blocks from the IND station—was nearly impossible to find.

Yet how nice it would be not to have to tiptoe around a house in fear of disturbing the people living in the apartment below. How nice not to have to smell a neighbor's on-ion-laden casseroles every time one opened the front door.

Money could be useful when it came to housing, she admitted. And certainly there was nothing ostentatious about Seth's house, no matter how many screenplays he had had to write to earn the down payment. Laura shouldn't brand him a traitor to the cause just because he happened to own a lovely home.

Roaming back to the kitchen, she shut off the coffee maker and searched the cabinets until she found a mug. The sound of approaching footsteps startled her, and she spun around to discover Seth entering the room. He had on a pair of baggy beige trousers and he was slinging on a bright red shirt. Laura glimpsed the lean, tan expanse of his hairless chest and turned away, inexplicably bashful. "Did I wake you?" she asked, busying herself with the coffee grounds. "I'm sorry."

"No apologies necessary." He raked his fingers through his sleep-tousled hair and grinned. "Early to bed and early to rise, makes a man healthy, et cetera."

"Are you wise?" Laura asked, turning back to him. He was buttoning his shirt, and she felt a strange mixture of relief and deflation that his torso was no longer in view.

He shrugged, then reached into the cabinet for another mug. "Two out of three ain't bad." He set his mug on the counter beside hers. "How'd you sleep?"

"Like the proverbial log. I'm sorry I was such a dead-head yesterday, Seth."

"No big deal. It takes most people a while to reset their inner clocks." Appropriating the role of host, he nudged her toward the table in the breakfast nook and filled the mugs. "I expect you to make up for it today. What can I get you for breakfast?"

"What have you got?"

"No fresh bagels, alas." He swung open the refrigerator door and related its contents to her. "Eggs, bran muffins, pita bread, Famous Amos cookies, and I think I've got some cereal somewhere."

"Bran muffins sound delicious," she said. Seth pulled a box of muffins and a tub of whipped butter from the refrigerator and carried them to the table.

"So what's on the itinerary for today?" she asked, watching while he distributed plates, knives and napkins. She liked being waited on by him, and she didn't offer any assistance in getting breakfast onto the table.

"This morning, I've got to drop the scene I rewrote off at my director's house," he told her. "After that, whatever you want. Homes of the Stars, Mann's Chinese Theater, Sunset Strip, the La Brea Pits. I bet you want to see Watts, too."

"Why on earth would I want to see Watts?" Laura asked. "I didn't come all this way to look at slums. I see plenty enough of them at home."

"I meant Watts Towers." Seth bit into his muffin and smiled. "The towers are a must on the tour. Some crackpot Italian immigrant built them out of scrap...you'll see. The first time I saw them I freaked out."

"Then we'll go there."

Seth leaned back in his chair, extending his long legs beneath the table, and sipped his coffee. "On a totally unrelated subject, Laura, is that a nightgown you're wearing?"

She glanced down at herself. There was nothing even remotely suggestive about the loose-fitting cotton gown, but she felt her cheeks color, anyway. "It isn't a three-piece suit," she joked nervously.

"The reason I ask," Seth said, "is that I've heard complaints from a certain quarter that you won't allow Rita to sleep in the nude until she's sixteen."

Astonished that Seth would mention such a thing, she scowled. "Since when are you interested in Rita's nudity?" she asked hotly.

He laughed. "It isn't Rita I'm interested in—it's this whole 'I am the mother—I lay down the rules' trip. I can't believe that an over-the-hill flower child like you would really play the heavy with her."

Laura suffered a momentary defensiveness, but as she studied Seth across the table, taking note of his genial smile and sparkling eyes, she realized that he was asking only out of curiosity. Having never been a parent, he evidently wanted to know how Laura handled the job.

She took a leisurely drink of her coffee, using the time to gather her thoughts. When she lowered the mug, she found Seth still watching her, still brimming with curiosity. "I don't know that I'm playing the heavy," she began, then exhaled. "It's just that things are so different today than they were when we were young, Seth. Kids are pressured in a thousand different ways to be grown up, to be sexual. I see it constantly in my work, and it's awful. They never have a chance to be just plain kids." She ran her finger around the rim of her mug, meditating. "I don't know where Rita got the idea of sleeping nude, but I suspect she read about one of her idols, a rock star or something, sleeping in the raw and thought it was a neat idea."

"It is a neat idea," Seth observed.

"For an adult, sure. But she's not an adult. She wants to wear cosmetics, spike-heeled shoes, musk colognes. She dreams about dating a boy who shaves, a boy who drives— in other words, a boy who's a lot older than her. Most thirteen-year-old girls do, so it's not like she's weird. But I'm her mother, and it's up to me to counter all the pressure she gets from other sources. I don't see any good in her growing up too fast."

"So you don't let her drink or do drugs, either," Seth surmised.

"I certainly don't." Laura exhaled again. "Maybe she does those things behind my back. I don't know. I can only hope. It's scary being a mother. I'm so crazy about Rita. I worry about whether I can protect her from all the danger in the world—and then I worry that I'm overprotective. It sounds so trite to say that I only want what's best for her, but it's the truth."

Seth contemplated what she'd said, and his smile grew tentative. "When I was growing up, my parents had a list of laws a mile long. I used to swear that if I ever became a parent, I'd never hand down so many rules and regs to my kids."

"So did I," Laura admitted with a laugh. "It's different once you're a parent yourself, though. After I had Rita, I felt much closer to my own mother. I could empathize with what she'd gone through raising me. I could understand it."

"Were your parents upset that you didn't marry Rita's dad?"

Laura rolled her eyes as she reminisced. "'Upset' is an understatement. They were apoplectic. They were furious that I was living on the commune, and then that I had Rita. But...wounds heal. Love conquers. My father passed away a few years ago, but we were very close again by the time he died. My mother and I are still close now."

"I'd probably be closer with my folks if I had a kid," Seth confessed. "Both my brothers have families. My mother never passes up an opportunity to lecture me on the virtues of settling down. One of her pet questions is, 'When are you going to settle down?' As if I were bouncing off the ceiling or something."

"When *are* you going to settle down?" Laura asked.

Seth comprehended that she was teasing him, and he responded in kind. "After I've run out of starlets."

"We're talking decades, huh."

"At the minimum." He pushed his chair away from the table and stood. "Let's shake a leg. Zeke is probably panting to get his hands on the new Jacuzzi scene." He carried the dirty dishes to the sink, then lifted the dog's water dish from the corner of the floor and filled it with fresh water. "Barney gets room service," he explained before heading for the back door off the kitchen.

"And I don't?" Laura griped.

Seth winked. "You aren't a dog, Laura," he murmured with a seductive grin before striding outside in the direction of the doghouse.

His smile unnerved Laura, and as soon as she reached the guest bathroom she gave her reflection a careful examination in the full-length mirror attached to the door. By no stretch of the imagination could her nightgown be considered sexy. The lacy trim around the neckline gave it an almost girlish appearance. Seth's insinuations were definitely uncalled for.

No, they weren't, she refuted herself as she stripped and stepped into the shower. That she hadn't made love with him in New York, that she had asked to stay in the guest room— none of it did anything to dispel the sexual undercurrent that passed between her and Seth. Even if he hadn't been aware of her reaction to the sight of his bare chest, *she* was acutely aware of it. She was aware of his every graceful movement, his every sly smile, the untamed glint in his eyes. Why else would she have been jealous of a mere voice on an answering machine?

She showered quickly, wrapped a towel around herself and hurried across the hall to her room, shutting herself inside. Confronted by the sight of the broad bed in which she'd spent the night alone, she was again forced to acknowledge the attraction she felt toward him. She knew that all she had to do was quirk her finger and he would be tearing off his clothes, happy to satisfy her every urge.

Every urge but one. As long as he was still writing tripe, she feared that she might never be able to give herself completely to him. She feared that possibility, and so, she suspected, did Seth.

She dressed in a cotton skirt with a calico print and a gauzy white blouse, fastened her silver hoop earrings to her ears and made a futile attempt to brush out the tangles in her hair. When she emerged from the bedroom, she spotted Seth standing by the desk in his office, gathering a stack of papers into a folder. He turned from his desk to greet her, and she saw that he was wearing sunglasses. With regular lenses, not mirrors. "All set?"

"All set."

They left the house and climbed into the Porsche. The sun had risen high enough to cast long, mysterious shadows through the canyon, but the morning was brisk. Laura wondered where the famed Los Angeles smog was, but she said nothing, appreciating the clean, dry aroma of the air.

"Zeke is a first-class jerk," Seth warned her as he navigated the winding roads. "He's directing the picture. His favorite word is 'beautiful.' Everything is beautiful with him—my ideas, my writing, my typewriter ribbons. Don't let him get to you."

"If he tells me I'm beautiful, I'll thumb my nose at him," Laura promised.

"If he tells you you're beautiful, it'll be the first time I've ever heard him say something sensible," Seth countered, downshifting around a sharp curve in the road. "He lives in Beverly Hills. Or should I say, *beautiful* Beverly Hills."

All Laura knew about Beverly Hills was what she had seen on television, most particularly what she'd seen as a child watching *The Beverly Hillbillies*. " 'Swimming pools, movie stars,'" she intoned, quoting from the series' theme song.

"Something like that," Seth concurred with a chuckle.

Laura didn't notice any swimming pools as they entered the exclusive enclave nestled within Los Angeles and cruised down a broad boulevard lined with towering palm trees. She assumed that the swimming pools were behind the houses, out of view. The houses themselves were predominantly white stucco, with red Spanish tile roofs. They were unabashedly huge, oppressively opulent. She much preferred Seth's community to the neatly manicured lawns and massive homes past which they were driving now.

"Where are all the people?" she asked. It suddenly occurred to her why the neighborhood looked so stark. Not a pedestrian was in sight.

"There they are," Seth said, pointing to a slow-moving bus with huge tinted windows. "Taking the tour, looking for stars. Hello!" he hollered, waving wildly at the tourists in the bus. "Go ahead, Laura, wave at them. They'll think you're famous."

Laughing, Laura complied.

Seth steered onto a circular driveway in front of one of the Spanish-style houses, coasting to a halt by the oak double doors. "This shouldn't take long," he predicted as he gathered up his file and swung his legs out of the car. Laura got out, too, and accompanied him to the front door.

A young woman uniformed in a black dress and white pinafore answered their knock. "Yes?" she said automatically, then smiled at Seth in recognition. "Ah, Señor Stone," she welcomed him with a heavy Spanish accent. "You are expected."

"Pretentious, huh?" Seth whispered as he followed Laura and the maid into a tiled foyer that was easily as large as Laura's entire apartment.

A silver-haired gentleman in a silk bathrobe appeared from a broad hallway, a long black cigarette in one hand, a cup of coffee in the other. "Hello," he hailed them, smiling broadly. "Early for you, Seth, isn't it? And who is this beautiful lady?"

Seth gave Laura a subtle poke in the ribs, and she stifled the reflex to giggle at Zeke's choice of adjective. "Laura, meet Zeke Montgomery, Ax Man's alter ego. Zeke, an old friend of mine, Laura Brodie."

"Old? I'd hardly call her 'old,'" Zeke gushed, handing his cup to the maid and taking Laura's hand. "It's a pleasure, Laura. Can I get you something?"

She considered his question cryptic, but thought it best not to ask for clarification. "No, thank you," she said.

"You've caught me with my croissants down, I'm afraid," he apologized, gesturing at his robe. "But we're scheduled to shoot the Jacuzzi scene in an hour, so I'm glad you got here when you did." He released Laura's hand to accept the folder from Seth. He thumbed through the pages without reading them. "Did you come up with a solution for Miss Prissy?" he asked Seth.

"Yeah," Seth replied. "I have her spot Lance through the window, do a fantasy trip and pull off her bikini while she's spying on him. It's pretty steamy, Zeke, but the motivation is there."

"Beautiful." Zeke took the folder back from Seth. "As long as we get her down to the bare essentials. Motivation," he huffed, shooting a glance at Laura, as if he expected to find an ally in her. "These prima donnas take one acting class, and they think they've got to play every role as if it were written by Chekhov."

"Well." Seth took Laura's hand and angled his head toward the door. "I've got to take Laura around to see the sights. This is her first time in our part of the world, so..."

"Don't let me keep you," Zeke said graciously, indicating with a flick of his hand that the maid should escort them out. "I'll be in touch if I need more from you, Seth. But this will probably do the trick with Darla. It sounds beautiful. Thanks for smoothing the waters—if such a phrase is applicable in the context of a Jacuzzi." He laughed hard at his own joke, and Laura was exceedingly happy to be ushered out of the house.

"Yuck," she groaned once the oak double doors were shut behind them. "What a sleaze."

"It's mostly affectation," Seth said, defending the director. "The guy comes on pretty strong, but he does good work. Always gets his pictures in on time and underbudget, which goes a long way in the business." He opened the car door for Laura, then jogged around to take the wheel. "Onward," he said, igniting the engine. "You haven't lived until you've seen Rodeo Drive."

"What's Rodeo Drive?" Laura asked.

"It's something you haven't lived until you've seen."

He turned down another boulevard lined with palm trees. Or maybe it was the same one they'd driven on before— Laura couldn't tell. "It certainly is white here," she mumbled.

"Are we speaking architecturally or racially?"

"Both, I imagine."

Seth chuckled, then turned another corner. "This is Rodeo Drive. The most expensive shops in the world. I'm amazed they don't make you pay to drive on the street."

Laura stared out the window at the exclusive shops and boutiques. Rolls Royces and Jaguars were parked along the curb, and the pedestrians—at last Laura saw people actually walking on the sidewalks—were to a person tall, thin and gorgeous. She ought to have been put off by the sight, but she was too amused by the glitter and affluence on display. "Hey!" She sat taller and stared at an extraordinarily blond woman entering a jewelry store. "Wasn't that that actress—you know, the blond one?"

"What blond one? They're all blond ones," Seth quipped.

"The one from *Charlie's Angels*."

Seth gave her a mocking look. "Don't tell me you're a *Charlie's Angels* fan!"

"Oops!" Laura laughed. "My dirty secret is out. I'm not a big fan of cop shows, but give me a cop show where three women get to do all the derring-do, and I'm a sucker for it."

"Laura, there are dimensions to you that I've never even suspected."

"Enough!" she protested, sitting back in her seat and succumbing to more laughter. "Okay. I've seen Rodeo Drive. Now I've lived."

Seth accelerated. "Next stop, Watts. From the sublime to the ridiculous, or vice-versa."

Watts was nothing like the slums Laura was used to back East. Although the houses were small and rundown, they *were* houses, complete with yards, grass and fences. Compared to the dreary tenements crowding the poor neighborhoods of most eastern cities, Watts struck Laura as a reasonably cheerful place.

Right in the midst of the neighborhood stood the towers, a pocket park decorated with bizarre sculptures and spires composed of refuse: broken bottles, scraps of metal, seashells, a society's discards welded together with cement and shaped into benches, bridges and soaring cone-shaped towers. "Incredible," Laura murmured in awe as she and Seth wandered through the tiny park and examined the colorful structures.

"See?" Seth ducked under a graceful span, pulling Laura behind him into one of the open towers. "Great works of art can be created from trash."

Laura understood Seth's unspoken message—that he, too, might be creating artistic screenplays even though they were trashy. But she derived another message from the magnificent towers and from the explanatory pamphlet she had obtained at the entrance gate to the park. "The man who built all this may have been a crackpot, Seth, but what a dreamer! He spent the better part of his life turning his dream into a reality. It wasn't practical. It wasn't reasonable—it was probably dangerous. But he didn't give up. He held on to his dream and made it come true. That's what makes this place so wonderful, Seth."

Seth studied her, his eyes hidden behind his sunglasses, his expression inscrutable. But she knew her comment had struck home. "The guy had a dream, sure," he granted. "He also had talent...."

"So do you."

Seth turned away, then craned his neck to view the looming peak of the tower in which they were standing. The multicolored concrete girders climbing to the sky dwarfed him, giving him an almost slight appearance.

Laura had intended her statement as a compliment, but she knew he hadn't taken it as one. She moved closer to him and wrapped her arms around his waist, hugging him from behind. "Poor Seth," she whispered. "This'll teach you to invite your conscience for a visit."

He rotated within her arms to face her. "Is that what you are? My conscience?"

"I'm your friend," she swore. "Is it the same thing?"

"Damned close," he admitted. He struggled with his thoughts for a moment, then said, "It isn't like I never tried, you know. I've got a drawerful of Watts Towers in my office at home, but nobody wanted them. Maybe I haven't got the kind of talent it takes."

"Or maybe the people who didn't want them were nobodies, just as you said."

He laughed wistfully. "How can you be good and bad for my ego at the same time?"

"I'm your friend," Laura repeated.

"Yeah." He gazed past her for a long, silent minute, then brightened. "Let's go step on some stars," he suggested.

"Stepping on stars," Laura quickly learned, meant walking on Hollywood Boulevard and literally stepping on the star-shaped implants paved into the sidewalk to honor Hollywood's luminaries. Seth took this part of the tour to heart, bowing to the stars that bore the names of performers he admired and stomping on those he abhorred. "This guy was an A-1 fink during the blacklisting," Seth muttered, scuffing his sandal across one star. "Now this one's politically sound," he went on, carefully skirting another star rather than treading on it.

"Isn't one of these drugstores where that actress was discovered?" Laura asked.

"Lana Turner? You're thinking of Schwab's," Seth informed her. "How come you want to see that? Would you like to perch on one of the stools and wait for a talent scout to discover you?"

"I doubt I'd make much of an impression," Laura conceded with a laugh.

"Don't belittle yourself. You're going to be on TV tonight."

"Tonight?"

"Tonight's the night *Evening Potpourri* is broadcasting the piece on the *Dream* party," he reminded her.

Laura smacked her forehead lightly with her hand, as if to jar her memory. "Is that tonight? Oh, Seth—make sure I call Rita so she won't forget to turn it on."

He checked his wristwatch. "It'll be on back East three hours ahead of us. We'll give her a call around three."

They stopped for lunch in Malibu at a restaurant built on the end of a pier. Through the broad windows Laura could watch the beachcombers and sun worshippers gathering on the clean white sand. It took some effort to remember that April hadn't yet begun. Yet watching the golden-skinned bodies of the frolickers on the beach caused her a twinge of envy. She'd spent enough of her life in northern New York State to have been disabused of the notion that blizzards were pretty. To live in Southern California, where it was balmy all year, where one could cruise along winding canyon roads and step on stars whenever the urge struck, might not be such a terrible thing.

As soon as they were seated, Seth spotted a waitress delivering to an adjacent table two festive-looking drinks embellished with tiny paper parasols. When the waitress approached him and Laura, he asked, "What's that drink they're having?"

"Piña coladas," the waitress informed him.

Seth turned to Laura. "You want one?"

She shook her head. "I don't think so."

"How about a strawberry daiquiri?" He peered up at the waitress. "Does a daiquiri come with an umbrella?"

"Sure, if you want one."

Seth glanced at Laura, who shook her head again. "I really don't want a drink," she declined. "It's too early for me. You can have a daiquiri yourself, if you want an umbrella."

"I'm not in a daiquiri mood," he complained. "Maybe a beer. What beers have you got?" he asked the waitress. She proceeded to rattle off a few brands, and Seth cut her off as soon as she mentioned Dos Equis. "I'll have one of those," he requested. "With an umbrella."

Suppressing a grin, the waitress departed. She returned shortly, carrying a brown beer bottle with a pink paper parasol protruding from its open neck, and a chilled glass mug. "Perfect!" Seth crowed.

"What's it perfect for?" Laura asked, amused.

Seth pulled the parasol from the bottle and took a swig of beer. Then he stood, circled the table to Laura's chair and planted the toothpick-thin stem of the parasol in the dense curls at the top of her head.

"Seth!" she protested, twisting beneath his hands. "What are you doing?"

"Experimenting," he answered blithely. "You've got the thickest hair I've ever seen. I want to see if it's thick enough to support an umbrella." He arranged her hair around the umbrella, then stepped back to appraise the effect. "Magnificent, Laura," he decided, resuming his seat. "Now you're set for all kinds of weather."

"Even if 'it never rains in Southern California,'" she joked, groping through her hair for the parasol and untangling it. She extended the parasol to him. "Here, you wear it."

"I haven't got enough hair."

"I noticed," she chided. "You ought to grow it back."

"Do you think so?" He ran his fingers through his cropped hair and shrugged. Then he pushed the parasol back to her. "It's for you," he insisted. "I get the beer and you get the frills."

Grinning, she wedged the parasol behind her ear, balancing the delicate pink rice-paper circle against her hair. "There. Doesn't that look better?"

Seth squinted thoughtfully. Then he smiled. "Actually, it looks gorgeous. Did I tell you I've got a thing about umbrellas? Remind me to show you my Mickey Mouse umbrellas when we get home."

"I'd love to see them," Laura confirmed. "Do you wear them in your hair?"

"One behind each ear," he explained, shaping his hands into circles and lifting them above his temples like Mouseketeer ears. Then he whistled the Mickey Mouse Club song. Convulsed in laughter, Laura had a hard time concentrating on the menu's listings when the waitress returned for their orders.

After lunch, Seth drove her to the area of Sunset Boulevard known as Sunset Strip. Dingy rock clubs and nightclubs bordered the curving sidewalks, which teemed with street life. "You want to see the grimy underbelly of the city?" Seth goaded her. "There are probably more hookers here per square foot than in all of Times Square."

"They look so young," Laura murmured sadly as Seth pointed out a couple of skinny girls loitering on a corner.

"They *are* young," Seth confirmed. "Runaways, mostly. Prepubescent waifs with stars in their eyes."

"What's being done for them?" Laura asked.

He shot her a wry look. "Uh—oh. I smell the blood of a social worker."

Laura refused to let him rile her. "It's pathetic, little children selling themselves that way. Somebody ought to help them."

"I don't mean to sound hard-hearted, Laura," Seth debated her, "but not all of us are geared to saving the unfortunates of the world."

"I wasn't talking about you," Laura said. "I was only speaking generally. Look at them." She spotted another girl, wearing fishnet stockings and gobs of makeup on her eyes, leaning against the outer wall of a record shop, her gaze following a pair of strutting T-shirted men as they walked past her. Her heart brimming with pity, Laura turned from the dismal sight and rummaged through the collection of tapes in the glove compartment. She found "Sergeant Pepper" and shoved it into the cassette deck. The familiar rock music, and especially "Lovely Rita, Meter Maid," quickly restored her spirits.

It was nearly four by the time they reached Seth's house, and he ordered Laura to telephone her daughter at once so Rita wouldn't miss the seven o'clock broadcast of *Evening*

Potpourri. Laura made herself comfortable in his office at his desk while he lounged on the reclining chair, and dialed the Gonzalez number. A girl's voice sounded through the wire. "Hello?"

"Courtney?" Laura guessed.

"This is," Courtney replied, using one of the baffling telephone locutions Rita and her friends had recently adopted.

"Hi, Courtney, it's Rita's mother. Is she there?"

"Oh, yeah. Sure. Hey, Rita?" She hollered so loudly Laura had to pull the receiver away from her ear. "It's your mom!"

Laura heard some muffled shrieks and laughter, and then her daughter's voice. "Ma? Is that you? Are you in California?"

"Of course I'm in California," Laura said with a laugh.

"Wow! Hey, Courtney, she's in California!" Rita announced to her friend. More shrieks and laughter ensued.

"Rita." Laura demanded her daughter's attention. "You can talk to Courtney when it's not costing a fortune a minute, okay? How have you been?"

"Fine, Ma. We gave each other pedicures today. You won't recognize my feet when you get home."

Laura suppressed a grimace. "Have you been good to Courtney's mother? No misbehaving?"

"Ma-a," Rita groaned.

"All right. I don't want to talk long, because at seven o'clock you're supposed to watch *Evening Potpourri*. Tonight's the night I'm going to be on."

"Wow! Okay, Ma. Is Seth going to be on, too?"

"Yes, Seth's going to be on."

"All right! How's it going with you two, anyway? Kissie-kissie?"

"None of your business, Ms. Buttinsky," Laura retorted, though she was smiling.

"Yeah, well, you know what they say. If you can't be good, be careful," Rita advised her mother. "Becky Lo-Caffio said if you get pregnant when you're too old, you can have a baby with three eyes or something."

"I don't even want to know why you and Becky Lo-Caffio happened to be discussing such a topic," Laura muttered. "But rest assured, Rita, I have no intention of giving birth to any three-eyed babies in the near future."

"That's a real relief, Ma, you know? Hey, Courtney, turn on *Evening Potpourri*! My ma's gonna be on! And Seth, too! Tell your brother he can stuff the Mets up his zit nose!"

Laura didn't bother to suppress her grimace this time; the imagery was simply too gross. "It's been charming talking to you," she grumbled once she was sure she had Rita's attention again.

"You, too, Ma. I helped Mrs. Gonzalez with the dishes this evening, okay?"

"Good for you."

"And tomorrow Courtney and I are gonna tweeze our eyebrows. I better go and watch the tube. I don't want to miss Seth."

"I'm sure you don't. Take care, honey. I miss you."

"I miss you, too. Bye!" The line went dead, and Laura hung up.

"So?" Seth called over from the chair. "How's Rita doing?"

"I'm not going to recognize her feet when I get home," Laura reported, then laughed. "She's doing fine. She can't wait to see you on TV."

Seth appeared surprised. "She can't wait to see *me*?"

"I think she has a crush on you, Seth."

"She does?" A pleased smile lit his face. "My very first groupie!"

"I highly doubt that," Laura scoffed, then bit her lip. Had she sounded too sharp, too jealous? Hoping to make amends, she stood and crossed to the door. "I tell you what. Why don't I cook you dinner tonight? I'm psyched to try out that microwave oven of yours."

SETH FINISHED ADJUSTING his VCR to tape the show and joined Laura on the couch in his basement den. He had watched *Evening Potpourri*, a video magazine, only a few times before, mostly by accident while he was running through the buttons on his cable box. But this was one show he intended to tape. For posterity, he contemplated with a self-deprecating laugh. For the same posterity as the file cabinets full of chest-thumping screenplays that no producer worth his salt would spit on.

He was in a reflective mood, thanks to the excellent Bordeaux he and Laura had shared over dinner and were finishing off now as they waited for the show to begin. Thanks, also, to the tour they'd taken of the city, to the pitiful sight of those underage prostitutes lining Sunset Strip like malnourished cattle at an auction. Thanks to what Laura had said about those girls and what she'd said about the crazed sculptor who had dreamed up Watts Towers.

Did she honestly expect Seth to write a script about teenage runaways? He could think of few themes more depressing—and besides, that particular sordid subject had been done to death in made-for-TV movies. If Seth were ever to write something Laura would approve of, it wouldn't be about prostitution. He'd never even talked to a prostitute. He couldn't imagine what went on in their minds.

There had been a time when he believed he *could* imagine what went on in the minds of ethnic street gangs, suburban racists, crass industrial polluters. He had been in his twenties then, full of hubris, ready to take on the world with his pen. But he knew that if he ever bothered to reread the scripts he'd written then, he'd be embarrassed by them. When you were young and foolish, you believed you could write about anything. He wanted to think he knew better now.

The television show's theme music began, and Laura tapped her wineglass to his. "Here's to the boob tube's latest stars," she joked. "I usually don't drink much, Seth, but I can't help thinking I ought to be drunk to watch this."

"Then go to it," he encouraged her, taking a sip of his own wine. He looped his arm around her shoulders and turned to the television. "He-e-ere's Connie," he boomed in a fair Ed McMahon imitation as Connie Simmons, the reporter who had attended the *Dream* party, appeared on the screen, positioned in front of the birthday cake.

"Oh, no! There's that photograph, in the background!" Laura hooted, pointing at the black-and-white photo of the six of them, young and grungy, hoisting Julianne into the air in front of the building where the basement office of *The Dream* had been located.

"'Enterprising students,'" Seth groaned, latching on to a phrase the reporter used in her introduction. "Was that what we were?"

"'Foolhardy' would be more like it," Laura commented. "Julianne looks fantastic, doesn't she?" For now Julianne was standing beside Connie, talking about *Dream*'s origins.

"Julianne's got class," Seth remarked.

"And it helps being tall. Tall people always look better on TV. You're going to look great, Seth."

His image appeared on the screen to prove Laura's claim. Posing in his mirror sunglasses, the collar of his white blazer turned up and his smile inexplicably wicked, Seth chatted amiably with the reporter. "That's right, screenplays," he told her. "One thing about *The Dream*—working on it taught me how to type."

Laura exploded in laughter. "Type? That's what you told her?"

"I can't deny that I said it," Seth confessed, waving toward the screen. "You just saw for yourself."

The next person Connie Simmons interviewed was Andrew. "I think it's fair to say that we're all essentially the same people we were back then," he declared. "The outer trappings may have changed, but I think we're all still dedicated, hard-working and idealistic. One learns to accommodate reality, but that doesn't mean one has to rearrange his soul."

"Once a professor, always a professor," Seth critiqued Andrew. "Leave it to Dr. Collins to make the rest of us sound like pea-brains."

"Here comes Kim," Laura said, silencing Seth. "Oh, God, she looks even better than Julianne."

"Kim has a habit of looking better than everyone," Seth pointed out. Laura nodded and leaned forward to listen.

"Journalism, public relations, speech writing. It's all connected," Kim was saying in her languorous Southern drawl. "If it weren't for my work on *The Dream*, I doubt I would have had the career I've had. It's all been one form or another of communication."

"Platitudes," Seth snorted.

"Shut up, pea-brain," Laura scolded him. "Let's watch Troy."

"Now there's a guy with guts. I thought I was dressed like a maniac, but look at him. Blue jeans and boots. *That's* class."

The reporter had just asked Troy about his decision to live in Canada. He seemed uneasy, shifting slightly and clutching a cup of punch in one hand and a lit cigarette in the other. "A lot of people moved to Canada in the late sixties and early seventies," he mumbled. "For a lot of different reasons. I'd rather not talk about it."

Seth sat up straighter. "I thought for sure they'd edit that out," he said. "I mean, he answered more discreetly than I would have, but still—it's not like he's recanting, saying he's sorry he dodged the draft."

"Maybe he isn't sorry," Laura posed.

"I'm sure he isn't. But that's not fashionable these days. It's in to be patriotic, you know."

"Maybe he's a patriotic Canadian," said Laura. Before Seth could respond, Laura appeared on the screen. She let out a pained cry. "I look like a blimp!"

"You look gorgeous," Seth consoled her, squeezing her shoulder. "Buck up, Goodyear."

Laura socked him in the arm, then turned back to the screen. She had been so nervous during her interview with Connie Simmons that she couldn't even remember what she had said, and she listened to the broadcast with curiosity. "I was never a great writer," she addressed the microphone. "But I always felt very strongly about my subjects. I think that's what social work is all about—making a profession out of feeling strongly about your subjects."

"Ugh. How pompous," she moaned.

"No, it's not," Seth said. He meant it, too. Laura had always felt strongly about things, and she still did. If any of them had managed to avoid 'rearranging their souls,' to borrow Andrew's phrase, it was Laura. Seth wondered whether she had even bothered to learn how to accommodate reality.

The show broke for a commercial, and Seth switched off his VCR with the remote control. He turned to Laura, who was staring at the television, her elbows on her knees and her head propped in her hands. "Would you like me to replay it?" he asked.

"Maybe later," she said pensively.

He tried to interpret her poignant smile, and the strange glow in her large, dark eyes. She didn't seem to be enjoying her TV stardom in the least. "You looked nothing like a blimp,'' he said, hoping to cheer her up. "You looked great.''

"Don't humor me, Seth. I looked fat.''

"You looked beautiful,'' he contradicted her, totally earnest. "You *look* beautiful. You were too skinny in college. Now you look..." Thinking about her having chosen his guest room to sleep in, he drifted off.

"I look what?'' she pressed him.

His eyes pored over her. He wondered whether his longing was apparent. He hoped it wasn't. She obviously was too troubled by what they'd just viewed on TV to be receptive to the ideas simmering inside Seth. "What's really bothering you?'' he asked. "It isn't just the way you looked on the show, is it?''

Maybe she *had* sensed his longing. Her dark gaze held his for a long moment, then shifted away. "Seth...I enjoyed using your microwave,'' she confessed.

Taken aback by her non sequitur, he scowled. "What does cooking have to do with anything?''

"Don't you see?'' She sighed. "I have this image of myself—we all do. You're the fun-loving rascal. I'm the purist. When I lived on the commune, I learned to bake bread in a wood-burning oven. I rejected things like microwaves and Porsches. And...and now I feel like a hypocrite, because I really like those things. I like your car. And your oven. Maybe I'd even like your movies, if I ever saw one.''

"I'm corrupting you,'' he apologized, though he was secretly pleased. If Laura could actually like such symbols of financial success, then maybe she didn't disapprove of him as much as he feared.

"No, Seth. You aren't corrupting me. You're just making me face certain things about myself.''

He arched his arm around her and cushioned her head against his shoulder. "All you have to face is the fact that you're human. You're allowed to like cars and appliances—and even bad movies, if they're fun. It isn't a crime."

"What if I get spoiled? What if I never want to go back to the life I used to live?"

Actually, Seth found that possibility immensely appealing, but he treated Laura's question with the solemnity it deserved. "None of us can go back, Laura. We can only go forward."

"I know." She nestled deeper into his shoulder and captured his hand in hers. "Growing up is hard, isn't it," she mused philosophically.

"To paraphrase George Bernard Shaw, it's preferable to the alternative." He kissed her brow. "Growing up isn't so hard when you're in the company of friends."

"One friend in particular," she murmured, tightening her hold on his hand. She didn't say anything more.

Chapter Eight

"Anything else I can get you?" the clerk asked.

Seth surveyed the assorted items he had deposited on the counter: a yet-to-be-assembled kite shaped like a butterfly with rainbow-striped wings, a board game called Organized Crime, a Velcro dart board that you were supposed to throw Velcro balls at—things had changed a lot since the time Seth had purchased his Spiro Agnew dart board.

"That'll be all," Seth told the clerk. Reaching into the hip pocket of his jeans for his wallet, he spotted a glass fishbowl filled with old-fashioned metal kazoos. "Wait!" He halted the clerk before the young man could hit the Total button on the cash register. "I'll take two kazoos, too." He crossed to the fishbowl and pulled out a yellow one and a blue one. He tried them both out, testing their timbre as he carried them to the counter for the clerk to ring up. "Hmm," he grunted, handing the blue one to the clerk. "This one needs to be tuned."

The clerk laughed and punched a few more buttons on his cash register. "That'll be forty-three ninety-five."

"Ouch," Seth yelped, though he handed over his credit card without hesitation. "Why can't I ever walk into this store without spending a fortune?"

"Some people leave here without parting with a dime," the clerk told him. "I guess you're just one of the weak-willed ones."

Seth grinned at the clerk's good-natured reproach. After signing the receipt, he pocketed his wallet, gathered the bulging bag into his arms and left the toy store.

The afternoon was balmy and breezy. If tomorrow turned out to be like today, he and Laura would be able to take the kite down to a beach and fly it. He doubted that she would be interested in trying it out today. The way things were going, he'd be lucky if he could get her out of the La-Z-Boy for dinner.

The way things were going... He issued a silent curse and started up the Porsche. The way things *weren't* going was the way he had hoped they would go. He wasn't sure what he had expected from Laura's visit, but having her beg him to let her read some of his old film scripts wasn't it. They had argued about it throughout their late-morning breakfast, Seth assuring her that the scripts were boring and pedantic, Laura insisting that she wanted to read them, anyway. He had given in, dug the old scripts out of his file cabinet and left her ensconced in the recliner with the damned things heaped on her lap.

All right. She'd read them; she'd see for herself that Seth wasn't cut out for writing that kind of stuff. She would get off his case, play Organized Crime with him, or Velcro darts, and tomorrow they'd fly a kite. He hadn't invited her to California to give him a hard time.

"Liar," he muttered aloud. He had brought her to California for just that reason. He had invited her because he was drifting, his mooring all but lost, and he wanted her to drag him back to shore. If she had to give him a hard time to do it, those were the breaks.

The hitch was that she was drifting, too.

At a red light, he glanced to his left and stared at a café on the corner. It was a classic California fern bar—lots of glass, natural wood and hanging plants. He had been there several times on dates. The bartender on the premises happened to make one of the better strawberry daiquiris in this part of the universe.

There was a pay telephone at the rear of the café, next to the rest rooms. Seth could park, hop inside, give Troy a ring and ask his old buddy for advice.

Except what sort of advice would Troy give him? He would probably lecture Seth on phallic symbols and gun control and then admit that he was in as much of a bind as Seth was. Troy hadn't figured out how to construct a solid life for himself. And he'd never indicated that he was much of an expert when it came to matters of the heart. How could he possibly help Seth?

Better to drive straight home, Seth resolved as the light turned green and he gunned the Porsche's engine. Better to go home, where he would undoubtedly find Laura making a bonfire with his old scripts.

He steered away from the coast and into the hills, playing the gear stick with as much virtuosic flair as Rampal his flute. Perhaps tomorrow Seth would let Laura take a turn behind the wheel. She had already admitted that she liked his car. For someone who relied on the New York City subway system as her main mode of transportation, piloting a Porsche ought to be a real thrill.

He was surprised when Barney didn't come bounding through the brush in welcome at the sound of the car's tires crunching up the driveway. Shrugging, Seth braked, shut off the engine and rummaged through his parcel until he located the yellow kazoo. Wedging it between his teeth, he locked the car and entered the house. Inside the door, he paused and listened. Not a sound, neither Barney nor Laura.

He proceeded down the hall to his office and stopped at the open doorway. Barney was fast asleep on the rug beside the recliner, where Laura was still seated. She might have been asleep, as well; she sat motionless, her head at a funny angle against the leather upholstery, her gaze fastened to the window. The stack of scripts lay unopened on her knees.

He took a deep breath, then let loose with a fanfare through the kazoo: "Tootle-di-TOO, di-TOO!"

Laura and Barney jumped in unison. The dog peered up at Seth, whimpered drowsily and dropped his head to his paws, closing his eyes once more. He was used to Seth's grand entrances.

Laura, however, needed a little more time to recover. "Good God," she gasped, settling back into the chair and laughing. "You scared me. What is that thing?"

"A kazoo," he told her, marching into the room. "I got one for you, too, so we can do duets." He dumped the bag on his desk and groped inside it for the blue kazoo, which he presented to Laura.

She studied it intently, then put it in her mouth and blew on it. No sound emerged.

"You've got to vocalize into it," he instructed her, then lifted his own kazoo to his lips and hummed a few bars of "Lovely Rita, Meter Maid."

"Oh." She tried again, singing this time, and the kazoo emitted a nasal, cartoony melody. "Aha!" she exclaimed, clearly delighted. She hummed a little more into the kazoo and smiled at the sound. "I've always wanted to learn how to play a musical instrument."

Seth leaned against his desk and watched her expectantly. He didn't know what he was waiting for—some sort of transformation, a glimmer of prideful joy at her mastery of the kazoo? Her mood did seem to change, but not in a way he could have foreseen. She lowered the kazoo and turned her attention to the binders on her lap. Her eyes be-

ame strangely distant, an intriguing glow emanating from
heir profoundly dark irises. When she lifted her gaze to
iim, she was smiling tenuously. "Can we talk?" she asked
olemnly.

Uh-oh. The boom was about to fall, and he braced him-
elf by slumping into his swivel chair, removing his sunglasses and folding his hands docilely in his lap. "Shoot."

"These are wonderful. Especially the one about the black
amily in the white middle-class neighborhood," she said,
apping the top binder. "*Good Fences*. It's fantastic, Seth.
There's so much of you in it."

"There is?" he joked, finding her reaction a bit extreme.
'Where? I'm not black, and I'm not a closet racist."

"Yes, but the way you tell the story, Seth. It's so—so
passionate."

"Passionate? There isn't a single nude scene in it."

"Seth, I'm being serious." She kicked down the footrest
and stood, then glided across the room to him. "Seth, it's a
beautiful story—they all are. I'm not using that word the
way your director does. I mean, they're *beautiful*. I'm very
grateful you shared them with me."

She was so earnest he couldn't make any more jokes. Her
eyes still glowing, she slid her hands beneath his arms and
urged him out of his chair. Then she gave him a warm
hug.

His arms reflexively circled her, returning her embrace.
"If everybody responded to my work the way you do, I'd be
a very happy man," he murmured.

"If everybody had the chance to see a film like *Good
Fences*," she claimed, her voice slightly muffled by the fabric of his shirt, "they'd respond the way I'm responding.
Oh, Seth, reading it . . . it was like finding you again, finding the Seth I know and love. You just can't keep ignoring
what's inside you."

"I don't ignore it," he contradicted quietly, running his hands soothingly up and down her back. "What's inside me is all this kazoo music just dying to get out."

"Seth." She drew back an inch, then cupped her hands around his cheeks so he was forced to look at her. "There's more in you than kazoo music, and you know it. There's kazoo music, and there are symphonies. You can do it all, Seth. You're wonderful."

She had never looked lovelier to him than she did then, her entire face radiating her certainty, her faith in him. Impulsively he bowed to kiss her, and she didn't stop him.

IF HE HADN'T KISSED HER, she would have kissed him. She had spent the past few hours reading his scripts, devouring them, falling in love with Seth.

Was it because he feared rejection that he had kept his finest work hidden in a bottom drawer of his file cabinet? Was it because he preferred to remain detached from his professional endeavors, putting as little of himself as possible into them, taking his money and running? Or was it because he honestly hadn't realized how superb his early scripts were?

More than just the screenplays themselves had transported Laura. She was overwhelmed by the discovery that Seth was everything she had always believed him to be, everything she had hoped. The writing had been rough in spots, some scenes too obvious, others too muddy. But the sentiments in them moved her deeply. Seth's soul was in those scripts, and seeing into his soul, experiencing the sheer goodness of it, exhilarated Laura.

Her mouth moved with his, her hunger growing as he pulled her more firmly to himself. "You know what we're doing, don't you?" he whispered when he finally slid his mouth from hers. His breath was uneven, his body obviously aroused.

She nodded.

"We don't have to if you don't want to."

"I want to," she said steadily. "Do you really think I came all this way just to sleep in your guest room?"

His mouth opened and then shut as he worked through his thoughts. "As a matter of fact, yeah, I was beginning to think that."

"Well, why didn't you say something, you ninny?" she scolded him. "Why did you take me to the guest room if you didn't want me to sleep there?"

"Because...because we're friends, Laura," he said soberly. "Because friends owe each other the right to make choices."

"All right, then," she whispered, pressing her lips to the warm hollow of his neck. "I'm making my choice."

He slid his hand beneath her chin and lifted her face to his, then peered into her eyes, as if to seek confirmation in their glittering depths. Apparently he found what he was looking for. A shy, enchantingly dimpled smile danced across his lips, and he clasped Laura's hand in his own and led her out of the office.

His bedroom was at the end of the hall. Like the other rooms, it was large and airy, the open windows allowing a gentle, fragrant breeze inside. He walked with Laura as far as the bed, then turned her to face him and kissed her brow. "Do you mind if I lay down a couple of ground rules first?"

Ground rules? She smiled nervously. If Seth was about to recite a few kinky preferences, she would be appalled, to say the least. "What sort of rules?" she asked.

"Once we hit the bed, I don't want you harassing me about my work."

"Why on earth do you think I'd do that?"

"You did it when I was on your bed," he reminded her, grinning. "It was a real turnoff. And frankly—" he brushed her lips with a light kiss "—I would like to remain as turned on as I am right now."

"I'll do my best on that score," Laura promised, mirroring his grin. "What's the next rule?"

"That we be careful. Out of respect for Rita, of course."

"Of course," Laura agreed. "I'd hate to have a three-eyed baby at this stage of my life."

"What?"

"Don't ask," Laura said with a laugh as she headed for the door. "I'll be right back."

She raced down the hall to the guest bedroom, trying to ignore the acceleration of her pulse, the heated expectation drumming through her body. She had anticipated this moment with Seth enough to have brought along her diaphragm, yet she had packed it inside an inner pocket of her suitcase, as if she were hedging her bets, unsure of whether she would actually use it.

As soon as she was ready she returned to his bedroom. He had already removed his shirt and shoes, but at her entrance he stopped undressing to give her his full attention. "Come here, lovely Laura," he murmured, extending his arms to her. She happily obeyed. He kissed her soundly, then smiled. "Do you believe in love at four thousand five hundred seventy-first sight?" he asked.

She trailed her fingers across the well-toned muscles of his chest. "As a matter of fact, I do," she admitted.

"Glad to hear it." He tugged her blouse free of her jeans and unbuttoned it. He seemed shocked to discover that she was naked beneath her blouse, but his surprise quickly dissolved into pleasure as he cupped his hands under the round, heavy swells of her breasts. "Flower child," he murmured.

"Hmm?"

"You aren't wearing a bra."

"Does that make me a flower child?" she questioned him, laughing. "I've never worn a bra. I guess you didn't notice that the first four thousand five hundred however many times you looked at me.''

"For at least the first three thousand of those times, you didn't need one," he recalled. "You were pretty flat-chested in college."

"Do you think I need one now?"

"No," he said decisively, then chuckled. "Especially not right this minute." He bent to kiss the warm crevice between her breasts.

His kiss ignited them both, and within an instant, it seemed, they had disposed of the rest of their clothing and tumbled onto the bed. Laura had never been particularly taken by bulging muscles on a man, and she found Seth's lean, lanky build incredibly attractive. She wanted to touch him everywhere, to stroke his streamlined muscles and hard flesh. Her hands moved insatiably across his body, savoring its sleek, firm lines.

He reciprocated, his fingers roaming over her breasts, along her slender waist, around the feminine softness of her bottom and thighs. "Did I happen to mention that I find you beautiful?" he asked, reaching as far as the crease behind one knee and tickling it.

She moaned softly, bending her leg around his hand to hold it in place. "I don't remember. You might mention it again."

"You're beautiful," he obliged, the words drifting across her skin on a gust of breath as he slid his lips down her throat to her collarbone.

"So are you," she complimented him. Her voice dissolved into another moan as his mouth ventured lower, skirting the full flesh of her breast before centering on her nipple.

"We're all beautiful people out here," he joked.

"No..." She drew in an erratic breath as her entire nervous system responded to the assault of his tongue. "You're different, Seth. Don't lump yourself with all the others. You're unique." His mouth roved to the other breast, and she twisted to accommodate him. Her hand rounded the broad ridge of his shoulder and stroked his back. "You have a gorgeous body."

He lifted his head to gaze down at her. "Do you think so?"

"I wouldn't have said it if I didn't."

He nodded, acknowledging that, whatever else Laura was, she was always brutally honest. "According to the statistics, I'm supposed to be past my prime," he pointed out, grinning wickedly.

"You've always been one to flout tradition," she parried. "I bet you aren't past your prime at all."

"An interesting bet," he mused, rising beside her and pressing his lips to hers. He nibbled tenderly at her lower lip, and his hand rose from the back of her leg to tangle in the mound of hair between her thighs. "A very interesting bet, but I don't think I'm going to take you up on it," he whispered.

"Please don't," she breathed, moving urgently against his hand. What little patience she had burned away beneath his provocative caresses, and she drew him onto her, demanding him.

He bound himself to her, then paused to catch his breath. His eyes bore down into hers, and she basked in their luminescence, their glittering array of color. She studied the dimples lining his cheeks, the brilliance of his smile, the tightness in his jaw as he struggled for control. "I was thinking—" he began, and then his voice broke off as his tension increased perceptibly.

"About what?"

He issued a shaky laugh. "About flying a kite with you."

"A kite?" she asked, bewildered.

"This afternoon." He inhaled sharply as his body reacted to the involuntary rocking motion of her hips. "I bought a kite, and I thought we'd..." He groaned, nearly surrendering. Shoring up his willpower, he inhaled again and continued. "I thought we'd fly it down on the beach this afternoon."

"Is that what you'd rather be doing right now?" Laura asked with a teasing smile.

His body answered for him, surging within her, succumbing to the longing that encompassed them both. He enveloped her, filled her, simultaneously giving and taking, following and leading.

She closed her eyes as waves of delight spread through her, fluid and honey sweet, buoying her, carrying her to the edge of sensation and then beyond. For an immeasurable moment, she lost all consciousness of where she was, who she was, and then Seth drew her back to reality with the wrenching force of his own release.

A low, helpless groan rose from his throat as he sank onto her. Her hands floated consolingly up his back and into the silky blond hair at the nape of his neck. His lips brushed her temple and he exhaled. "It was better than I expected," he whispered.

"Oh?" She drew back so she could view him. His face reflected exhaustion and utter contentment. "What did you expect?"

"Something wonderful," he answered. "But nothing *this* wonderful. I didn't know... I didn't think it was possible...."

His extravagant words elated her. She, too, hadn't known that it was possible to love someone so fully. She had loved Neil, but that had been so long ago, and she'd been so young. It was nothing like what she felt now, lying in Seth's arms, gazing up into his shimmering eyes and reading in them his resplendent satisfaction.

Then she noticed a change in his expression, a faltering, a flicker of doubt. "What, Seth?" she asked anxiously. "What's wrong?"

Brushing her hair back from her cheek, he wrestled with a pensive smile, then forced out the words. "I'm not— Laura, I don't know whether you were making love with the guy who wrote *Good Fences* or with *me*, the guy who wrote *Ax Man Cuts Both Ways*."

He looked so somber, so unnecessarily insecure, that Laura felt the need to make light of his remark. "You wrote *Ax Man Cuts Both Ways*?" she gasped with pretended horror. "I must be in the wrong bed!"

His smile widened only the slightest bit. "That's what I'm wondering," he confessed.

His worry was so genuine that she couldn't make any more jokes about it. It pained her to think that she could have undermined his confidence in himself.

Yet hadn't she? Wasn't that just like her, coming on so positively, behaving holier-than-thou, impugning his work while availing herself of the fruits of his labor, his oven, his car, the airline ticket that had brought her to him? She had been a hypocrite, afraid to admit that she loved him until she had read his old scripts and found in them the justification for her love.

She suddenly felt awful. She eased out from under him and rolled onto her side, staring at the window, abashed. "Why do you put up with me, Seth?" she groaned. "I'm so insufferably—"

"Braless," he completed. "I'm a sucker for jiggling jugs."

She shrieked at his deliberately crass phrase and tried to punch him. He easily caught her hand and pinned her to the bed below him. Staring up into his humor-filled eyes, she surrendered with a reluctant laugh. "You're disgusting, Stoned."

"And you love it," he goaded her.

"I wouldn't go that far." She attempted to look disappointed in him. "It's no wonder you write junk like *Coed Summer*. 'Jiggling jugs,'" she sniffed.

He scowled. She could sense his subtle withdrawal from her, and she wished she could retract what she'd said, specifically the word "junk." She had only been ribbing him, after all.

But she couldn't blame him for taking such teasing to heart. Most of the time, when she was criticizing his work, she wasn't ribbing him at all. "Am I harassing you?" she asked timidly.

"You're walking a fine line, Brodie."

She would salvage the moment. She had to. She loved Seth, and she had to restore his confidence. Managing a natural-looking smile, she swung off the bed.

"Hey—I didn't mean—"

"I'll be right back," she promised him, scampering out of the room. She dashed down the hall to his office, lifted *Good Fences* from the pile she'd left on the recliner and hastened back to his bedroom. She tossed the script onto the bed and climbed on beside Seth. "Read it," she ordered him.

"This minute?"

"Yes."

He sat and eyed her dubiously. "You sure you wouldn't rather fly a kite on the beach?"

"Read it, Stoned," she said sternly, placing the binder on his knees and opening it to the first page for him.

"Is there going to be a surprise quiz when I'm done?" he asked. At her glower, he smiled meekly and lowered his eyes to the script.

Laura curled up on the mattress, rested her head on Seth's shoulder and watched while he read. She wasn't bored; in fact, she could think of nothing she would rather be doing.

Even if Seth were sleeping she would enjoy lying beside him, admiring his physique, contemplating the shadowed contours of his smooth chest, the sinewy shape of his calves, the play of dusk's half-light through his hair.

But more engrossing to her than the sight of his naked body was his studious composure as he read. From his rapt expression, she could tell that he hadn't looked at *Good Fences* for a long time, maybe not since some myopic producer had rejected it a decade ago. Every now and then his eyebrows would arch in amazement at a perfectly constructed speech, a turn of phrase, a vivid image. Every now and then he'd gnaw on his lower lip or wrinkle his nose in disgust. But his attention never flagged. He perused the script without a break, without a quibble.

It took him much less time to read it than it had taken Laura. When he was done, he folded the binder shut and set the manuscript on the night table. Then he turned to her and found her still watching him. He laughed. "If you thought that was fun, perhaps I can arrange for you to watch some paint dry tomorrow."

"Quit stalling," she chided him. "Tell me what you thought."

"You can see for yourself," he said wryly. "The thing moved me to tears."

If she'd had infinite faith in him before, she entertained a sliver of doubt now. "You don't think it's beautiful?"

"I think . . ." He reflected for a minute. "I think it's well done for what it is."

"And what is it?"

"An uncommercial property."

"What's uncommercial about it?" she persisted. "Explain it to me, Seth. I don't know much about the film business."

He rolled his eyes. "That's obvious," he muttered. "All right. It doesn't have any nude scenes, for one thing," he said, echoing his earlier comment about it. "Nowadays, if you can't score an R-rating, it's the kiss of death. There's no sex in this script, and no violence—"

"No violence?" she exclaimed. "What about the emotional violence the family endures? The cruel rejections, the phoniness of the supposedly liberal neighbors? What about the bigotry the kid experiences in school? That scene where he tries out for the basketball team and he isn't good, and his classmates taunt him and say all those horrible things to him, calling him 'Globetrotter' and all that? Seth, that's an incredibly violent scene!"

"Maybe to you and me and the three other people in the world who like subtlety," Seth maintained. "But let's be real, Laura. I couldn't sell this thing if there were a famine in L.A. and I stuffed slabs of steak between the pages."

She eyed the binder then Seth. "What would you have to do to it to make it sellable?" she asked.

He snorted. "Shred it, for starters."

She ignored his sarcastic assessment. "You'd have to rewrite it, sure. It's got some rough spots—even I could see that. But you're pretty much done with that *Ax Man* script, and I'm sure that's going to pay you enough to keep the Porsche in gasoline for a while. Why don't you fix up *Good Fences* and see what you can do with it? "Ten years is a long time—you said it yourself. Maybe things have changed since then. Maybe, now that you've built yourself a reputation, someone will be willing to take a chance on it."

"You think so, huh," he muttered.

Laura sensed that he was half-convinced. "I think so," she maintained.

Seth stared at her for a long while, as if absorbing her certainty. A tentative smile cracked his face. "It does have some good things going for it," he admitted.

Laura felt a thrill of triumph ripple through her, as arousing as anything she'd felt while they were making love.

And indeed, this was a kind of lovemaking, too. Making Seth confront himself and his talent, making him recognize his abilities, restoring his faith ... they were as valid, as vital to her love for him, as anything else they might share. She wrapped her arms around him and gave him an exuberant kiss.

"Go to it, comrade," she exhorted him. "Save the world."

Chapter Nine

"I had an abortion."

Laura flinched. She stared at Sandra Miller, who was seated on the other side of the desk in the cramped cubicle that served as Laura's office. Sandra's baby was balanced precariously on her knee, leaning toward the desk and trying to swipe Laura's stapler. Sandra smiled anxiously. She looked far younger than her sixteen years, and for a brief moment Laura wanted to cry.

She didn't, however. To do so would be unprofessional. Not that Laura felt that one had to adhere strictly to the codes of professional behavior in every instance, but today, also seated in the crowded cubicle was Susan Trevor, the reporter Julianne had sent to write an essay on a day in the life of a typical New York City social worker and her clients. Laura had to maintain a calm facade in the presence of the scribbling journalist.

"I get it," she said to Sandra, forcing a smile. "It's April Fool's Day."

"Huh?" Sandra appeared befuddled. "Is it?"

Laura sighed, accepting the fact that Sandra's announcement hadn't been a joke. "Would you like to talk about what happened?" she asked.

"I don't know." Sandra shrugged, hoisting her baby higher on her lap. "You were on your vacation, see, and you know. Dennis came to call on me, and he has this way about him, and he says, 'Get an abortion.' So I did it."

"It was your boyfriend's idea, then?" Laura confirmed, jotting a note into the file folder spread open before her on the desk.

"Yeah. I guess he was right. I mean, what am I gonna do with two of his babies when I can't even get him to help me out with one? So I did it."

"How do you feel?" Laura asked.

"You mean, like how do I *feel*?" Sandra shrugged again. "Okay, I guess. It didn't hurt too much or nothing. I mean, it hurt a little, you know? But it's all over now. The doctor, The doctor, he said I was okay."

Laura lowered her gaze to the folder. "Why didn't you tell Mrs. Sprinks?" she asked, naming the social worker who had covered for her while she was away. "She didn't leave me any information about this."

"I don't know. I figured, who is she? Just some strange lady. I wasn't gonna talk to her about it." Sandra angled her head slightly as she measured Laura's reaction. "I thought you'd be glad, Miss Brodie. I mean, like you said, I got to take responsibility and all. I thought the new baby, well, it would mean a bigger check from the welfare, but Dennis, I thought he was talking sense."

"You thought he was talking sense when he insisted on 'pure' sex," Laura snapped, then took a deep breath to compose herself. "We discussed the idea of an abortion the last time I saw you, Sandra," she reminded the girl. "You were dead set against it."

"Well, you don't know Dennis. You don't know how he can be. I mean, he started talking sense," Sandra said, justifying herself. "I thought you'd be glad."

"What would make me glad," Laura said grittily, "is if you would start taking responsibility for yourself, Sandra. You've got to stop doing everything Dennis tells you to do. You've got to think for yourself. Having an abortion is a very big decision, and one you'll be living with for the rest of your life. All I can say is, I hope you made the right choice." She suppressed the urge to shudder, and offered a limp smile. "Did you write up your budget for this week?"

Sandra handed over the budget she had prepared. Many of Laura's clients had little notion of how to run a household, let alone run one on the skimpy allowance welfare provided. One of Laura's duties was to help them organize their finances. This was an area in which she frequently had major disagreements with her clients; she found it difficult to understand why they would rather spend their meager funds on cosmetics and record albums than on rent and utilities.

Sandra was fairly disciplined when it came to budgeting, though, and as Laura reviewed the figures in front of her, she let her mind drift. She suffered a transient pang of guilt for having been in California when Sandra obviously would have benefited from having Laura to talk to. But she didn't dwell on it. She had earned the time away from work. She simply wasn't going to shoulder Sandra's traumas.

Still, a vague anxiety continued to eat at her, even after she'd finished her session with Sandra and updated the file. It saddened her to think that her client was raising one child and aborting another when she ought to be attending high school, giggling, getting crushes on boys, watching MTV. She ought to be living a life like Rita's.

If Seth were around, he would tell Laura to stop worrying about trying to save the world—and he would probably be right. She couldn't help all the people all the time. Maybe it was enough to know that she did help Sandra some of the time, that Sandra's life was better for having known Laura.

But Sandra alone wasn't the cause of Laura's uneasiness. Nor was it the presence of Susan, who seemed like an intelligent, pleasant young woman. What was bothering Laura was the understanding that she didn't want to be sitting in her office in downtown Brooklyn, helping Sandra, at all. She wanted to be back in California.

She missed the summery weather, the fresh, dry air, the tangy desert aromas of Topanga Canyon. She missed the sight of people lolling on the beach in bathing suits at the end of March. She missed the statuesque palm trees of Beverly Hills and the luxury cars on Rodeo Drive, the restaurants with their strange sandwiches concocted out of mashed avocado, alfalfa sprouts and cream cheese on seven-grain bread. She missed sprinting with Barney up and down the driveway and test-driving the powerful Porsche.

She missed Seth.

She was a fool to have fallen in love with him, knowing that at the end of the week she would have to return to New York. Friendship could endure over three thousand miles, just as it could endure over fifteen years. But love...

"I'm sorry," Susan was saying, and Laura dragged her attention back to the journalist. Sandra had just left the office, and Susan apparently felt free to express her opinion. "I have to agree with your client. Why wouldn't you be delighted that she's had an abortion? It's one less unwanted child in the world, right?"

Laura shoved her chair back from the desk and stood to return the file to its drawer. "My personal views on abortion don't belong in your article," she claimed. "Abortion is a fact of life for my clients, and that's how I deal with it. I suppose it's good when a client has an abortion for the right reasons, just as it's good when a client decides to keep her baby for the right reasons. But the truth is, clients who do things for the right reasons are few and far between in this office.''

"What would you do if Rita got pregnant?" Susan asked. She had spent the entire day with Laura, and over lunch she had gathered some personal information about her subject, including the fact that Laura had a daughter. "Off the record, of course."

"Off the record? I'd kill her," Laura declared, then laughed. Susan laughed, too. "No, I wouldn't kill her," Laura said unnecessarily. "I would hope that she had become pregnant by choice, that she wanted the baby, and that she was ready, willing and able to be a good mother to it." She pulled her purse from the bottom drawer of her desk, then locked the desk for the night. "Rita's a good girl. Then again, so is Sandra Miller. She's just confused."

"Rita or Sandra?" Susan asked.

Laura grinned sadly. "Both, I suppose."

"Aren't we all?" Susan mused. She slid her camera onto her shoulder by its strap and accompanied Laura out of the office. "Is it all right if I come again tomorrow? I feel as though I've barely scratched the surface today."

"Sure. Tomorrow I'll be making house calls, so wear good walking shoes. I usually see Sandra at her place, but she had insisted on making this extra appointment. Now I know why."

A brisk gust of wind tugged at Laura's corduroy blazer as she left the building, and she turned up her collar against the early evening chill. If she were in California, she wouldn't be wearing the blazer at all, or stockings. She loathed stockings.

When Susan offered her a lift home in her car, Laura gratefully accepted. At the moment she probably would have loathed the subway, too.

"Ms. Robinson told me you were in Los Angeles last week," Susan mentioned as she maneuvered through the dense traffic.

"That's right," Laura said. She had told Julianne she was going to be visiting Seth when Julianne had called her to set things up with the reporter.

"I love Southern California," Susan confessed. "I know New Yorkers aren't supposed to admit to that. I laughed through *Annie Hall*, but even so, Woody Allen was kind of unfair to that part of the country, don't you think?"

"Yes," Laura concurred. "I had never been there before, but I liked it." She wondered whether she would have liked it as much if she hadn't been with Seth, then decided that was irrelevant. Seth and Southern California were incontrovertibly linked in her mind.

"My roommate in college came from Santa Cruz," Susan went on. "I visited her family out there a couple of times. It's a gorgeous part of the state, not far from Big Sur. Did you get that far north?"

"No."

"You ought to see it next time you go to California," Susan suggested.

If there is a next time, Laura responded silently, then remonstrated with herself for thinking so negatively. Why wouldn't there be a next time?

Because Seth hadn't called her since she'd left three days ago, that was why. Because, although she and Seth had had a wonderful time together, he had his own life out there, a very different life from Laura's. He had his career and his seven hundred starlets—a bevy of beautiful, compliant women who had no reason to harass him about his work. Surely he didn't want to have his conscience, in the person of Laura, harping on him at close range.

Her visit had entailed more than harping, of course. It had entailed some splendid times. One day they had driven, with Laura at the wheel, to a town called Solvang, the location of a restaurant reputed to have the best split-pea soup in the world. Not that Laura was wild about split-pea soup, but Seth had insisted that she consume a bowl of the stuff. Actually, she suspected that he had only been looking for an excuse to allow her to navigate his sports car on empty, out-of-the-way roads. The drive, she had to admit, had been far more exciting than the soup.

Another morning, they'd played catch with a football in Seth's driveway. Barney had romped back and forth between them, slobbering all over them and the ball. Keyed up by the game, Barney had then taken it upon himself to gallop into the underbrush surrounding Seth's house, sending Seth and Laura on a wild chase and giving Laura the opportunity to explore the region's flora in greater detail than she might have liked—particularly the shrubs that featured thorns. After their hectic chase, it had taken Seth nearly an hour to pull all the twigs and seeds from Laura's hair. "Just like those orangutans at the Prospect Park Zoo," he had observed, peppering his meticulous grooming of her hair with screeches and mugging and scratching beneath his arms. He'd completed his interpretation of orangutan behavior by pretending to discover in Laura's snarled tresses an array of insects, which he popped into his mouth, just as the orangutans had done when they'd groomed each other at the zoo. "Mmm! Lip-smacking good!" he'd squawked as Laura erupted in laughter. "Love them beetles!"

Yet another day, they'd taken the kite he had bought down to the beach and lofted it. Its rainbow-hued butterfly wings had cut daringly across the sun, and she and Seth had raced the length of the beach again and again, until they were both winded. Then they'd collapsed on the sand, and

Laura had griped about how the passage of years had destroyed her stamina. Seth had boasted that his stamina was as strong as ever, and had attempted to prove his claim by rolling onto her and showering her face with kisses. If it hadn't been for the few other beachcombers present, Laura was certain that he would have made love to her right there, beneath the warm California sky.

But Seth didn't really need Laura. He could play ball with Barney whether or not Laura was with him. He could take drives, eat pea soup and fly kites. He could have a healthy sex life without her, she was certain.

If he truly felt strongly about her, he would have called by now. He had called her often before she went to California; his failure to contact her since her departure vexed her. She supposed she could call him, but Seth knew as well as she did that long-distance phone calls were an extravagance she would have difficulty accommodating. When he drove her to the airport to catch her flight back East, he had promised he would spare her the expense of telephoning him. "'Don't call us. We'll call you,'" he had quoted with a grin.

So why hadn't he called?

"That's my place, right by the fire hydrant," she said, pointing her building out to Susan. "I really appreciate the lift."

"No problem," Susan assured her. "Would you like me to pick you up tomorrow morning?"

Laura shook her head as she opened the passenger door. "I know I'm out of your way, and you'll have enough trouble fighting the rush-hour traffic. I'll meet you at my office."

"Okay. See you then," Susan said, pulling away from the curb once Laura had shut the door.

Rita was seated on a kitchen counter, her legs hanging over the side and the telephone receiver pinned to her ear, when Laura entered the apartment. "No!" she was squealing into the phone. "Is he really? I'll die!"

Laura waved and hung her jacket in the coat closet. Not wishing to interrupt her daughter's conversation, she attempted to communicate in sign language that Rita shouldn't be sitting on the counter.

Rita deliberately ignored her, hooking one bare, gaudily pedicured foot under the other thigh and clutching the receiver. "Like, how fat are we talking? *Fat* fat? Or just a little chubby-cheeks fat?"

Laura lifted Rita's dangling leg to get to the silverware drawer. As usual, it was stuck. Rita squirmed, trying to give her mother some room to yank the drawer.

"A lardo, huh," Rita said glumly. She pulled on one of her brassy hexagonal earrings and sighed. "Maybe I should forget about him. You know who's really cute? This guy Jim Morrison. He's this awesome fox who used to sing with that old band the Doors. Only he's dead... Who said that? Becky LoCaffio? She's a slime. Oh, yuck. Guess what?" Rita reported into the phone. "My ma just pulled this thing out of the fridge for dinner. It's got lentils in it." She covered the mouthpiece with her hand and said to Laura, "Courtney says lentils are gross."

"Then tell Courtney she isn't invited for dinner tonight," Laura replied, sliding the casserole dish into the oven to heat and then preparing a salad.

Back into the phone, Rita said, "I better get off. Ma is making one of her healthy meals. I might just gag. Later, Courtney." She hung up the telephone, jumped off the counter and pouted. "You know what she told me? She said they had this special on MTV with the Monkees, and Mickey Dolenz is fat."

"We can't all age gracefully," Laura said, nostalgically recalling the slender figure she had boasted in her youth.

"Yeah, so I was thinking. You know Jim Morrison from the Doors?"

"He's dead," Laura remarked. "It's better to be fat than dead, don't you think?"

"Becky LoCaffio said maybe he isn't dead," Rita told her, sliding two paper napkins from their package and carrying them to the table. "She said some people think he's just pretending to be dead and he's actually living in France or something. But she's an idiot. You can't believe half of what she says. So how was work today?"

"All right," Laura said laconically. She didn't want to trouble Rita by telling her how upset she was about Sandra Miller.

"How did it go with the reporter?"

"It went well. Susan's a nice woman."

"Did you tell her about Seth?"

"Of course not." Laura wrenched a chunk of lettuce from the head and tore it with near violence into the salad bowl. It was hard enough trying not to think about him without having Rita mentioning his name every chance she got.

"I bet she'd be impressed. I bet she'd write something in her article about how you spent a week with a guy who writes movies."

"That's not what the article is going to be about, Rita." Laura sighed, then managed a smile. "How was school?"

"The usual. Do you think Seth will call tonight?"

"Not if you keep tying up the phone," Laura pointed out.

"I won't, I promise." She pulled two plates from an upper cabinet and set them on the table. "I hope he calls."

"So do I," Laura said before she could stop herself. Her eyes met Rita's for a brief instant, and then she averted her gaze. She could hide her frustration about her work from her daughter, but not everything.

Rita approached her mother from behind and gave her a bracing hug. "You'll see, Ma. He'll call. He's a good guy."

"I love you, Rita," Laura whispered, feeling her eyes grow moist. Sometimes Rita drove Laura insane, but . . . if only every mother were blessed with a daughter like her, Laura knew the world wouldn't be in such dire need of saving.

"IN TOWN? Now?"

"For a few more hours," said Andrew. "I was here to take care of some business, and I finished earlier than I expected. I thought maybe we could meet for lunch before I have to catch the red-eye back to Boston. Although I imagine it's kind of late for lunch by now . . ."

"That's okay," Seth assured him, clicking off his typewriter. "I haven't eaten. Where are you?"

"At the Best Western in West Hollywood. Do you know where that is?"

"It's only minutes away," said Seth.

"How many minutes?"

Seth laughed. Leave it to Andrew to demand a precise answer. "Beats me. If I don't show in a half-hour, give up."

"One half-hour," Andrew repeated. "Should we synchronize our watches?"

"Skip the watches. Count seconds, Andrew—one-Mississippi, two-Mississippi, up to eighteen hundred. By the time you're done, I'll be there."

He dropped the receiver back into its cradle, surveyed the mess of papers on his desk and the half-completed page rolled into his typewriter and shook his head. Andrew's call, as unexpected as it was, couldn't have come at a better time. Seth needed to get out for a while.

Standing, he shook his head again, trying to clear the fog from his brain. What time was it? What day? He definitely had to take a break.

He was out the front door before he realized that he didn't have on any shoes. And he wouldn't have realized that if Barney hadn't bounded gleefully through the shrubs and drooled all over his bare feet. "Sorry, pal," he muttered, retreating from Barney's exuberant greeting and sending him back into the yard with a friendly whack on the rump. Seth hadn't been giving Barney the usual amount of attention, and while Barney had been reasonably good-natured about having to fend for himself, he wasn't going to put up with such neglect forever. "Be grateful I'm still feeding you," Seth called after his dog, who had vanished around the side of the house. More than once since Laura had left, Seth had forgotten to feed himself.

He hurried back indoors to get his sandals from the bedroom closet and caught a glimpse of himself in the mirror above his bureau. He hadn't shaved since Laura left, either, and a thickening blond stubble decorated his jaw. What the hell, Seth consoled himself as he bolted from the house again. Andrew was an erstwhile beard man himself; he wouldn't object to Seth's ungroomed appearance.

Where had the time gone to? Where had Seth been? The hot wind rushing through the Porsche's open windows as he cruised along the twisting back roads reminded him that the world beyond his office still existed. He viewed the scenery with an alien fascination, as if it were something he'd never seen before.

The world still existed, filled with people. People like Darla Dupree, Zeke Montgomery and all the other clowns stupid enough to think that movies like *Ax Man Cuts Both Ways* mattered. People like Andrew, one of those lucky few who had their feet on the ground and their heads screwed on straight. People like Laura, who might not have her feet on the ground or her head screwed on straight, but who had heart and soul.

He would have to talk to her and tell her what he was doing. She would be so proud of him, so pleased. He had tried to call her once and gotten a busy signal, which he had decided to blame on Rita. Wasn't it true that teenage girls were always yakking on the telephone? A few other times, when his energy had petered out for the day and he'd put the typewriter to bed, Seth had considered phoning Laura, until he'd remembered the time. Lately he was working so obsessively that he often wasn't ready to call it quits until after midnight—much too late to call anyone, even without the three-hour time difference.

But he would call her soon. Now that Andrew had lured him away from his office for a couple of hours, perhaps Seth wouldn't be quite so compulsive about what he was doing. He wouldn't keep waiting until midnight before he withdrew enough from his work to think about Laura.

He arrived at the motel in under twenty minutes; even if he'd been living a hermit's existence for the past three days, he hadn't yet forgotten how to pilot his sports car like a pro. After parking, he jogged across the asphalt lot and into the impersonal lobby. He headed straight for the desk. "I'm supposed to meet someone who's staying here—Andrew Collins. *Dr.* Andrew Collins," he added because he liked the sound of it. He wondered whether Andrew was into his Ph.D. enough to register at a motel with his full title.

"Collins," the clerk echoed, scanning the register. He nodded, lifted his desk phone and rang Andrew's room. "There's a gentleman here to see you, Mr.—uh—Dr. Collins." Seth grinned.

The clerk had barely hung up, when Andrew strode into the lobby. Clad in pressed khaki slacks and a crisp cotton shirt, he looked appropriately collegiate as he crossed the room to Seth. "Seth! You're early. I was only up to four-teen-hundred-Mississippi."

Seth gripped his friend's hand in a robust soul shake. "Hey, man, it's really you! Why didn't you let me know you were going to be in town?"

"I would have, Seth," Andrew explained contritely. "But it was all planned at the last minute, and I'm out here for a ridiculously short time. I arrived yesterday afternoon, met a contact for dinner, met someone else this morning and I'm supposed to be back at the airport in two hours."

"I'm so glad you could squeeze me in," Seth mumbled with phony obsequiousness. "Two hours, huh. I don't know the hot spots in West Hollywood, but there's probably a McDonald's or something we could go to."

"The restaurant here isn't too bad," Andrew noted, pointing to the coffee shop off the lobby. "It isn't great, but in the interest of saving time..."

Seth eyed the glass-fronted eatery and shrugged. "I can tell just by looking at it that it must have gotten a three-star rating from Michelin. Have they got a liquor license?"

"Yes."

"My kind of place," Seth said agreeably, following Andrew into the restaurant.

They ordered hamburgers and Dos Equis beers. Waiting for his beer to arrive, Seth rubbed his jaw and smiled at the scratchy sound his beard made against the calloused surface of his thumb. He had made a serious effort to grow a beard once, in high school, but he had decided that the scraggly growth simply didn't suit him. Some guys looked good in beards, but Seth wasn't among them.

Andrew had looked good in his beard, but he looked better without it. He looked squarer, perhaps, more conservative, but, then, that could also be attributed to his neat attire and his shorter hair. Andrew was beginning to go gray, just a few strands at the temples, but enough to give him a nearly venerable appearance.

"So, tell me, Dr. Collins, what brings you to this part of the country?"

"What is this *Dr.* Collins stuff?" Andrew shot back. "You make me feel like I ought to be wearing a stethoscope around my neck."

"I'm impressed by you, that's all," said Seth. "You're a hotshot Amherst professor who covers six thousand miles in two days on business."

"You must travel a lot of miles on business, too," Andrew guessed.

Seth shook his head. "Not really. Occasionally I'll get shipped to some location for rewrites—if it's out of the state, it's usually Mexico, where production costs are cheaper. When I fly East it's almost always for pleasure." He thought for a moment of Laura, and of how much he'd like to fly East for the pleasure of being with her again. As soon as he was done, he promised himself. As soon as he had something he would be proud to show her.

The waitress arrived with their beers, and Seth lifted his mug in Andrew's direction. "A toast. Here's to your making more business trips to California."

"I sincerely hope not!" Andrew sipped from his mug, then smiled. "Not business trips, I mean. This sort of thing is exhausting. I had to cancel a bunch of classes to do it, and I've spent more time speaking Spanish in the past twenty-four hours than I did in four years of Spanish classes at Columbia."

"Hey, come on!" Seth protested. "I know some people think Southern California is like a foreign nation, but we do speak English here, most of us."

"Not the people I was meeting with."

"Chicanos?" Seth asked.

Andrew shook his head. "Salvadorans. I'm doing some research on El Salvador, and I was put in touch with a few refugees living here."

"Research, huh," Seth mused. The waitress delivered their hamburgers, and he reached for the bottle of ketchup on the table. "Are you going to write another book?"

"Maybe," Andrew replied noncommittally.

"If you do, tell me. I'll make sure all my friends buy a copy."

"If you made your friends read the books I write, I highly doubt that they'd be your friends for long," Andrew maintained with a modest smile. "I'm not looking to make the *New York Times* Best Seller list with my publications. Just trying to get tenure. Publish or perish, and all that."

"Tell me, Andrew," Seth ventured, genuinely curious. "When you're writing these publish-or-perish books, do you toe the line? Do you try to be objective, or do you push your own opinions?"

Andrew mulled over Seth's question. "I think . . . what I probably do is push my own opinions under the guise of objectivity," he conceded. "Of course, I'd like to think that my opinions are sound, based on an objective analysis of a given situation. But we all come from where we come from, Seth. I can't deny that I've got my biases."

"Same biases you had in '72?" Seth asked. "What's going on in El Salvador, anyway? I have trouble keeping up with all the global crises."

"It's depressing how many there are." Andrew chuckled. "In '72, I was much more concerned with Southeast Asia than with Central America. But my biases are probably the same. I still have a soft spot in my heart for such concepts as 'One man, One Vote'—although I suppose it ought to be 'One Person, One Vote.' Better yet, 'Power to the People.'"

"Once a fist-waving revolutionary, always a fist-waving revolutionary," Seth concluded. Regardless of his preppy clothes and his posh college affiliation, regardless of his eagerness to win tenure, Andrew obviously hadn't sold out. Seth wanted to believe that he remained as true to his principles as Andrew had. Today he had good cause to think he had.

Andrew seemed able to detect Seth's rejuvenated sense of himself. "Tell me what you've been up to," he demanded. "You're looking great."

"I am?" Seth guffawed. "I look like Rip Van Winkle." He took a hungry bite of his burger and tried to recall the last time he'd eaten. A stale cruller at his desk that morning, that was it. And coffee. Lots of coffee. He felt as if he'd been drinking coffee nonstop for three days.

"Are you working on a new film?" Andrew asked.

"Yeah." Seth took another bite, chewed and reconsidered his answer. "Not a new one, really. It's an old script I'm tearing apart and rewriting. I've got to tell you, Andrew, it's one of the most thrilling things I've ever done."

"Really? Another *Ax Man* opus?"

"No. I just finished one of those. This is different." He wondered whether his excitement about his reworking of *Good Fences* was apparent to Andrew, and then realized that it must be. Why else would Andrew have told him he was looking great? "This one's important, Andrew," he went on, energized by the mere thought of the excellent work he'd accomplished in the past few days. "It's about racism in the eighties. No barking dogs, no George Wallace barring the schoolhouse door. It's a human story, Andrew. Subtle. One of the subtlest things I've every written."

"You're really involved in it," Andrew stated.

"Involved in it? I'm drowning in it, man, and having the time of my life." He couldn't stifle his enthusiasm. "I've never felt so good about anything I've written before. I tell you, if this ever makes it to the screen—"

"If?" Andrew pounced on the word. "I thought you had the Midas touch out here in Hollywood, Seth. Don't tell me there's a chance this masterpiece *won't* make it to the screen."

"There is," Seth acknowledged. "And you know something? I don't care. I'm writing the damned thing, anyway. It's that important to me."

Andrew leaned back in his chair. The overhead light glanced off the lenses of his glasses, temporarily making his eyes invisible to Seth. He smiled enigmatically. "Who else is it important to?"

"Laura," Seth said automatically, then frowned. "How'd you guess?"

"It wasn't very hard." Andrew's smile expanded. "You look like someone in the throes of terminal passion, Seth. Possibly you're just feeling passionate about your current project, but I've known you a long time. I figured it was just as possible that someone special had inspired you to new heights." He took a sip of his beer. "Tell me about her, Seth. Tell me about this Laura. Is she one of your Hollywood nymphets?"

"Laura?" Seth almost choked on his sandwich. "No, yo-yo, it's *Laura*. Laura Brodie." As if there were no other Lauras in the world.

"Laura Brodie?" Now it was Andrew's turn to choke on his food. "From school?"

"Of course from school. She's turned me upside down—or maybe I should say, right side up. She's done wonders for me, Andrew. Made me rethink things, made me repent my sordid past. Gave me the courage to thumb my nose at psychopaths and Ninjas." He reached for his mug, fingered its smooth glass handle, ruminated. "It was great seeing everyone last month, Andrew. You and Troy and the ladies...."

Andrew nodded in agreement. "I've spent a lot of time worrying about Troy," he revealed. "It was reassuring to learn that he's made a fine go of it in Montreal. It's one thing to move away from home, but quite another to move to an entirely different country, a different culture. I'm glad he came to the party. I really wanted to see him. And Julianne, too. She's such a fine woman."

"And Kimberly," Seth added. "I didn't know thirty-five-year-old women could look that cute."

"Cute," Andrew snorted disdainfully. "Yes, she did look cute."

"Hey, I know you and she were never bosom buddies, Andrew, but give it a rest, man. Kim's done spectacularly with her life. She's tooling around in the halls of power, rubbing elbows with senators, and nary a hair out of place."

Andrew shrugged. "She was always good about maintaining appearances."

"It's more than appearances, and you know it."

Andrew pondered Seth's assertion, then relented with a shrug. "Okay. I'll admit she's doing better than I might have given her credit for."

"And looking better than any woman has a right to."

"If you're so madly in love with Laura, why are you so hung up on Kimberly's looks?" Andrew challenged Seth.

He grinned, unperturbed. "Kim's cute. Laura's beautiful," he distinguished. The mere mention of her name caused an infatuated smile to illuminate his face. "She believes in me, Andrew. She believes in my ability to write good things. I didn't believe in myself, but then she came and turned me around."

"Turned you right side up," Andrew corrected.

"That, too."

"Well, good for you. And good for her." He reflected for a minute, then grinned slyly. "Does this mean you're giving up on all the nymphets?"

"It might," Seth confessed, mirroring Andrew's smile. "Darla Dupree, queen of schlock, asked me out for last night, and I turned her down. Tell me what it means when you'd rather be shut up in your office, reworking a screenplay, than messing around with the likes of Darla Dupree."

"It means, you should have sent her over to the West Hollywood Best Western," Andrew scolded him. "I would have appreciated the company."

"I would have done just that," Seth insisted, "if I'd known you were in the neighborhood. Nah," he contradicted himself. "Darla isn't your type. A mental midget, if you'll forgive me for sounding like an intellectual snob. Darla has a lot going for her, but brains isn't it. You always were a brain man, Andrew."

"True enough." He checked his wristwatch and grimaced. "Much as I hate to eat and run... I do have a plane to catch."

"You old jet-setter, you," Seth taunted him. He groped for his wallet. "Let me cover this, okay? I feel bad that you didn't let me play host while you were in town."

"I'd rather put it on the motel bill," Andrew said, refusing Seth's offer. "This whole trip is being paid for by the organization that's funding my research."

"Generous organization," Seth observed. He himself had traveled on plenty of open-ended expense accounts, but he had always assumed that things were different in academia, where money was tight and every dime had to be accounted for.

"I'm not complaining," Andrew said. "They treat me well. May they only grease the wheels of the tenure machine. I'd feel a lot more secure about flaunting my oh-so-objective opinions if I knew I could count on having a job after I shot off my mouth."

"Job security isn't everything," Seth argued. For the first time since he'd begun making money as a script writer, he was laboring on a screenplay that came with no contract, no guarantees, no assurances. After sweating blood over it for weeks, he might have nothing more to show for it than a bouquet of "thanks, but no thanks" notes from every producer in town. He might never receive a cent in return for his efforts.

But he didn't care. More was at stake than money, and if he could earn Laura's respect, he would consider himself paid in full. If he could earn Laura's respect...and his own...

Even before finishing the script, he'd already rediscovered his self-respect. And for that he had to thank Laura.

Chapter Ten

The jolting ring of a telephone in the middle of the night was certain to frighten anyone, and Laura was no exception. She had been awakened by telephone calls numerous times before, but that was because she often collapsed into bed before ten o'clock, a habit Rita considered embarrassing, if not worse. But the last time someone had called Laura after midnight, it had been her mother, telling Laura that her father was dead. At times like that she thought wistfully of her life on the commune, where there were no phones bearing such mournful messages.

Her eyes struggled to make out the hands on the alarm clock by her bed: 2:30. The phone rang again, its shrill peal screeching along her nerve endings and causing her to shiver with dread. She sat up, gulped in a deep breath and reached for the phone. "Hello?" she whispered.

"Laura? Did I wake you up?"

Seth. A million emotions flooded her—relief and rage predominant among them. "What do you think?" she retorted. "Do you have any idea what time it is?"

"I know, I know," he mumbled, sounding not at all contrite. "It isn't exactly early here, either. But I've been snowed under, and it's all your fault, and I love you for it."

"What?"

"Listen," he said offensively exuberant. "I've been working on *Good Fences*. Do you remember it? About the racial problems in the middle-class town. I tore the thing to shreds, and I'm piecing it back together again. In the draft you read, Laura, I don't know if you remember it, but it had 'novice' written all over it. So what I did was, I cut down to the bare bones and figured out what it was I had here, and now I'm rebuilding the entire thing. For instance—" Through the wire she heard paper rustling "—in this new version, the basketball scene, remember, where Joshua tries out for the school team and all...I've moved that until later in the script, so it occurs closer to the climax. It gives the story a better shape. At least, I hope it does. And the block association scene, what I did there was—"

"Seth." Her joy at hearing from him gave way to anger. "Do you honestly think I want to be analyzing your script at two-thirty in the morning?"

"Umm..." He measured her tone. "I guess not, huh."

"A very good guess, Seth."

"Well, I'm sorry I didn't call you earlier, Laura, but I was on a roll here, really smoking on this thing. I'm excited about it, and I thought you would be, too."

"I would be, at a reasonable hour."

"Do you want me to call you back?" he asked, belatedly considerate.

"What for?" she grumbled. "I'm already awake." Her anger slowly dissipated, leaving room for joy to return. "What did you do with the block association scene?"

Seth laughed. "It's all your fault for living so far away, Laura," he complained. "If you were here, we could be discussing this like normal human beings."

"Well, I'm not there," Laura pointed out, wondering whether that fact disturbed Seth as much as it did her.

"Yeah. So why don't you come back?"

She smiled hesitantly. Did he want her to come back only because he needed her reliable criticism on his screenplay? Or for some other reason, some better reason? "You know, Seth, you could have called me sooner," she chided him. "You told me not to call you."

"I miss you," he said, ignoring her comment. "Why don't you come back?"

"I miss you, too," she confessed.

"Then it's settled. I'll arrange a ticket for you—"

"Seth, nothing's settled," she cut him off. "I can't keep doing disappearing acts at work. In fact, I shouldn't have done the last one. One of my clients was in big trouble and I wasn't there for her."

"Trouble? How big?"

Laura exhaled. She had gone to Sandra's apartment for her regular weekly visit that afternoon and found Sandra wallowing in despair. Dennis had said he was only joking, she told Laura between sobs, and he no longer wanted to have anything to do with a woman who would get rid of his child the way she had. Laura had tried to console Sandra with the observation that Dennis wasn't much of a caring father for the child she had already borne him, and suggested that he had merely been looking for an excuse to break off his relationship with Sandra. Privately Laura thought that Sandra would be much better off without Dennis in her life, but she knew she wouldn't be able to convince her heartbroken client of that.

It was too late at night for her to go into the whole sad story with Seth. Laura was too tired. If only he were with her, if only they could discuss it, as he said, like normal human beings....

Once more she was forced to acknowledge the futility of maintaining a relationship with him over such a long distance. He might think she could drop everything on a whim and fly out to see him again, but she couldn't.

"Earth to Laura, are you there?"

"I'm here," she answered. "Seth, it's just....my client is going through a rough time, and I feel so helpless about it."

This time the silence was on Seth's end. Finally he spoke, his voice steady and calm. "You stay there. I'll come."

"What?"

"All I need to know is, have you got a typewriter?"

"No," she said. "I used to have one, my old college portable. But it broke during the move to Buffalo. I never bothered to get a new one."

"It doesn't matter. I'll bring mine. I'll be in Brooklyn tomorrow. Or if not tomorrow, the next day. I'll see what I can arrange, plane-wise and Barney-wise."

"Could you really come so soon?" she asked.

"Is the Pope Catholic? I'm going crazy here without you."

She felt her heart race at his implication. He *did* miss her, as much as she missed him. Yet, after so many days of hearing nothing from him... "You should have called, Seth. When I didn't hear from you, I thought—" She broke off.

"You thought what?"

"That maybe you didn't want to talk to me, or something," she mumbled.

He could easily interpret what she was saying. "You thought I didn't care? You thought I don't love you? Brodie, what's wrong with you? You're always so sure of yourself."

"No, I'm not," she admitted. It took enormous courage to reveal her intimate doubts, but she loved Seth too much to keep her insecurities hidden from him.

"Okay. Watch my lips. I love you."

This time her heart seemed to stop beating altogether. She simply sat, dazed, dizzy with joy.

"What happened?" he questioned her silence. "Did I put you back to sleep?"

"No." She inhaled, coming back to life. "No, Seth. But I couldn't watch your lips."

"You'll be able to soon enough," he promised. "Only if you're close enough to see them, they won't be doing much talking. I'll see you a.s.a.p., Laura."

I love you, too, she mouthed, not daring to speak the words aloud. It was still possible that Seth wanted to see her only to garner criticism on his revised manuscript. That he could hop on an airplane and fly across the country at a moment's notice indicated that he was rich, not necessarily that he missed her as much as she missed him. Even his confession of love couldn't put her doubts fully to rest. "What about *Ax Man Cuts Both Ways*?" she asked him.

"What about it? Shooting starts next week, and I'm sure as hell not going to rewrite any more Jacuzzi scenes if I can help it. If it's all right with you, I'll give Zeke your number so he can reach me if there's an emergency on the set. Or maybe I'll give him the number for Dial-A-Prayer. It would serve him right if he couldn't reach me."

"Give him my number if you want," Laura said. "I don't mind."

"And I'm not going to sleep on the living room sofa, by the way," Seth said before hanging up.

"Of course not," Laura addressed the dead air on the telephone. Sleeping with Seth had been one of the nicest aspects of her stay in California, much nicer than driving the Porsche or flying a kite on the beach. Much, much nicer than learning how to play a kazoo.

SHE LEFT WORK shortly after six the following afternoon. Some days went that way, each client demanding extra time, paperwork piling up and staff meetings dragging on. Just before she'd been about to depart from her office, Susan had arrived to hand-deliver a draft of the article she'd written for *Dream*. "Why don't you read it through and give me your comments?" she had offered. "I know you and Ms. Robinson are good friends. She'd shoot me if I didn't give you first edit on it."

"She wouldn't shoot anybody," Laura had refuted Susan. "She's a pacifist." Secretly Laura suspected that Susan was presenting her with the article not because she feared for her life, but simply because she was a thoughtful person. "I'll call you as soon as I've read it," Laura promised.

Tucking the folder beneath her blazer to protect it from the evening drizzle, she jogged around the corner from the subway station and down the street to her building. In the lobby she pulled out the folder and checked to make sure the pages inside it hadn't gotten too soggy, then continued to the elevator and upstairs. Laura judged from the smell in the corridor that Mrs. Cobb in 5-D was cooking something with enough chili powder in it to ignite a forest fire. Wrinkling her nose at the aroma, Laura unlocked her own door.

She heard Rita chattering energetically and wondered whether she would once again find her daughter lounging on the kitchen counter with the telephone receiver growing out of her ear as she bemoaned the blight old age had cast upon yet another over-the-hill rock star. But her voice was coming from a different direction, and when Laura reached the arched doorway to the living room, she discovered Rita and Seth seated on the sofa, so engrossed in their conversation they weren't even aware of Laura's arrival.

"You're here," she announced in astonishment. Although Seth had mentioned that he might get to New York by that night, Laura hadn't actually believed that he would. Didn't long trips take time to plan? Didn't airlines like to wait until one's check cleared before issuing a ticket? Didn't dogs have to be delivered to kennels or willing neighbors?

Whatever magic Seth had performed to get himself to Laura's apartment in less than twenty-hours didn't matter. All that mattered was that he had done it.

He was dressed in one of his bizarre outfits—a cotton shirt of forest green, a vest the same screaming red color as his sneakers and a pair of pleated gray slacks. But Laura didn't care what he was wearing; no one had ever looked so wonderful to her. He sprang off the couch and strode across the room to welcome her with a lusty hug. "Cool it," she whispered jerking her head in Rita's direction.

"It's okay, Ma," Rita calmly assured her mother. "I'm on to the whole thing. He put his suitcase in your bedroom."

"You're presumptuous," Laura chided Seth.

"She's savvy," he countered, poking his thumb in Rita's direction.

"I'm cool," Rita declared, rising to her feet, as well. "You know what else he brought? His typewriter. *The* typewriter. The one he writes his movies on."

"It was all I could do to keep her from kissing it," Seth confided to Laura. "It's about time you got home, pal. Your daughter is famished. Another ten minutes, and I was going to take her out for a hot fudge sundae."

"You hear that, Ma? A hot fudge sundae," Rita chorused. "We can go out for pizza first, and then ice cream after," she resolved, dashing out of the living room to get her slicker.

"Hello," Seth murmured once he and Laura were alone. He kissed her gently, and her mouth instantly softened beneath his. He slid his tongue enticingly along her lower lip, then pulled back and smiled.

"How did you get here so soon?" she asked.

"Are you complaining?"

"No."

His smile expanded. "Where there's a will, et cetera," he said about his seeming wizardry. Laura felt a flush of pleasure wash through her. Seth wouldn't have had such a strong will to see her if he didn't truly love her.

"Hey, you guys!" Rita hollered from the doorway. "Enough kissie-kissie. I'm gonna die here."

"Sure, lardo," Laura teased, separating from Seth and leading him from the room.

The pizza place was crowded, with throbbing rock music pouring down on them from ceiling speakers. It gave Laura a mild headache, and she thought the pizza was much too spicy and greasy, but Rita didn't seem to mind in the least. Her only complaint was that no one she knew from school happened to enter the place. "I'd just love for someone to see me here with Seth," she declared. "You know Tara Drake, she once met Weird Al Yankovich by accident, like two years ago, and she still hasn't shut up about it."

"And you haven't shut up about Seth," Laura reminded her.

"Yes, I have," Rita defended herself piously as she pulled another gooey wedge of pizza from the round tin pan at the center of the table. "I'm eating, aren't I? I never talk with food in my mouth."

After dinner they headed down the street to an ice-cream parlor. Seth and Rita ordered hot fudge sundaes, and Laura a dish of sherbet, which she had trouble finishing. Yet seeing how much fun Rita was having with Seth and he with her was more satisfying to Laura than even the most sinfully caloric dessert. The sherbet was extraneous as far as she was concerned. The happiness she felt having Seth with her was more than sweet enough.

Rita begged to watch television once they got home, but deciding that she'd been lenient enough for one evening, Laura chose to be a mother and ordered Rita to do her homework at her desk. "I've got to do some work, too," she informed Seth, gathering up the folder Susan had given her. "I promised I'd read this right away."

"What is it?" he asked, taking the folder from her and leafing through the pages.

"It's the article about me that Julianne is going to run in *Dream*. The reporter wants my opinion of it before she submits it."

"It must do your ego good to know your opinion is in such demand by us lowly scribes," Seth teased her. "I'll let you read her masterpiece tonight, as long as you promise to read mine tomorrow."

"Heavens, so many masterpieces all at one time," Laura clucked, kicking off her shoes and dropping onto the sofa. Seth turned on the television to a baseball game and settled on the faded upholstery beside her.

While he watched the game, she read. The article was indisputably well written, accurate, moving but... Why didn't she like it? Why didn't it thrill her? Why did such a clear, literate depiction of her work leave her feeling so discomfited?

"Well?" Seth asked, noticing that she had stopped reading. "Today *Dream*, tomorrow *Donahue*?"

"I don't think so," she said, attempting to smile. She tossed the folder onto the table and sighed. "She makes me look... I don't know."

"Like an angel?" Seth guessed.

"Like a social worker," Laura corrected him. "A good social worker."

"Which you are."

"Oh, Seth..." She sighed again. "I *want* to save the world. But as hard as I try, I just can't seem to do it. Lately I've been feeling as if maybe the world doesn't want me saving it. I feel like I can't give my clients the help they need. And if I can't, what's the use?"

Seth scrutinized her downcast expression, then gingerly brushed his index finger along her cheek to her chin and cupped his hand beneath it. He lifted her face to his. "How long have you been like this?"

"Like what? Burned out?"

He kissed her brow. "Everybody burns out sometimes. I imagine that for someone doing the kind of work you do, burnout must be a common occurrence. It's nothing to feel hopeless about."

"I don't feel hopeless, Seth."

"Guilty?" he suggested. "Guilty that you haven't saved the world?"

"Maybe," she admitted.

"Forget the world," he whispered. "If you've saved one or two people, you're doing more than your share. And trust me, Laura, you *have* saved one or two. I'm speaking from personal experience." He kissed her forehead again, then slid his lips down her nose to her mouth. His kiss momentarily deepened, and then he twisted toward the doorway. "When is Rita's bedtime?"

Laura glanced past Seth at Rita's closed door. The dark crack under it indicated that Rita had retired for the night. She turned back to Seth. "I think the coast is clear," she murmured.

They tiptoed out of the living room. Laura thought it was an odd role reversal, a mother sneaking around with her boyfriend behind her daughter's back. But no matter how cool Rita claimed to be, thirteen years old was an awkward age for any girl, let alone a girl whose single mother was entertaining a lover in their home. Laura preferred to be discreet.

As soon as they had shut themselves inside the master bedroom, Seth attacked the buttons of Laura's blouse. "God, but you're sexy," he murmured as he slid the blouse off her shoulders. He skimmed his hands over the firm swells of her breasts, then let his fingers fall to the waistband of her skirt.

Her lips shaped a giddy smile. "Nobody's ever told me I was sexy before," she admitted.

"You've been hanging out with the wrong people," Seth asserted, then contradicted himself. "No, you've been hanging out with the right people. I'd just as soon no one else caught on to how sexy you are. Truth is—" he slid her skirt over her hips, then eased down her panty hose. "—I want you all to myself."

They quickly finished undressing and stretched out on the bed. Seth kissed her slowly and thoroughly, his tongue playing over hers, teasing and taking. His hands moved over the ripe curves and indentations of her body, and she was instantly engulfed in the luxuriant sensations she had known the last time they were together, the spreading warmth, the stunning surges of longing. She had experienced such intense pleasure only once before in her life, with Neil. Yet making love with him had been very different. It had been more physical, somehow, more imperative. With Seth she was loving a friend. With Seth there was understanding, trust, comfort.

She touched him as he touched her, with quiet assurance, understated power. She felt his desire rising within him, expanding through him, paralleling her own desire. She relished the tensing of his lean muscles along his back and across his abdomen, the uneven tempo of his breathing, the urgent pressure of his thigh wedged between hers, his hips surging against hers.

He didn't have to tell her that he found her sexy; it was obvious in his movements, in the tender assault of his fingers and lips. He didn't have to apologize for wanting her all to himself; she was completely, willingly his.

"I really did miss you," she whispered, trailing her fingers along the flat expanse of his stomach.

"You don't have to miss me now," he swore, closing his teeth gingerly about her earlobe. "I'm here."

She sighed, an inchoate sound of agreement.

His hand drew a long, unbroken line from the nape of her neck forward, along her collarbone, down between her breasts, across the pliant flesh of her abdomen and through the curling tendrils of hair below. He found her damp and eager, and her body tensed at his welcome touch. She didn't need to speak for him to know everything she could possibly tell him at that moment. Words weren't necessary to communicate her every secret, her every pulsing want. Her body revealed what Seth already knew.

Their bodies merged, moved together, found each other. Passion wove a timeless web around them, trapping them in its rapturous spell and then propelling them up the steep path to its peak. Laura arrived, Seth right behind her, their souls suddenly free to unite for a fleeting, exquisite instant.

Spent, Seth rested wearily upon her, his body heavy as it unwound. His hands rose to her hair, and he tangled his fingers deep into the soft curls. He grew still, and for a minute Laura suspected that he had fallen asleep.

He dispelled that thought by speaking. "You're a wonderful mother, too."

Surprised that he would refer to Rita at such a moment, she opened her eyes and slid out from under him. He opened his eyes, as well, their luminous blend of green and gray complementing his radiant smile. "Oh? What makes you say that?"

"I like Rita. She's turned out nicely."

"Thank you."

His lips flexed as he pondered his words. "I probably have no right to ask, Laura, and you're going to think I'm unforgivably possessive, to say nothing of nosy, but..." He drifted off uncertainly.

"But...?"

"Tell me about her father," he requested. "I want to know."

Laura lapsed into silence. She didn't find Seth's question unreasonable. If he loved her as much as she loved him, then he did have a right to ask. She simply wasn't sure of how to answer. "What do you want to know?"

"What was he like?"

"He was pretty quiet," she recalled. "The strong, silent type—only he wasn't terribly strong, as it turned out. He came from West Virginia and he had a wonderful mountain drawl. He had majored in literature in college, and he read a lot. He was a big Hermann Hesse fan."

"He sounds like a weenie," Seth remarked.

Laura smiled reflectively. "He wasn't. He was very good-looking. Just look at Rita—whatever doesn't resemble me, she got from him."

"Did you love him?" Seth asked tentatively.

"Of course I loved him. Do you think I would have had a baby with him if I didn't?"

"Do I think you would have had a baby with someone who walked out on you?" Seth countered, apparently trying not to appear too condemning.

"I wasn't expecting him to walk out on me," Laura replied. If Seth didn't approve of what she had done, that was his business. Laura had never felt the need to justify her past to anyone, and she wasn't about to now. "If you want to know the truth, I don't think Neil expected to walk out, either. But he was afraid of responsibility. He liked the idea of having a baby more than the reality of it."

"What made you so responsible?" Seth asked, sounding genuinely fascinated. "How come you didn't want to walk away from it all yourself?"

"I loved the reality of it," Laura told him simply. "I loved being a mother. I loved Rita."

"But it must have been tough at times."

"It was," she admitted. "But I don't believe in walking away from tough situations. I believe that if you live with your choices, if you commit yourself to them, you'll be all the better for it. And I believe that when someone needs you—the way Rita needs me—you...you have to be there."

"Of course," he whispered. He leaned forward and kissed her lightly. "Of course that's what you believe."

IF WAKING UP TO DISCOVER YOURSELF fully exposed to a thirteen-year-old girl was humiliating, even worse would be to face that thirteen-year-old girl after having made love to her mother the night before. Seth gratefully took Laura up on her suggestion that he roll over and go back to sleep when she and Rita awoke early the next morning.

He rolled over, but he didn't go back to sleep. It was difficult to sleep through a noisy altercation between mother and daughter over Rita's insistence that she wear mascara to school. Without mascara, according to Rita, a girl could just about die. Laura's assertion that the cosmetic caused eye infections struck Seth as a creative approach to the problem, but, then, thirteen-year-old girls probably didn't care as strongly about eye infections as about fitting in with their peers.

He didn't know much about teenage girls, but he was willing to learn. He had grown up the youngest of three boys, so he'd never had the opportunity to deal with young girls close up. When he himself was thirteen, he had considered females an alien breed. As he recollected, they were by and large vapid; the most pressing issue in their lives was what they were going to do with themselves now that Ringo Starr was married. They danced with each other at parties and they wore funny-looking stockings with patterns woven into them. On occasion, he had been obliged to kiss a few of them, since when the girls weren't dancing with each other at parties they were organizing rounds of Spin-the-Bottle and Post Office. "Special delivery from Nancy Shea to Seth Stone!" someone would squeal, and he'd be dragged into a closet where Nancy was waiting, reeking of some cloying perfume, and they'd push their mouths together amid the winter coats and think they were very mature.

For all Seth knew, Rita might also play Post Office at parties. But he doubted it. She *was* savvy. She was smart. He had almost been glad that Laura got home late from work the previous day, because it had given him the opportunity to talk to Rita. She had asked him his educated opinion of the music of the Monkees and Wang Chung, but she had also asked him his educated opinion of the Middle East. Admittedly their discussion hadn't been scholarly, but at least she knew about the world. "I read that in Iran the women have to wear masks," she'd declared. "I mean yuck! Like, how is a guy ever gonna ask you out if you're wearing some dumb mask, you know?"

He remained in bed until he heard the front door close, signaling that Rita had left for school and Laura for work.

Then he rose, donned the jeans he'd brought with him and stumbled out of the room.

The coffee in the pot was still hot, and Laura had left open a cabinet door to reveal boxes of shredded wheat and Grape Nuts. "Figures," he sniffed disdainfully, swinging the cabinet shut. He wasn't a big cereal fan, but when he did eat cereal, he liked it sweet. Frosted Flakes, Sugar Smacks, Fruit Loops—Laura would probably string him up if she ever found out that he ate such stuff. Then again, Rita would probably cheer for him. She had wolfed down that hot fudge sundae like a pro last night.

Perhaps he was being too optimistic, but he was fairly certain that Rita liked him. He wasn't exactly clear about why winning her affection was so important to him, but he definitely knew that it was.

He gulped down some coffee and orange juice, took a shower, got dressed and lugged his typewriter, his script and a ream of clean typing paper to the kitchen table. Until he'd walked into Laura's apartment, he hadn't been able to get his mind off *Good Fences*—even during his flight to New York he'd reread several scenes and slashed them up with a pen. He had never worried so much about any of his other screenplays, but this one... He wanted it to be perfect. Every word, every camera angle, every punctuation mark, utterly perfect.

Undaunted by jet lag, he plunged into his work. The constant purr of the typewriter's motor energized him; the concave plastic surfaces of the keys inspired him. That he was in an unfamiliar environment, without his trusty thesaurus, without his supply of red rubber bands, which he liked to shoot across his office when he was blocked, didn't faze him in the least. He had his characters, his situation and plot. He had his ideas and he had confidence. He didn't need anything else.

Hunger forced him to take a break after a few hours. Rummaging in Laura's refrigerator, he found a casserole dish containing some leftover lentil stew. He scooped some into a bowl and ate it cold. It couldn't compete with pizza, he decided, but for healthy slop it wasn't half bad.

Rita arrived home from school at three-thirty, and she nearly pounced on the typed pages stacked beside the typewriter. "Oh, Seth, what's this?" she bellowed. "I told Courtney you were actually going to write something at our house, and she almost didn't believe me. But look at all this! You wrote this *here*! In *my* kitchen! What is it? Is it about Ax Man?"

"No, Rita," he said, slumping in his chair and rolling his head from side to side to loosen the muscles of his neck. "This one's going to be a *good* script."

"Yeah?" She abandoned the pages to open the refrigerator door, poured herself a glass of milk, then shut the door. "You know who you ought to cast in it? Emilio Estevez. He's *fine*, Seth. I saw him in this movie, *The Breakfast Club*. It was an R movie, but Courtney's family gets cable and we saw it on TV."

"He's white," Seth pointed out. "This film is about a black kid, not a white one."

"Todd Bridges," Rita recommended. "From *Different Strokes*. He's a fox, too."

Seth considered her suggestion and smiled. "That's an interesting idea," he agreed. "You've got the makings of a casting director, Rita."

"Yeah? No kidding?" Rita danced in a circle around the table. "Maybe that's what Courtney and I will do. We were gonna open a boutique in the East Village, but I hear the rents are awesomely high there."

"If you became a casting director for the movies, you'd have to move to Los Angeles," Seth noted.

Rita stopped moving and stared at him. Her eyes were uncannily dark and piercing, adorned with lashes so thick that mascara wasn't necessary. Whatever she might have inherited from her father didn't include her eyes. They were identical to Laura's.

As he met her penetrating gaze, he contemplated what he'd just said. Rita would have to move to Los Angeles. With Laura. Of course.

Evidently Rita also understood the full implications of what he had suggested. She folded her slender body onto a chair facing him, raked her short hair with her fingers and studied him quizzically. "Let's talk, Seth," she said.

"About what?"

"What's going on with you and Ma? You want her to move in with you, or what?"

He tossed the question back to her. "How would you feel about that?"

"If she moved in with you, where would I live?"

"With us," he insisted. "I've got a big house. There's a bedroom in it for you. And I've got a dog. A dalmatian. Do you like dogs?"

"They're okay," Rita said with a shrug. "I'd rather have a car."

"I've got one of those, too," Seth told her. "A Porsche. You're too young to drive it now, Rita, but when you get older, I'll teach you how."

"Yeah?" She mulled over his offer. "What about Courtney?"

"I'll teach her, too, if she wants me to."

"No, I mean, what about her? She's my best friend. If I lived with you, Seth, I'd never get to see her."

"Of course you would. You could come back east to visit her. And she could come out to California to visit us there."

"On an airplane?"

"Flying beats walking."

Rita drank her milk and meditated. "What does Ma have to say about all this?"

"I haven't discussed it with her yet," Seth admitted. He hadn't even thought about it until ten minutes ago. Yet it was such a terrific idea, such an obvious one, that he was amazed he hadn't come up with it sooner.

Rita swung her feet back and forth as she considered Seth's words. "Ma is kind of weird, Seth, you know? She might not go for it. I mean, like, you'd lay it out for her, tell her about all the neat people who live in Los Angeles. You'd explain the whole thing to her, and you know what she'd do? She'd say something like, 'I can't leave my clients.'"

"Do you think she'd say that?" Seth asked, mildly alarmed. He had known Laura longer than Rita had, but Rita knew her better. And what Seth knew about Laura led him to believe that Rita might just be correct. Laura was attached to her work. She cared about her clients; she fretted over them. She felt guilty when one of them went through a rough time while she was out of town.

"You know my mother," Rita snorted. "El Weenie Supremo. She would probably worry about California being too cool. Look at the way she dresses, right? Move her out there, where everybody is rad, and she might just hate it."

"Not everybody is rad out there," Seth cautioned Rita, wondering whether she, and not her mother, might have difficulty adjusting to the West Coast. "Some people are neat and some are dorks. What's wrong with the way your mother dresses, anyway?"

Rita glared at him in horror. "You think she dresses right? I think she looks like an A-1 flame. To say nothing of her hair...."

"I think your mother is beautiful," Seth argued. "I love her hair."

"She's old," Rita grunted.

"Are you trying to talk me out of this plan?" Seth challenged her. "Or are you on my side?"

"I'm on your side, Seth," Rita said quickly.

"Okay, then. Leave everything to me."

Easier said than done, he ruminated as Rita grinned and bounced out of the kitchen. He turned back to his typewriter, but for the first time in days he couldn't even bring himself to read what he had just written, let alone write anything more. He couldn't concentrate on *Good Fences* when he had just decided that he wanted to live with Laura.

Maybe he hadn't just decided it. Pondering the idea, he couldn't shake the comprehension that he had known all along that he wanted to live with her. He loved her. He desired her. And he needed her—a whole hell of a lot more than any of her clients did.

He grew restless waiting for her to come home from work. He prowled the kitchen, the hall, the bathroom. He gave his reflection a harsh assessment in the mirror above the sink. He had shaved that morning after his shower, but perhaps he ought to shave again. Perhaps he ought to shower again. At the very least, he ought to tuck in his shirt.

He had never asked a woman to live with him before, and he tried to figure out how nervous he should be. What had it been like the first time he'd asked a girl out on a date? Well, he and Nancy Shea had already been kissing in closets for two years before they'd gone on an official date, so naturally Seth had been relaxed about it.

Why shouldn't he be relaxed this time, then? He had known Laura for over fifteen years. They were friends. The worst that would happen was that she'd say no. Which would be pretty bad, but he'd cross that bridge when he got to it.

Much to Seth's relief, she arrived home at five, clutching her mail. "Look what I got—a letter from Kim!" she announced, waving the pink envelope beneath Seth's nose. Then she ripped it open.

"Belmont?" Seth was strangely relieved by the delay. He was too edgy to jump right into the issue of Laura's moving in with him. "What does she have to say for herself?"

Laura pored over the neat script and frowned. Then she sighed. "Poor Kim. She's been working with a lawyer, finalizing the details of her divorce."

"Her divorce?" Cripes. Nothing like a divorce to put a hex on talk about living together. "How come she's getting a divorce?" he asked.

"Obviously because her marriage is a failure." Laura set down the letter and sighed again.

"I always thought she was a 'happily ever after' type," Seth mused.

"We all think we are, don't we?" Laura reread the letter, then folded it and inserted it in the tattered envelope. "She sounds as if she's holding up, under the circumstances. But it's a lousy break. You think you can trust your heart, and then reality intrudes and things go wrong. I feel so bad for her, Seth."

Cripes was right. This was definitely not the appropriate introduction to the subject he wished to talk over with Laura. "I feel bad for her, too," he noted, trying to remain optimistic. "But things don't always have to go rotten. Sometimes they can work out okay."

"You're right," Laura agreed, brightening. She gave him a hearty hug. "Lord, it's good having you here, Seth. You know how to cheer me up. So, how was your day?"

He felt his gut tighten into a knot, but he resolutely ignored the sensation. *Relax,* he admonished himself. *She's a friend.* "Let me help you with your jacket," he offered, sliding her blazer off her shoulders with uncharacteristic chivalry.

"What's the matter?" Laura asked suspiciously. "What did you break?"

Abruptly Rita bolted out of her bedroom and shouted, "Hi, Ma. What's for dinner?"

Seth laughed and eyed Rita. "Go back to your room and starve for a while," he ordered her. "Your mother and I have to talk."

"Huh?" Then Rita remembered what she and Seth had discussed earlier, and she grinned slyly. "Oh, yeah. *That*." She spun around and darted back into her room, slamming her door shut behind her.

"Why do I have a sinking feeling in the pit of my stomach?" Laura asked skeptically, stepping out of her shoes and shoving up the sleeves of her sweater. "What have you two been cooking up?"

"Nothing fattening," Seth said to put her at ease. Stupid, really. It didn't even put *him* at ease.

She studied his face, absorbing his anxious expression, trying to interpret it and gradually coming to look pretty anxious herself. "Well?" she prodded him.

"How would you like to move to California?" There. He'd said it.

"California?" Laura echoed. "What's in California?"

"*I'm* in California, you twit."

"You mean, you want me to live with you?"

This wasn't going quite as well as he might have hoped. Why did Laura look so startled? Why didn't it seem as obviously right to her as it did to him? "I want you and Rita both to live with me. Rita loves the idea. She wants me to teach her how to drive the Porsche."

"You asked Rita before you asked me?" Laura asked, stunned. "Why?"

"I thought Rita was going to be the tough one to convince. I was sure you'd be easy." He reached for her hands, gathered them in his, lifted them to his lips. "I want you with me. We can make it work. I need you with me, not three thousand miles away. I know it's a big question, Laura, but things don't have to go rotten between us the way they did for Kim." No, too negative. He drew in a deep breath, then squeezed her hands. "I want you with me. You're good for me. Okay?"

She lowered her eyes to her hands clasped within his. He wished he could read her mind, wished he could guess at her reaction. "I'm good for you," she echoed uncertainly. "Like cod liver oil."

"Like sunshine," he corrected her. "Like a light through the shadows. You're helping me to find my way, and I need that."

She appeared curiously pained by his words. She broke from him and turned away, her eyes averted. "You want me with you to help you with your work," she summarized in a constrained voice.

"Of course I do. You've done wonders for me, professional-wise."

She shook her head. "That's not enough, Seth."

He gazed at her, at the resplendent fall of her hair down her back, at the way each hand gripped the opposite elbow, as if she were hugging herself, holding herself in. Did she think her assistance in steering him straight was the only reason he wanted her?

He reached for her shoulders and rotated her face to him. "I love you, Laura," he swore. "Is that enough?"

Her eyes lit up as they met his. "More than enough," she whispered.

"Are you sure? Would you like me to serenade you with something romantic? 'You Are the Sunshine of My Life' or something?"

"Wait a minute and I'll get my kazoo," Laura joked, but she didn't move from him. Instead she curled her fingers around his neck and pulled him closer. "I can think of a lot of practical reasons we ought to take the time to analyze this fully," she admitted. "But right now, Seth, I don't want to be practical. I just want to say yes." She rose to kiss him. "All right?"

He smiled. He was definitely relaxed, now, relaxed and elated both. "You *are* easy, aren't you."

"Easy, maybe. But don't forget, I don't believe in free love."

"That's all right," Seth reminded her, wrapping his arms around her in an exuberant hug. "I'm rich, pal. I can afford you."

Chapter Eleven

The practical considerations came later. One was her job. As burned out as she might be, she wasn't sure she was ready to give up on her career and turn her back on her clients.

Rita was another consideration. Although she was unrestrained in her excitement about the notion of moving to California, Laura worried whether Rita would truly like the place—or the move itself, a move away from her friends, her school and her community. Rita had had a rather unsettled childhood, and Laura wanted to provide her daughter with as much stability as possible. California was awfully different from Brooklyn. And if things between Seth and Laura didn't work out, if, after moving in with him, Laura and Rita had to move out...

That was the biggest consideration, of course: things between Seth and Laura. She loved him, and she was fairly secure in his love for her. Still, neither of them had even breathed a hint of "forever after" or "till death do us part." Not that Laura was obsessed by the legalities of the situation—although they, too, were a legitimate practical concern, if Laura lost the medical coverage and pension that came with her job. She recognized the possibility that her relationship with Seth might not work out, might not last. And then where would she and Rita be? Legal, sanctified marriages frequently didn't work out, either, but at least a married woman had some protection, some recourse.

In her youth Laura had never worried about such issues. She decided she wanted to live on a commune, and so she did. She decided she wanted a baby, and she had one. She didn't lose sleep over her finances; she wasn't wealthy, but she and her daughter never went hungry. She had faith that things would work out. Somehow they always did.

She was no longer young enough to rely on faith alone. Or maybe it had nothing to do with her age; maybe it was a matter of responsibility. If Rita were an independent adult, Laura wouldn't think twice about taking her chances with Seth, hoping for the best and trusting in love and luck. But Rita wasn't an independent adult. She depended on her mother to plan ahead, to steer a straight course for their tiny family. It would be unfair for Laura to take chances when Rita's future hung in the balance.

So, after the euphoria of Seth's invitation wore off, Laura proposed that she and Seth take things slowly. Rita's spring vacation from school was approaching. Laura would pull as many strings as necessary to obtain a few days off from work coinciding with Rita's holiday, and they would travel west then and try out the arrangement.

"You're so damned sensible, Laura," Seth griped, but he agreed to her plan, on the condition that she would let him stay with her in Brooklyn until she and Rita could accompany him back to California. Laura found nothing objectionable about that. On a practical level, that would give Rita more time to get used to the idea of her mother and Seth as a couple, and...

The hell with all the practical considerations. Laura wanted him to stay because she loved him.

"IT'S GREAT!" Rita shrieked, leaping out of the car. She had already expressed the same opinion of the taxi drive to JFK Airport, the airplane flight and the drive from Los Angeles International Airport to Topanga Canyon. Flying was great. The Porsche was great, even though the back seat was barely large enough for her to fit in. The hot, dry weather of Southern California was great. And now, Seth's house was great.

"You guys are probably wasted," Seth noted, unloading their luggage and his own from the car as Laura joined her daughter outside the car. "Why don't I get you settled, and then I'll scoot down to the Morgans' house for Barney and my mail."

"I want to go, too," Rita declared. "Who's Barney?"

"My dog." Seth unlocked the front door to the house, and Rita ran inside. "Oh, Ma, look at this living room!" she hollered, racing the length of it. "Isn't it great?"

"A vocabulary of one word," Laura muttered. With Seth beside her, instead of a genial-looking old man full of horror stories about airplane disasters, she had survived this flight to California better than her last one. But she still felt a touch queasy and worn out.

Seth appraised her and then her energetic daughter. "I tell you what," he suggested. "You go lie down for a while, and I'll take Rita with me. We've got to buy some groceries, too. Whatever I've got here has probably gone bad by now."

Laura was too exhausted to argue. She gratefully accepted Seth's offer and staggered through the house to his bedroom to sack out.

Barney's rambunctious barking roused her from her nap a couple of hours later. Dragging out of the bed, she stumbled to the bathroom and splashed some cold water on her face to revive herself. Then she followed the sound of Seth's and Rita's voices down the hall to the kitchen, where she discovered them unloading groceries from paper bags.

"Now that we've bought all this food," Seth said, stacking cans of dog food in one of the cabinets, "I think we ought to go out for dinner. Rita needs to taste real Mexican food. Remember that ace joint I took you to?" he asked Laura. "I figure I can stop off at Melinda's house on the way," he continued. "I want to drop *Good Fences* off for her to read."

He had already filled Laura in a bit about his agent, the woman who had told Seth when he was just starting out that she would gladly represent him if he would write violence for her. Laura wondered whether Melinda would care for Seth's new script, in which there was no overt violence at all, and no sex.

Whatever the woman's taste, whatever her sense of commercial viability, she had made plenty of money from Seth's screenplays. Laura believed that, having sold so much of his bad writing, Melinda owed it to Seth to sell something good.

For it was good. No question about it. Laura had read the revised version and been enthralled by the alterations Seth had made on the earlier draft. If she had liked *Good Fences* the first time she'd read it, she liked it even more now, in its new and improved version. It was so strong, so vital—she couldn't believe that anyone wouldn't be taken with it.

Not surprisingly, Rita was captivated by Melinda's Malibu beach house, which stood on stilts above the surging ocean. She was equally captivated by Melinda, a bleached-blond, middle-aged woman who chewed gum, called Rita "honey" and promised Seth that she would read his script overnight. "You really think this is special, huh?" she said, popping her gum in her molars. "And not a single decap in it?"

"Not a one," Seth told her. "Brace yourself."

"What's a decap?" Rita asked once they were in the car again and on the way to the Mexican restaurant.

"A decapitation," Seth replied. "Each of my *Ax Man* flicks had at least one decap in it. *Victory of the Ninjas* had two. I've developed a reputation in the industry as being one of the best decap writers around."

"What a laurel," Laura muttered, grimacing.

"At least I've got a head to wear it on," Seth joked.

"I think it's great that you're the best," Rita claimed. "Mrs. Tashki, she's my home-ec teacher at school, she's always saying, 'Find out what it is that you do well and be the best you can be at it.' If Seth does decapitations well, I think it's great that he's the best."

You think everything Seth does is great, Laura mused silently. She was thrilled that Rita adored Seth, but...Laura wanted Rita to like him not because he was the best decap writer in the business, but because he was talented and sensitive; not because he had a gorgeous house, but because he rained affection on his pet dog. Not because he owned a snazzy sports car, but because he was magnanimous enough to let his loved ones drive it. Not because he had made a mint writing trashy scripts, but because he possessed the wisdom and the vision to write a script like *Good Fences*.

Witnessing their playful banter over dinner, however, Laura cautioned herself that she ought to be thankful Rita liked Seth at all, even if her reasons weren't those Laura would have preferred. Things could be worse.

After dinner they returned to Seth's house and descended to the family room to watch television. "Wow!" Rita exclaimed, spotting the VCR on the lower shelf of the television cart. "You've got one of those!"

"I've got one of those," Seth confirmed, crossing the room to turn on the set.

"Do you rent dirty movies?" Rita asked.

Seth laughed. "I *write* dirty movies," he reminded her. "The last thing I want to do at the end of a day toiling in the trenches is watch a movie just like the one I've just been writing. However..." He switched on the VCR and rummaged through his modest collection of video cassettes. "Here's an oldie but a goodie." He inserted the cassette and returned to the sofa, taking a seat next to Laura.

Rita appeared disappointed that she wasn't going to get to view something X-rated, but her disappointment waned as soon as the screen lit up with the introductory titles for *Evening Potpourri*. "You taped this?" She crossed her legs on the sofa cushions and leaned forward. "The show you and Ma were on?"

"Do we have to watch this?" Laura protested, although she already knew the answer. Seth was lounging next to her with his arm around her shoulders and his feet kicked up on the coffee table. He showed no interest whatsoever in turning off the tape.

Within a minute Julianne appeared on the screen, describing *The Dream* with utter poise. Then Seth appeared, and Rita whistled and clapped. "You were a scream on this show, Seth," she recalled. "Most men wouldn't have the guts to admit they knew how to type. Don't you think Seth is liberated, Ma?"

"If he weren't liberated, do you think we'd be here now?" Laura responded, complimenting Seth. "After all, this is the man who wrote the most feminist Ninja movie in creation."

"This guy was boring," Rita remarked as Andrew appeared on the show. "He reminds me of a social studies teacher."

"He *is* a social studies teacher—of sorts," Seth told her.

Rita sniffed. "Which one is she?" she asked her mother as the camera focused on Kimberly. "That other lady, she looked kinda stuffy, but this one, Courtney and I both thought she was beautiful."

"She is," Laura said.

"Like, she ought to be in the movies or something—oh, yeah, here comes the fox." Rita sighed as Troy came into close-up. "He's so fine. He ought to get together with the blond lady. They'd look so good together."

Seth apparently found such a pairing absurd, and he guffawed. "Kim is a purebred Southern belle," he explained to Rita. "Troy is an inner-city outlaw."

"They always got along pretty well," Laura remembered. "Troy seemed to like Kim more than Andrew ever did."

"That's because Troy is mellow," Seth opined. "Ah, now here comes the star."

Laura cringed, bracing herself for her own appearance on the screen. As with the last time she had watched the show, she thought she looked obese and sounded like a prig. She shot a surreptitious glance at Rita, curious about her daughter's reaction.

"You did good, Ma," Rita said simply as soon as Laura's turn had ended.

Laura turned to Rita, astounded. "Do you really think so?"

"Sure I do," Rita replied, inspecting her polished fingernails. "You didn't do anything embarrassing."

Coming from Rita, Laura considered such a comment the highest praise. She impulsively leaned toward her daughter and kissed her brow. Rita recoiled with a bashful snort. Kissing one's daughter, Laura acknowledged—now *that* was embarrassing!

Rita's energy began to wind down at around nine-thirty, and once Seth reminded her of the fact that it was after midnight in New York, she didn't balk at Laura's command that she go to bed. As soon as Rita was settled in the spare bedroom, Laura and Seth retired to his room, undressed and climbed into bed.

"Seth," Laura murmured, cuddling against his warm body and savoring the familiar strength of his arms around her.

"Mmm."

"Seth, we've got to talk."

"Shoot."

She ran her finger in an abstract pattern across his chest as she collected her thoughts. She replayed in her mind Rita's excitement about Seth's house, his car, his agent, his VCR. The words came easily to her. "You live a very different life from what we're used to."

He pulled back to look at her. "Meaning...?"

"Well, it's all so—so comfortable and—"

"You mean because I'm rich? You mean because I can afford things?" He sounded somewhat rankled. "Come on, Laura. Adjusting to a nicer life is a lot easier than adjusting to a harder one. You've already admitted that you like the microwave, pal, so you can't deny it now."

"I won't deny it," she conceded. "But, Seth...you like all these things, too. And if Rita and I move here, well..." She took a deep breath, then went on. "I can't expect you to support us. That's asking too much of you."

He relaxed beside her and stroked his hands consolingly through her hair. "It's not asking too much of me," he assured her. "Do you think I was kidding when I said I could afford you? Money isn't a problem. You know that."

She nodded. Seth's hand felt so good against her cheek, so comforting, his fingers moving gracefully along the curve of her face. She wished she could just close her eyes and will away her uneasiness.

But she couldn't. "If it isn't money," Seth pressed her, "What is it?"

She took another deep breath. "If I'm going to stay here, Seth, what am I supposed to do about my job?"

"Your job?" A short laugh escaped him. "Quit," he said succinctly.

Quit? Just like that? Walk away from her clients? How could she do something so irresponsible? How could she strand all those hapless young girls?

He seemed able to sense her unspoken thoughts. "You need a break, Laura. You're burned out. You know that as well as I do. You can't do those poor kids much good when they're driving you up the wall."

"Driving me up the wall? Seth, I care about them!"

"Of course you do. But then one gets pregnant, and you get exasperated. You feel as if she's failed you, and then you feel as if you've failed her. It's crazy. And when things get that crazy, it's time to back off for a while." His fingers raveled deep in her hair, and his smile grew distant. "Let me tell you a story about a lady named Shirley Stone."

"A relative of yours?" Laura asked, settling against the pillow and smiling expectantly.

"My mother. A far-out lady, as mothers go. I like ol' Shirley, Laura. She was a very good mother to her three sons, but you know what happened? She burned out."

"What do you mean?" Laura asked, fascinated. "What happened to her?"

"Three sons was what happened to her. Back in those days, when you and I were growing up, mothers were never supposed to burn out. They did, of course, but if they did, they weren't supposed to let on about it. Instead they got frustrated. They took their frustrations out on their kids or their husband. They ate too much, drank too much. You name it. Right?''

Laura nodded. She knew enough women of her mother's generation who had been afflicted that way. They had loved their children and they had cared for them, but they hadn't derived the satisfaction they'd needed from the job. "What did your mother do?" she asked.

"One day she said, 'That's it, guys. I've had it. I need a break.' And she up and left."

"She left!" Laura didn't bother to conceal her shock. "She walked out on her family?"

Seth chuckled. "Nothing that dramatic, Laura. What she did was she got a job."

"A job?" Laura had been expecting a more profound revelation than that. "Lots of women got jobs back then."

"For the money, mostly. Few of them were willing to admit that they got jobs because they were burned out as full-time mothers. But one thing about my mother, she never played games. She said, 'I need a break, and I'm taking one.'" He curled a strand of Laura's hair around his finger as he reminisced. "She got a job as a secretary. My father was horrified, naturally. First of all, what little Mom was earning threw us into a higher tax bracket, so her income was basically a wash. But worse than that, if Mom worked, people might think Dad wasn't earning enough on his own. I mean, Scandal City! Alan Stone isn't earning enough! The guy's manhood was on the line!''

"And?" Laura prompted him. She could easily understand why Seth was such a successful writer. He had her hanging on his every word, dying to hear how his parents had resolved their crisis.

"And Mom refused to back down. After a few weeks Dad got off her case, because the job—the break from being a homemaker—had so refreshed her that she was like a new person. Suddenly she was charming with me and my brothers. Suddenly she wasn't a shrew anymore. She lost ten pounds and looked terrific. Dad started whistling and smiling right around bedtime. Taking a break from being a wife and mother made her a better wife and mother.''

Laura waited for Seth to say more, but he presented her only with a smug grin. She had expected some earth-shattering revelation, and she felt deflated by his story's humdrum conclusion. ''That's all very interesting,'' she said dryly.

Seth leaned toward her and kissed the tip of her nose. ''Don't you get it, Laura? Nobody's saying you ought to stop being a social worker. What I'm saying is, if you quit for a while, you'll be a much better one when you decide to return to work sometime down the road. Take a break. You need it.''

Her lips spread in a wide grin. Yes, the story Seth had just shared with her was humdrum, but its moral was significant. Laura would be a better social worker if she allowed herself the chance to get away from it, to cleanse herself of all the frustration she had been feeling lately in her job.

But still, to allow Seth to support her and Rita... ''Are you sure I wouldn't be taking advantage of you, sponging off you like that?''

''I wish you *would* take advantage of me,'' he asserted. ''I want you to, Laura. Let me spend my money on something more worthwhile than a Porsche, okay? Let me spend it on you and Rita. And every night, you can give your thanks to your buddy Ax Man for making it all possible.''

''I didn't know this sort of thing was done nowadays,'' she mused, amazed by the appeal of Seth's suggestion. ''Women have fought so long to take their place in the work force. And here I'll be, living off you. What will I do with myself, Seth? Cook and clean the house?''

"Cooking's fun in a microwave," he pointed out. "And forget about cleaning. I hire a housekeeping service to do that for me."

"I've got to do something," Laura protested. She had never not worked in her life. The mere idea of doing nothing exhilarated her, but it also daunted her. Without a job, without a routine, without taking care of everything and everyone that needed taking care of, how would she survive?

"You can relax," Seth proposed. "You can take it easy. Do you know how to take it easy, Laura?"

She laughed. "I'm not sure. I may be too old to learn."

"Consider it your new challenge in life."

"I've never minded a challenge," she said with a chuckle before rising to kiss him.

Chapter Twelve

"You're up early," Seth said, entering the kitchen.

Laura was seated at the table in the breakfast area, sipping a cup of coffee and reading the morning newspaper. A corn muffin, sliced and buttered, lay on a plate at her elbow. She glanced at the wall clock and smiled. "It's eleven o'clock in New York," she explained.

"Then how come Rita isn't awake?"

"Rita needs an alarm clock and a cattle prod to get her out of bed," Laura informed him. "Thank you for buying muffins. I read the ingredients on that box of cereal you bought and almost threw up."

"It's terrific stuff," Seth argued, filling a bowl with Sugar Pops. "Nothing can beat it when you've got the munchies." He filled a cup with coffee for himself and joined her at the table. "My appointment with Melinda is at nine-thirty. You can let Rita sleep late if you want. She might wake up by the time I get home, and then we can all do something together."

"Actually, what I was thinking was we'd drive into town with you," Laura suggested. "While you're seeing your agent, I can show Rita the Sidewalk of the Stars or something. If that's all right with you."

Seth smiled. He loved the way Laura looked, her hair more disheveled than usual, her eyes uncommonly bright. He loved the way she looked and even more, he loved her idea. He was delighted that she took enough of an interest in Los Angeles to want to play the tour guide for her daughter. "It's fine with me. You can drop me off and take the car, if you want."

"You don't mind?"

"Not at all. I'd just as soon have you both out of my hair for an hour."

Laura seemed startled by his statement. "Are you sick of us already?"

"No, of course not." He took a long drink of the coffee, ignoring its scalding temperature. He wanted to remain calm; he didn't want Laura to notice how tense he was. But he should have known better. Laura was too attuned to him not to be aware that he was on edge. "All right," he admitted without prompting. "I'm nervous, that's all."

"Nervous? About what?"

"About seeing Melinda."

Again his words startled Laura. She reached across the table and covered his hand with hers, giving it a comforting squeeze. "She's your agent. She's been working with you for years. Why on earth should you be nervous about seeing her?"

"She's going to hate *Good Fences*," he predicted, trying to smother the urge to shudder. "I just know she is."

"She's going to love it," Laura refuted him, her tone low but reassuringly firm. "It's such a fine screenplay, Seth. She can't help but love it."

"You aren't the most objective person in the world," he pointed out, dismissing her flattery.

"Like hell I'm not. *Good Fences* is the best thing you've ever written. If Melinda doesn't like it, then get yourself a new agent."

"Easier said than done," Seth muttered. But he took heart in Laura's confident words. Her abiding faith in him was almost enough.

Almost. It was more than meeting with Melinda that had him panicked.

He respected Laura's opinion as much as he respected Melinda's, but Melinda was a professional. She wasn't in love with him. She didn't have to deal with Seth's soul; she dealt with reality, with the marketplace, with his output, his product. Not with his intentions, but with his words.

For the past few weeks, Seth had put all thoughts of reality and the marketplace aside. He had essentially forgotten that he was a professional. He had written not from his head but from his heart . . . and he'd written for Laura's heart, as well. He had written a screenplay he knew Laura would approve of. He had written it because he had wanted to live up to her concept of who he was.

Yet if her objectivity was questionable—and it was—then his own was even more questionable. Melinda knew what Seth's career was about. If she liked the script—and God, how he hoped she would!—then he had nothing to worry about. But if she didn't like it, he would have to respect her opinion. He would have to accept that he'd blown it. He would have to acknowledge that he'd aimed too high and fallen short, that he had limits.

And if he acknowledged that and accepted it, then he might lose Laura.

He took another long drink of his coffee, then dug into his cereal. What the hell. Either Melinda would approve of the manuscript or she wouldn't. Eating himself up about it wasn't going to change a thing.

Checking the clock again, Laura folded the newspaper and stood, announcing that if she and Rita were going to drive Seth to his appointment, she would have to get her daughter's rear in gear. She bounded out of the kitchen, and Seth watched her, wishing he were as cheerful as she was.

Laura could afford to be cheerful; she was ignorant of the film business, of the severe difficulty of getting something like *Good Fences* produced. Ignorance *was* bliss, he mused morosely, setting down his spoon. Even his favorite cereal didn't taste good that morning.

Laura had such an abundance of faith. If only Seth had half as much faith, he would rest assured that Laura would love him no matter what. He would understand that she would love him even if his magnificent opus was found to be little more than cow droppings in Melinda's esteem.

But his faith was a shaky thing. He remembered with acute clarity the first time Laura had revealed her love for him: it was right after she'd read the original version of *Good Fences*. Laura hadn't been able to love him, himself, alone. She had loved him not for who he was, but for who she wanted to believe he was. If the real world came crashing down on him with the news that all Seth was, and all he would ever be, was a skilled, successful hack, would Laura still be able to love him?

He doubted it.

He thought about what they had discussed last night in bed. For Laura, taking a break from saving the world was just that: a break. She would use her sabbatical to restore herself, to spend time with Rita, to plant a garden, or learn how to bake bread in his oven, or read. And then, in a few years—Seth was certain of it—she would be ready to save the world again. If not as a social worker, she would do it some other way. Laura had too much goodness inside her to keep it all for herself and Rita and Seth. She would want to share it with others. That was the way she was.

But Seth . . . for him, writing *Good Fences* had been the break. Now that his soul was restored, would he find himself with no alternative but to return to writing junk? He still wasn't totally convinced that writing junk was such a terrible thing. Yet Laura believed that it was.

He would be happy to spend the rest of his life with Laura, even if she never returned to any sort of professional work. And he would be happy to spend the rest of his life with her if she *did* return to work. But if he couldn't sell *Good Fences*, and if he never returned to *his* professional work—writing commercial film scripts—he wouldn't be able to support Laura and Rita forever. And if he *did* resume that sort of writing, he would lose Laura. She would walk. Not because he was a sellout, but because he wasn't as brilliant and talented as she wanted him to be.

He heard Rita's plaintive whine from the spare bedroom, then Laura's voice announcing that if Rita wanted to see Sunset Strip she'd have to shake a leg. "Sunset Strip?" Rita chirped, abruptly awake and elated. "No kidding?"

A half-hour later, all three of them were in the Porsche, weaving through the canyon toward the congested Coast Highway. "This," Seth quipped, trying not to let his anxiety get the better of him as his car's overpowered engine moaned in the bumper-to-bumper traffic, "is what we call life in the fast lane."

"Isn't it great that you can wear Hawaiian print shirts to work?" Rita babbled. "Remember, Seth—tell Melinda, 'Todd Bridges. He's your man.' "

"Whatever you say, Rita," Seth mumbled, wondering whether she, too, would lose interest in him if Melinda deemed *Good Fences* a first-class flop. Probably not, he reolved. As long as he wrote a part for Todd Bridges in his next *Ax Man* feature, he'd have Rita's undying adulation.

After forty-five sweaty minutes, he steered the car to a halt in front of an imposing black-paned skyscraper in the center of Los Angeles's business district. "This here's the place," he said, taking a deep breath for courage. He handed his keys to Laura and swung open the door. "Meet me here in two hours. It won't take any longer than that. Wish me luck."

"You don't need any luck," Laura bolstered him.

Right, he muttered to himself as he watched her assume the driver's seat and restart the engine. He remained outside on the paved plaza until the car vanished into the flow of traffic, and for a brief, excruciating moment, he imagined that she had actually driven out of his life.

He couldn't bear to lose Laura—and he couldn't bear the thought that his future with her might very well be resting on what Melinda had to say about his script. Praying with all his heart that Melinda would greet him with a bottle of Mumm's and a slap on the back, he steeled his shoulders and valiantly approached the building.

"A HALF-HOUR ISN'T long enough," Rita complained as Laura prodded her out of the Tower Records shop on Sunset Boulevard. "I could have spent all day in there."

"You could spend all day staring at a single record album," Laura commented. "But I promised we'd meet Seth at his agent's office building in twenty minutes. We're running late."

"I thought you were going to take me to see some of the other sights," Rita sulked, folding herself into the passenger seat of the Porsche.

"And I thought that spending a half-hour in one of the world's largest record stores would satisfy you for the time being. Didn't you think that life-size poster of Sting was cute?"

Rita gaped at her mother. "You like Sting?"

"I think he's sexy," Laura admitted.

"He looks a little like Seth, the way he wears his hair. And the color, too," Rita observed. "He's a fox."

"Who? Sting or Seth?"

"Both," said Rita. Laura nodded in enthusiastic agreement.

As the car neared the building that housed Melinda's office, Laura spotted Seth loitering in the sprawling plaza in front of the building—it was hard to miss him when he was wearing such a brightly colored shirt. She downshifted, taking pride in her smooth manipulation of the gear stick, and cruised to a stop at the curb. He loped across the plaza to the car, and she and Rita climbed out, rearranging themselves so Seth could drive.

He smiled and kissed Laura's cheek as he took the key from her. "Well?" she asked expectantly as he fastened his seat belt and revved the engine.

"Let's drive a little," he said.

His reticence troubled Laura, but she didn't probe. She was by nature a patient person. She would wait until Seth was ready to give her a full report on his meeting with Melinda.

He drove onto the Coast Highway, but didn't take the turnoff at Topanga Canyon. Instead he continued north on the road bordering the twisting coastline, past sun-glazed beaches and dramatic houses, farther and farther from the heart of the city. After making one or two observations about the spellbinding scenery—and the good-looking guys on the beach—Rita subsided in the back seat, also respecting Seth's brooding silence.

Eventually he pulled off the road at a stretch of sand far enough from the city to be sparsely populated. An elderly man with a long-handled metal detector paced the beach, searching for hidden treasures. Two handsome women in daring maillots lay supine on beach towels, baking their skin, oblivious of the treasure seeker as well as the three people in the sleek black Porsche that had just parked in the graveled lot beside the sand.

Seth opened his door, and Laura took that as a signal to open hers, as well. Rita practically pushed her out of the car, shoving the back of Laura's seat forward and leaping out. "Oh, wow!" she shrieked. "This is beautiful!"

"Yes, it is," Laura agreed, inhaling the briny ocean scent and smiling.

"Go ahead, Rita," Seth urged her. "Go stick your big toe in the Pacific."

Rita needed no more encouragement. She yanked off her shoes and darted across the sand to the water's edge.

Seth took Laura's hand and guided her onto the beach at a leisurely gait. He was breathing deeply, too, filling his lungs with the clean, refreshing shore fragrance.

"Melinda hated it," Laura guessed. Even her patience couldn't last forever.

Seth shot Laura a quick look, then turned to gaze at the curling gray-green surf. "Yeah. She hated it."

Laura studied his harsh, angular profile. She knew he must be heartbroken. He had put so much of himself into the script. If his agent hated it, Seth would undoubtedly take such a rejection personally. "I'm so sorry, Seth," she murmured.

"That's the breaks, pal," he said stoically.

"Why did she hate it?" Laura asked. "What did she say?"

He shrugged. "I was in with her for a long time, Laura. We walked through my career, practically through my entire life." He turned to Laura, his eyes tinged with a sadness that nearly broke her heart. "The script is too quiet, she said. Too tame, too understated. Themes with a capital T aren't enough to carry the day. The bottom line is, I just don't have it."

Laura refused to succumb to his pessimism. "You don't have what, Seth?"

"I don't have..." He groaned. "I don't have the talent for it. What I can do, I do well. But what I *can't* do is write a human interest script that anyone in his right mind would be willing to produce. *Good Fences* is too soppy, she said. Too milky. It just won't make it."

"That's her opinion," Laura emphasized.

"Her opinion is worth a hell of a lot," Seth countered. "She's smart, Laura, and knowledgeable. Don't belittle her opinion just because you don't happen to agree with it. Melinda got me started, gave me guidance, helped me to find my talent and develop it. She isn't an idiot."

"She isn't infallible," Laura argued. "Just because she thinks—"

"She *knows*, Laura. All she did was put into words what I already guessed. I'm not—" He stared past Laura at the smooth seam of the horizon and exhaled. "I'm not good enough. I'm not good enough to pull off a script like *Good Fences*, and I'm not good enough for you."

His voice cracked slightly on those final few words, and Laura felt something crack inside herself, as well. "For me? What do I have to do with it?"

"You? I wrote the damned script for you!" His temper flared for a moment, but he resolutely swallowed his anger and returned his aching gaze to the horizon. "I wrote it be-

:ause you asked me to. You pushed me into it, Laura. You ested me."

"Tested you?" She felt as if the sand were slipping beneath her feet, as if the world were no longer able to support her. How could Seth have thought such a thing? How could he have imagined that she was testing him?

She had urged him to write the script because she loved him. She loved him, and she thought he would enjoy writing something he could believe in. That was all.

She tried to ignore the irrational fear that clutched at her. "Seth," she said, daring to touch his arm. Her fingers curled about the muscle, and she took strength from the solid feel of him. "You don't honestly think I was testing you, do you?"

He twisted his head to peer down at her. "I wrote that script because I wanted it to be good for you, Laura."

"And I wanted it to be good for you," she countered. "I wanted you to write it because I knew you'd make something wonderful out of it."

He sighed, his gaze drifting downward, studying the ripples in the sand at their feet. "I didn't make something wonderful out of it. I flopped. You had faith in me, Laura, and I failed."

"I still have faith in you," she insisted. "And you didn't fail. Melinda might think you did, but that's only her opinion. Not yours, and not mine. Maybe..." She took a deep breath. Once again she was going to make a suggestion, based in total ignorance, about Seth's career. But she wasn't really ignorant. About the movie business, maybe, but not about Seth. "Maybe it's time to find another agent."

"Another agent?" he exclaimed, evidently astonished by Laura's naïveté. "You mean, quit Melinda? After all she's done for me?"

"You don't have to quit her if you want to keep writing the stuff you've been writing all along," Laura said, making a distinction. "That's what she wants. It's easier for her to sell trash than to sell something worthwhile."

"Perhaps writing trash is all I can do," he said grimly. "Perhaps you're giving me more credit than I deserve. Wake up and smell it, Laura. Be real. I'm not cut out for saving the world. I am what I am, and all that."

How could he be so negative? How could someone who had written something as lovely as *Good Fences*, someone with a brain like Seth's and a heart like his not know who he was? "Seth," she said steadily, "you are a brilliant, immensely talented man. I don't give a damn what your agent thinks of one script. *I* know it's the best thing you've ever created. And you know it, too. If she doesn't know it, then it's her misfortune."

He studied her quizzically, as if he weren't sure what she was saying. She wondered at his puzzlement. What could be more obvious? Seth *was* brilliant and talented. After all this time he ought to be aware of that.

"Bypass her," she recommended, desperate to make Seth understand. "Bypass Melinda. You must know people in the industry. An independent producer, maybe. Some rich eccentric looking for an unusual project to invest in. Invest your own money. If I had money, I'd invest in *Good Fences*. Someone somewhere must have enough taste to take a chance on it."

"Just because you like challenges doesn't mean everybody does," Seth pointed out.

"I don't care about everybody," Laura maintained. "I care about you. Your stupid agent likes scripts with blood and guts in them, but she hasn't got the good sense to realize that what you showed her is full of *your* blood, *your* guts. You can't turn your back on it now."

She detected the merest glimmer of a smile on his lips. "Would you like me to find you a windmill to fence while you're at it?" he offered.

"I've already found one," she answered calmly.

"Laura." He twisted back to face the water. Rita had rolled up the hems of her jeans and was wading in the foam. He watched her for a moment. "She's probably dreaming about becoming a surfer," he observed.

"Yes," Laura agreed. "Rita has dreams, and she doesn't quit on them. That's one reason I love her."

"Why do you love me?" he asked solemnly.

"Because you're you," she replied. "Because you've got dreams, too, and because you've shared them with me. *Good Fences* is one of your dreams, Seth. Don't quit on it."

His hand tightened on hers. "You'd love me even if I were a failure, wouldn't you," he half asked.

"As long as you were a noble failure," Laura swore. "As long as you didn't give up. But, then, as long as you didn't give up, you couldn't possibly be a failure."

He pulled her toward him and wrapped his arms around her. "And why do I love you?" he whispered.

"I don't know," she answered tentatively. "You think I'm pushy, testing you, that I forced you to do something you didn't want to do." She shivered as the truth of her words sank in. If Seth honestly believed such things of her, how could he ever love her?

"I'll tell you why I love you," he said, bowing to kiss her brow. "Not just because you've got dreams, but because you knock yourself out trying to make them come true." He smiled. "You didn't force me to do anything I didn't really want to do, Brodie. If you think I'm that easy to push around, think again."

"You're not easy to push around?" she asked, permitting herself a slight smile.

"Try me and find out," he dared her.

"Hmm," she mused, her smile expanding and growing mischievous. "That's a challenge I can't refuse."

He studied her face, and his lips slowly spread into a grin. "Does that mean you're going to stick around?"

"Of course I am. I want to master that fancy oven of yours."

"Now the truth comes out," he grumbled playfully. "You love me for my microwave."

She shook her head. "Your Porsche, Stoned," she corrected him.

"I knew it!" he crowed, lifting her off the sand and exuberantly swinging her in a circle. "I knew you'd come to love that car of mine."

"More than life itself, Seth," she deadpanned.

Seth began to laugh, although he didn't lower Laura back to her feet. Clinging to him, her arms tight around his neck, she laughed, too. The sweet harmony of their laughter lifted on the wind and mingled with the muffled roar of the surf pounding the earth.

And they discovered, much to their utter pleasure, that it was possible to laugh and kiss at the same time.

Keeping the Faith

by
Judith Arnold

It renewed old friendships, kindled new relationships, but the fifteen-year reunion of *The Dream*'s college staff affected all six of the Columbia-Barnard graduates: Laura, Seth, Kimberly, Andrew, Julianne and Troy.

Follow the continuing story of these courageous, vital men and women who find themselves at a crossroads—as their idealism of the sixties clashes with the reality of life in the eighties.

You may laugh, you may cry, but you will find a piece of yourself in *Keeping the Faith*.

Don't miss American Romance #205 *Commitments* in July and #209 *Dreams* in August.

AR201

Harlequin American Romance

COMING NEXT MONTH

#205 COMMITMENTS by Judith Arnold

In the seventies they'd have called it "bad karma." Andrew Collins, self-avowed cynic of *The Dream*, and Kimberly Belmont, its resident optimist, seemed destined to remain antagonists forever. But shortly after the magazine's anniversary bash, something extraordinary happened. They'd become lovers. Was it an accident? Or a mistake? Catch the second book in the *Keeping the Faith* trilogy.

#206 FAIR GAME by Susan Andrews

Being a winner on *Love Life*, TV's popular dating game, meant that Julie Turner had to spend a week in Atlantic City with Marcus Allen, TV's heartthrob. To publicity-shy Julie it seemed more like a chore than fun, but how could she resist a man who whisked her away from the prying eyes of the media to a seaside hideaway?

#207 CHRISTMAS IN JULY by Julie Kistler

Kit Wentworth was furious. How dared Riley Cooper call her a lily-livered coward! The time had come for her to go home. But that meant seeing her family, and confronting the man who had prompted her exodus four years earlier.

#208 A QUESTION OF HONOR by Jacqueline Ashley

Helping people was a matter of honor to Frances McPhee. But traveling with her cantankerous old uncle Fergus and his companion to his Oklahoma cabin was pure torture. With Ash Blair's penchant for gourmet foods and pricey hotels—and his devastating charm—would Frances bring Fergus home safely without first falling in the poorhouse—or in love?

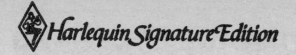

Carole Mortimer

Merlyn's Magic

She came to him from out of the storm and was drawn into his yearning arms—the tempestuous night held a magic all its own.

You've enjoyed Carole Mortimer's Harlequin Presents stories, and her previous bestseller, *Gypsy*.

Now, don't miss her latest, most exciting bestseller, *Merlyn's Magic!*

IN JULY

MERMG

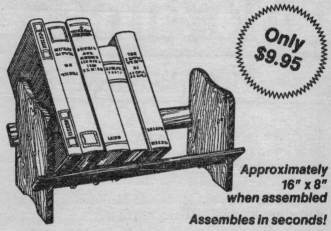

Take 4 books
& a surprise gift
FREE

All men wanted her,
but only one man would have her.

Desert Storm

Nan Ryan

Her cruel father had intended
Angie to marry a sinister cattle baron twice her age.
No one expected that she would fall in love with his
handsome, pleasure-loving cowboy son.

Theirs was a love no desert storm would quench.

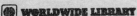